FORGING THE BLADE

Book One of the Mage Web Series

C. LaVielle

DRAGON'S EGG PRESS
Portland, Oregon
2021

Forging the Blade
Book One of the Mage Web Series

Dragon's Egg Press
Portland, Oregon, U.S.A.

Front cover illustration and design by Ture Ekroos
www.tureekroos.com

Back cover image: The Fool card from a deck produced in
Marseilles, France in the 18th century by François Chosson.
Image courtesy of www.taropedia.com

ISBN 978-0-9983260-3-0

First Edition 2016
Second Edition 2021

This book is for my mother
Helen Todhunter Mellinger
1910–1989

0

The Fool

The wind howled as the stormdragon touched down. Monstrous bat wings snapped as they caught the air. It bounded toward Darkfire, smashing aside full-grown oaks like they were saplings. Faceted ruby eyes gleamed as it reached for her with talons the size of swords. The lone wizard supercharged six magic darts and fired them in rapid succession.

"Take that, you scaly bastard!"

One shattered its right eye, two tore satisfying gashes in a wing, and the other three ripped through its chest. The dragon roared with rage and spat a column of golden flame, which the wizard repelled with a Shield of Solomon spell. She vaulted high in the air, her lithe form twisting to teleport past the beast and attack from behind...

"Molly?" There was a knock on her bedroom door.

Molly Adair groaned and hit pause.

"Just a sec," she said, running stiff fingers through her tangle of auburn curls and forcing her brain back into what she'd started calling "Zombieland."

Why wouldn't everyone just let her stay in WarCraft Universe? In that world she wasn't a fat, dorky sixteen-year-old with too many freckles. She was Darkfire, a powerful wizard with a 24-inch waist, gorgeous cleavage, and a wardrobe to die for. She went on quests for kings and queens and warlords, earned tons of ducats that she could spend any way she wanted, and had lots of friends. In WarCraft Universe her stomach wasn't all screwed up in a knot and her arms and legs weren't so numb and heavy that just crawling out of bed and dragging her butt into school was almost impossible. In WarCraft Universe, whatever it was that used to make her grin like a fool when she saw a kitten; and her heart sing when she scored a soccer goal; and her stomach do flip-flops when she talked to a cool guy, hadn't disappeared.

"Molly?" There was another knock.

It was Suzanne, her mother's lab tech. Molly didn't need a babysitter while her parents were at their stupid research conference. Like, she was a babysitter.

Mother said Suzanne wasn't a babysitter; she was just there to keep her company.

Yeah, right.

Babysitter or whatever, Molly didn't want one, especially not some chirpy chick with fantastic curves and perfectly applied eyeliner.

Suzanne, however, wasn't looking so chirpy at the moment. Her eyes were red and her eyeliner was smudged. "There's someone here to see you." She pointed to a tiny woman with perfectly cut, wispy, gray hair, choked back a sob, and hurried away.

Her visitor didn't look to be in much better shape than Suzanne. The knot in Molly's stomach twisted viciously. Something was wrong. But the woman just stood there and stared at her like she was the most fascinating thing on earth.

"Uh, come in," Molly said, stepping back from the door and hoping the stranger would quit gawking and tell her what was going on.

The woman blinked and stepped into the room, sharp eyes observing everything and then jumping back to the raging dragon and sexy wizard on the computer screen. Her lips compressed as she turned abruptly and sat on the bed. She was even shorter than Molly, but she dominated the room like a top-level magic user.

"My name is Estelle Adair," she said. "I'm your grandmother."

Molly plunked down on the desk chair. So this was the mysterious grandmother who never came to visit, but sent her cool books and generous checks every birthday and Christmas. Dad never talked about her, never shared a single photo of her. Why was she here now, looking like she was gonna burst into tears?

"Um, nice to meet you."

"And it's nice to meet you as well, although I wish it were under different circumstances. I've come to tell you that your father and mother are dead. Their plane went down over the Atlantic."

Molly stared at her visitor in disbelief which rapidly flared into anger. Who did she think she was, coming in here and jerking her around like this?

"No! You're lying. Go away!"

The woman's eyes widened with surprise and filled with tears.

"And you probably aren't even my Grandmother!"

Instead of leaving she stood and gestured for Molly to sit on the bed. A moment later, Molly was amazed to find herself meekly sitting on the bed while the stranger sat at her computer. She'd already minimized WarCraft Universe and her fingers were flying over the keyboard. An article popped up.

"Here. Read this," she said and left the room.

The knot in her gut burst into a thousand bits of agony as she read. According to *The New York Times* news feed, her parents' plane had, indeed, crashed over the Atlantic.

The woman returned and handed Molly her driver's license.

"Nooooo!" Molly shrieked as her world went black.

She was falling into endless screaming blackness.

She was in The Nightmare again. The terrifying dream that had shattered her sleep night after night for months. If she didn't wake up, she always crashed to her death.

Just like Mother and Dad.

She moaned and buried her face in her hands. The Nightmare had been about her parent's death, not hers. She had been so sure she was gonna die. The thought had paralyzed her, haunting every waking moment.

But this was even worse.

She should have figured it out and warned them instead of worrying about herself. Then they'd still be alive instead of blasted into bloody bits of fish food.

She shuddered and forced her room into focus.

Oddly enough, it was still there. The screen beside her still showed the horrid article. Its lower right hand corner told her that only a few minutes had passed. The stranger who was her grandmother was sitting on the bed.

Everything was the same.

But everything was changed.

Her parents were dead. And it was her fault. She hadn't told them about her dream. Now Dad would never hug her and call her princess again and her beautiful mother was gone forever.

"I'm so sorry," her grandmother said as she stood up and gently squeezed Molly's shoulder. "I'll come back a little later." Her voice and touch were muffled, like someone had covered Molly from head to toe in mummy wrappings.

The door clicked shut like a coffin lid and she curled up on her bed. She lay still and let her mind skitter in miserable circles. She was so full of gray emptiness that there was no room left for grief. Her parents were dead, yet she couldn't cry a single tear. What kind of monster was she?

She sat up and reached for the foot-tall, painted bronze statue of Xena Warrior Princess. She was striding across Molly's nightstand, one arm thrust forward and the other drawn back, ready to strike down evil with her sword. She was Molly's treasure. When she'd seen her for sale in a thrift shop at a price she could afford, she'd been ecstatic.

Now she couldn't even remember what ecstatic felt like.

Xena wouldn't be sitting here like a zombie; she would be weeping and raging and fighting to put things right.

Well, there was one thing Xena *could* do to make things a little better.

The cold, empty ache that curled and twisted inside her had become intolerable.

Molly gazed into the Warrior Princess's fierce blue eyes, rolled up her sleeve, and drew the inside of her forearm across the blade of her sword. She'd filed it to a sharp edge, but she still had to press hard, even though she was just opening an old cut.

Bright pain flashed up her arm; every nerve in her body sang. Gently replacing Xena on the nightstand she lay back on her bed with a sigh of relief and relaxed into the burn. Warmth eased the pit of her stomach. The colors of her quilt flashed into temporary brilliance and the drops of blood oozing from the cut glowed vivid red against the surrounding white scars.

Much better.

She didn't know what she was gonna do when summer came and it would be too hot to wear long sleeves. But her parents were dead. No one was left to care how many scars tracked up her arm.

One problem solved.

But Mother and Dad were still dead.

Even Xena could never fix that.

She stared at the ceiling letting her mind circle this fact like the tiny mongoose she'd seen on a nature show stalking a king cobra.

"Molly?" Her grandmother knocked gently on her door. "I've brought you a sandwich."

"I'm not hungry. I just wanna be alone, OK?" The last thing she needed was some stranger trying to cheer her up.

Time passed.

The light faded.

Her room filled with shadows.

As she stared into the growing darkness a feeling of dread seeped into her. It nudged and stroked the edges of her attention, gently caressing her into terror.

Something was watching her.

She could feel its eyes pinning her to the bed like a bug.

She scanned the room, her breath coming in shallow gasps.

There! In the corner by the dresser...

A shadow moved when the other shadows were still and was still when the other shadows moved. A bitter chill seeped out of it, raising every hair on Molly's body.

It glided toward her in terrible silence and she knew with a bone deep certainty that when it touched her she would die.

A part of her reached for it with a sigh of relief, but the rest of her cringed in fear. Cold sweat slicked every inch of her skin and shakes trembled through her.

This was it. She was gonna die.

But she wasn't gonna do it curled up and quivering in her bed.

Xena and Darkfire would never do that. They'd go out fighting.

Molly gathered every last bit of her strength and leaped up. She stood with her legs apart and her fists jammed into her waist so the thing couldn't see how bad she was shaking.

"Go away!"

To her vast relief, it faded like smoke curling off a blown out candle wick.

Except for its piercing red eyes.

They hung menacing and motionless for a few heartbeats and then blinked out.

Molly collapsed onto the patchwork quilt and shook.

Portland, Oregon

Four ghastly months later, Molly slouched in the blue plush chair beside her bed and glared out the window of her new room. The chair had appeared yesterday, the day after she'd moved in, and was the only thing that wasn't from her bedroom back in Massachusetts. In fact, the room looked almost exactly like her room back home except for one important thing. Xena was gone. Her grandmother had discovered the cuts the day after she arrived and gone ballistic. Molly was still trying to figure out how she knew they were there. Every sharp thing in the house had suddenly disappeared and she couldn't even get the knife drawer open, although it didn't have a lock as far as she could tell. So she took lots of walks and searched for sharp things.

Estelle had held her parent's memorial service in a church.

Why? They never went to church.

The place was crammed with tons of people she'd never met, and it was so hot and stuffy with grief that you couldn't breathe. Lindsay and Beth and a few other friends from the academy managed to show up, but they just mumbled a bunch of sorries and stared at her like she had a terminal disease. Then her grand-mother cleared out the house that Molly had lived in all her life, sold it, and moved her way out here to Portland. She hadn't even talked to her about it. When she'd protested, Estelle had said that there was no other choice.

The Nightmare still jolted her awake every night and the Shadow was a frequent visitor. The only time she got any relief from the fear and numbness was when she played WarCraft Universe, and she was only allowed two hours of that a day. Plus, Estelle had moved her computer out of her room. She'd stuck it down in the family room. How lame was that?

In hardly any time at all, the woman had turned Molly's rotten, useless life into a pure, living hell.

A warm August breeze curled in through the window as she sank back in the over-stuffed chair. It was gonna get hot. Good. She was always cold.

And with that thought, the temperature plunged to polar and an all too familiar terror overwhelmed her.

The Shadow was forming beside the nightstand.

It hadn't even waited till evening.

"Go away. Oh please go away," Molly whispered as cold sweat prickled out of her pores and her heart shrank into the farthest corner of her ribcage.

It swirled into a vaguely human shape and glided toward her. She was sure it was getting stronger and more distinct with each visit.

"I said 'Go away!'" She could barely form the words, much less get out of the chair.

It kept coming, its red eyes stabbing into hers, and she shrank back with a whimper. She was so tired of everything. Part of her had already checked out and what was left didn't give a shit. Maybe she should just quit fighting and let the Shadow take her.

"Noooo!" A tiny piece of her heart flared with anger, sending a surge of strength coursing through her.

Molly's jaw dropped in amazement as a pulsing beam of light shot in through one wall of her room and out the opposite one. The air around her shimmered and expanded slowly. When the shimmers touched the light beam there was a flash; and just like that, The Shadow disappeared.

Before she could even slump back in relief, a voice outside began yelling "Yeeeeeeeeeeeeee."

It was getting louder. "EEEEEEEEEEEEEEE—

"HA!" A figure burst through her bedroom wall; arms, legs, and Day-Glo-orange Converse high-tops flailing as it slid and tumbled along the light beam. The smell of a summer thunderstorm right after a lightening flash filled the room.

Molly moved her dumbfounded gaze from the perfectly intact wall down to the intruder. He was sitting cross-legged in front of her, furiously stabbing and swiping at the screen of a smart phone. At least she thought it was a he; it could have been a she, but Molly decided to stick with her original impression. His filthy leggings, khaki hiking shorts, and blue earth T-shirt were in shreds.

And he was floating two feet above the floor.

"Who are you?" Molly said, shrinking back into the chair.

"Tracy Bliss," he replied, still focused on his phone. "Shit. This is gonna be a mess," he said, poking at the screen. Two large, mottled brown feathers sticking out of his mop of ash blond hair swiveled and twitched like the antennae of an anxious moth.

This guy was a total freak out. She wanted to run far, far away, but she was paralyzed, heart thudding like crazy.

"Get out of my room!"

The intruder ignored her and held up the phone like he was about to take her picture.

His eyes were spinning like silver pin-wheels.

"Smile," he said, as the phone whirred and clicked.

"Noooooo!" Molly shrieked in terror as her body twisted and warped.

The chair disappeared out from under her.

Once again, she was falling through screaming blackness.

1

The Magician

olly landed with an undignified thud—alive, unhurt, and sprawled in the middle of a ruler-straight dirt road. The only sounds were her ragged breathing and an occasional chirp from some invisible bird. Huge trees soared skyward making her feel like she was in the aisle of one of those cathedrals she'd seen when she went to Europe last year with her parents. They'd traveled together for a whole wonderful, amazing week. The memory twisted her heart.

She gasped in surprise as Tracy appeared, sitting cross-legged above the road in front of her. And then her temper flared.

"You sent me here!" Molly shouted, "Take me back. Now."

"Can't."

"How come?"

"Cuz I didn't send you here."

"You did too!"

"Nah, I just helped a little."

"Then who did? Make them take me back!" Her heart was pounding like a drummer on meth.

"Can't."

"Well then how am I supposed to get back?" Molly struggled to her feet and jammed her fists into her hips, outrage and fear fighting for first place. "I haven't a clue where I am or where this road goes; and even if I did, I couldn't follow it 'cuz my shoes are back in Portland."

A ragged, brown leather backpack materialized on the trail beside her with a gentle pop.

She shrieked and jumped away from it. Tracy looked skyward as if praying for patience. His smoky gray eyes had stopped spinning, but the feathers in his matted hair still twitched and jerked. As he stood to face her, he fidgeted in time with the feathers.

Molly glared at him, grabbed the pack, unbuckled the main compartment, and found hiking boots and two pairs of boot socks. This was beginning to look suspiciously like a WarCraft Universe session.

So...an evil game-master had transported her into this universe and given her the backpack. It would have been nice if he'd let her develop a better character, like a wizard or a warrior or something. A short, overweight, out of shape, sixteen-year-old human female would totally not have been her choice, but it was what she was stuck with. She'd have to work with it.

"What's in that direction?" she asked, pointing to her right.

"Mountains."

"Nothing but mountains?"

Tracy nodded.

Mountains wouldn't help her find a way back.

"Good luck!" Unable to hold still any longer, Tracy clapped her on the shoulder and headed off toward the mountains.

Molly looked to her left. What would she find if she went that way? What if there were robbers or wild animals? There wasn't any food or water in her pack. Her palms pricked with sweat and her stomach clenched.

This was insane. She turned to ask Tracy to wait up.

The road to the mountains was deserted.

Nothing stirred in the cool, green forest.

Molly stared in terror at the empty road, which suddenly felt dangerous and menacing.

She didn't belong here.

She wished she was safe in her room in Portland. No, actually, she wished she was back in Concord, Massachusetts, with her parents still alive. They'd be at work now and she'd be hanging out at the pool or at the mall with Lindsay and Beth and getting psyched up for their junior year at Concord Academy. As she relaxed into that comforting vision, the empty stillness of the forest opened up around her. She felt herself peeling off from the present and drifting away into her daydream. The world around her disappeared, replaced by familiar images of her life in Concord.

Her body began numbing out and she felt The Shadow stir.

In a panic she squeezed her hands into fists, digging sharpened, pointed fingernails into her scarred, scabbed over palms. With brutal precision she reminded herself that her parents had been dead since May. And when she'd quit playing soccer, Lindsay and Beth had decided she wasn't cool any more and hadn't spoken to her since December. And she lived in Portland now with a grandmother who hated her. And she'd never see Mother or Dad or Lindsay or Beth or Concord Academy ever again. And if she didn't get moving she was gonna die of thirst.

The pain brought her back.

With shaking, stinging hands she put on the socks and hiking boots, shrugged into the backpack, and headed down the road.

Hours later, sweat was dripping off her chin and she had plenty of pain to keep herself focused. Her feet throbbed, her boobs hurt because she hadn't put on a bra this morning, and her black cut-offs were too short and her sweaty inner thighs rubbed together with every step and burned like crazy. Every bird call and twig snap in the looming trees made her jump.

Up ahead a shaft of sunlight speared through the branches, illuminating a path curving off to the right. In the middle of that path lay a perfect red rose. Dewdrops sparkled like diamonds on its velvety petals. As she reached down to pick it up, its scent eased her aching heart. But when her fingers touched the stem, the rose disappeared.

Things appeared and disappeared way too often around here.

As she turned back to the main road, a glowing white something appeared farther on down the side path.

Uh-huh, definitely like a WarCraft Universe quest.

The whiteness turned out to be a lily. Its fresh, clean scent reminded her of a spring day. Without thinking, she reached for the flower, only to watch it fade away.

A faint humming trickled down the path and she headed toward its source. Moments later she arrived in a garden full of white lilies and cascades of climbing red roses. A stone cube marked its center. The air was warm and sweet with honey-gold sunshine and the scent of roses and lilies. Hundreds of bees bumbled drunkenly from flower to flower, and a deep purr rumbled over, around, and under the hum of the bees. It emanated from a large, black cat, or maybe a very small leopard, lying on its back in front of the cube. Its paws batted at a butterfly that was fluttering by. If there had been words to the purr, Molly was sure they would have gone something like, "Warm sunshine on this tummy of mine makes life so fine." The scene was so charming and the cat looked so cute, that Molly couldn't help but giggle.

When was the last time she'd even smiled?

The cat sprang to its feet, back arched and ears back. It bared its fangs with a bone-chilling hiss. *Who are you and what are you doing in my garden?* The words hammered into her brain with brutal force, yet the beast's mouth hadn't moved. This world was impossible. Since when could animals talk into your head? Anger bubbled up inside Molly. What gave this nasty creature the right to threaten exhausted travelers? She snarled right back. "I'm not hurting you or your stupid garden. If you don't want company, then do something about those disappearing roses and lilies on the path back there."

The cat's eyes glinted dangerously and Molly braced for the attack. It was big enough to do some real damage. Stupid, stupid, stupid. Mother was always telling her that her short temper and sharp tongue would get her in real trouble one day.

Her mother was dead...

But the black beast's ears flicked into airplane wing position, then forward and up. *Then you're supposed to be here. What's your name?*

"Molly."

Everyone seemed to know more about what was happening to her than she did.

It made her nervous.

Molly who?

"Molly Adair."

Adair? Golden eyes studied her intently. The cat sat down on its haunches and began washing its paws.

I wish they'd tell me when they decide to send me someone.

"They?"

The Webmasters—powerful men and women with an atrophied sense of humor. I'm one of their guides. They send me all kinds of people.

So there *were* Game-masters, just like in WarCraft Universe, and they sounded like the sort of folks you wouldn't want to piss off. But Molly had a feeling that it was her grandmother who was behind all this. Oddly enough, the thought made her heart ache.

She started pacing. This totally sucked.

"I'll eventually get back, right?"

That depends on you. You might decide you don't want to go back, you might get lost, or you might get killed.

"Killed?" Molly stopped short and turned to face the cat. "Then can't I just 'res'?"

What?

"Like, come back after awhile and start over where I left off?"

Of course not. When you're dead, you're dead.

Molly dragged her fingers through her sweaty curls as she digested this unsettling piece of news. She might never see Portland again.

"Then, this isn't a game?" she asked, just to make sure she had everything straight.

I don't play games.

"I mean, like, this isn't someone's made-up universe and we're all here playing the characters we've picked out and developed?"

No—unless you are speaking philosophically. If so, I decline to comment. I'm not a philosopher.

Why wouldn't anyone give her a straight answer? Molly's stomach twisted into a knot and her temper exploded again. "Quit jerkin' me around. Is this place real or not?"

It's as real as the world you came from. The cat's ears folded back tight to its head. *But in case you hadn't noticed, things are a bit different here than they are there. And you're not there anymore—you're here.*

"And that's the problem, I want to be back there."

Why?

Molly began to reply, but stopped short.

"I don't know."

You need a better reason than that.

"Why do I have to have a reason? I just wanna go back, OK?" Molly and the cat glared at each other until Molly said, "Look, couldn't you start helping me, and by the time I know how to get back, maybe I'll have figured out why I want to go back?"

That's the first sensible thing you've said. You have a deal, Molly Adair. Allow me to introduce myself. My name is Asmodius.

"Pleased to meet you," said Molly. And to her dismay, she just barely stopped herself from bowing.

Are you hungry?

Molly's stomach unknotted and rumbled at the mention of food.

Thought so. I'll see what I can produce for you.

Molly caught her breath in surprise when a knife, fork, spoon, goblet, plate, and candle popped into existence on the cube. A baked chicken breast, brown rice pilaf, and broccoli appeared on the plate and the goblet filled with water.

How freakin' amazing! Things appeared and disappeared around here all the time, but here was someone who could actually make it happen whenever and however he wanted. He knew the rules.

A magical talking cat with an attitude.

This was going to be either really bad or really good.

"Cool! Um, how about a cheeseburger, fries, and soda instead?" She so wasn't gonna let this egotistical beast know how blown away she was.

When you learn the trick of making food appear on your plate whenever you wish, then you can have all the cheeseburgers, fries, and sodas you like, Asmodius replied, flicking his tail.

"Oh, right, like I'll ever be able to do that."

Au contraire, ma petite! That is the most basic magic any successful being learns. It's called making a living, manifesting your desires. And what ever happened to the magic words, "Thank you so much, this looks delicious."?

"Thank you," Molly said through clenched teeth. He made "manifesting your desires" seem so simple.

It wasn't.

All she wanted was to be safe and sound back in Massachusetts with her Mother and Dad where she belonged. How was she gonna manifest that?

You are most welcome. One last thing...

The candle wick burst into flame.

There. Ambiance is everything, don't you think?

"Oh, most definitely." Molly was surprised to find that she was grinning. She pulled her gaze away from the cheerfully burning candle, sat down, snatched up the large, wineglass-shaped goblet and drained it. It refilled the moment she set it down. Plain, fresh water had never tasted so good. Then she attacked her dinner. It wasn't a cheeseburger and fries, but it was still food, and food always made her feel better.

Well, shall we be going? Asmodius asked as she finished devouring her meal.

"Now? But I'm tired."

Remember to bring your plate, chalice, and silverware. You'll need them when you get hungry again, Asmodius said, and strolled out of the garden.

"Hey! Come back here!"

The cat ignored her.

—

Portland, Oregon

"You did what?!" Althea couldn't believe her ears. She was sitting in her friend's kitchen sharing a pot of green tea. A wall of windows opened onto a stunning view of Portland and the West Hills drowsing in the August sun.

Estelle Adair shifted in her seat. "I didn't think they'd take her so soon."

"You two just got here a few days ago! And how could you even imagine it would be a good idea to send a grieving sixteen-year-old off to Damia with no one but Asmodius for guidance?"

"She has The Chair."

"Pish, The Chair is a pompous idiot," Althea replied, and continued her rant. "They fight wars there at the drop of a helmet. I've heard there's one brewing now. She could be killed, raped, or lost. You may never see her again."

Her friend's ice blue eyes brimmed with tears, and her wispy, gray curls drooped uncharacteristically. Worry lines creased her brow and the corners of her mouth. But her spine was broomstick straight.

The two mages glared at each other across the table.

Estelle sighed and took a sip of tea. Dashing the tears from her eyes with the back of her hand, she regarded her old friend intently, as if trying to decide how much to confide. Estelle always avoided emotional, soul-baring conversations. They offended her pragmatic sensibilities. Apparently she decided to make an exception this time, and squaring her already square shoulders, she said, "Two months ago during a jump into the future I heard about the plane crash. I called David and warned him not to take that flight to the Amsterdam conference. All three of them were going. He wouldn't listen. He hated having me interfere in his life. I finally managed to talk him into leaving Molly at home."

Althea reached across the table and patted her friend's clenched fists. There had been a rift between Estelle and her only child. David left home when he started college and had never set foot in the house again. He called and then e-mailed occasionally, but he kept the width of the country between them, even after Molly was born.

Estelle blew her nose on a pristine handkerchief. "I wish they would have been willing to let me share more of their lives. I hardly know Molly. She's clueless about magic, which is worrisome because her aura positively bristles with mage energy. What's happening to all that power? I can't talk to her about it because she fidgets and glares whenever I try, and ignores me whenever possible. We fight constantly. All she wants to do is play computer games. She's as stubborn as her father."

And her grandmother, thought Althea.

She had never had children, but she'd listened to friends who were parents of teens wail and complain about pretty much these same things on countless occasions. This sounded like fairly normal teenage behavior to her.

"But this is more than normal teen angst and surliness," Estelle continued as if she'd read her mind. "She's cutting herself."

Althea gasped. Yes, there was definitely a problem.

"Again, she wouldn't talk to me about it, so I couldn't help her." Estelle set down her mug with a decisive click. "She has a tough, adventurous spirit that kicks at things to see what they're made of and how far they'll give. Having her moping around the house with nothing to do until school started would have driven both of us crazy."

Looking up at Althea, she continued, "I meditated and did several readings on the problem, and I always came up with the same answer—'Ask the Webmasters to take her on a trek through Damia. She needs a challenge to pull her out of this.'".

2

The High Priestess

o, where're we going that's so important it couldn't wait?" Molly asked as she limped down the dirt road after Asmodius. Her feet throbbed, her inner thighs were rubbed raw, and she had a headache. She didn't really care where they were going, but she felt like she should ask, like she was in a play and this was her next line.

I have a friend I'd like you to meet.

The occasional bird trilled briefly from the depths of the forest and afternoon sun slanted down through the trees, creating long, black shadows separated by brilliant bars of light; the air smelled cool and green and alive with possibility.

Ah, here we are. I believe she's camped just a bit farther on.

They turned left onto a narrow, overgrown path and arrived in a clearing inhabited by two peacefully grazing horses and a deep blue caravan. A white full moon bracketed by two crescent moons and surrounded by strange symbols floated on its side panel. The back door was draped with a gaudy tapestry and a slender woman sat on the steps in front of it. She was dressed in a rumpled white smock that revealed ample cleavage and a long blue cloak that trailed off past the wagon and into the forest. It rustled and shifted and, when the sunlight hit it just right, it sparkled.

"Ah, Asmodius, my friend," she said in a voice that sent shivers shimmying up and down Molly's spine, "who have you brought me this time?"

Greetings Madame Rue, this is Molly Adair.

Molly stared into an ageless face surrounded by a tangled mass of midnight black hair. Ebony eyes x-rayed her. The gypsy smiled a smile that wasn't a smile and a gold-capped eyetooth gleamed balefully.

This was not a nice woman. Not that she was evil or mean. No, that wasn't it at all. She was aloof and otherworldly, and gave the distinct impression that she had been places most people would never dare to go—and if they did, most of them wouldn't come back with anything resembling sanity. And she managed to convey, with one freaky glance, that she wouldn't hesitate to send Molly somewhere like that if she thought it might be a good idea.

"What'sa matter, Dearie, cat got your tongue?" Madam Rue's laugh echoed eerily through the clearing.

Dark fear boogied down in the pit of Molly's stomach. Asmodius was cranky and full of himself, but this woman was terrifying.

"Uh, afternoon, Ma'am," Molly said. "Asmodius says you might be able to tell me how to get back to my own world."

"Aye, Dearie, that I can. But a telling ain't cheap. You must first cross my palm with silver." She held out a skeletal hand tipped with long black fingernails studded with tiny silver stars.

What do I do? I don't have any money.

Check your pack.

Molly rummaged through her pack and found a collection of copper, gold, and silver coins in the side pocket. How much were they worth in this world? Was this a fortune or lunch money? With a shaking hand, she picked out a silver piece and placed it in the gypsy's palm. Madame Rue gave her a look that turned her insides to ice water. Her hand remained open and expectant. Molly quickly added two more silvers.

"Very generous," cooed the seer, slipping the coins into her bodice, "Now give me your hand."

The forest went still as Madame Rue held Molly's hand palm up and drew her cold, dry index finger over its lines. Molly shivered and looked up. The tapestry had turned to gauze. Shadowy shapes stirred and shifted restlessly behind it. Occasionally the fabric would twitch, as if they were impatient to be let out. A slender, elegant sword materialized out of the curtain and floated in front of it. The hilt was wrapped with a satiny, auburn cord and blood dripped in a continuous stream off its exquisite point. Her gut clenched with terror and, oddly enough, desire.

She couldn't take her eyes off that sword.

"You have started on a journey, but you don't know how to proceed." The woman's voice flowed through the forest.

Oh great, tell me something I don't know.

"Patience, Dearie, patience. A telling must be done in the proper order. I will tell you where you need to go, but…" She let go of Molly's hand, "I'll be needing a bit more coin. One of those wee gold ones will do just fine."

Molly placed one of her two gold coins in the gypsy's outstretched palm and glanced up at the curtain. It was a tapestry again, but it still twitched alarmingly. The sword had vanished.

"Um, what's behind the curtain?" Molly asked.

"Ah, now there be a question worth asking. And because you've been so generous with a poor, old woman, I'll even answer it. Behind that curtain dwell memories of things past, things present, and things yet to come."

"Whose memories?"

"Yours, mine, and everyone who's ever been and ever will be."

Molly snorted in disbelief. She'd seen some bizarre things in Damia, but this was impossible. However, she needed answers, so she played along.

"Cool. Where'd you find them?"

"I didn't," Madame Rue replied, "they found me."

But what if the gypsy *could* listen to all those memories? And what if Molly could somehow learn to do it? That would be so awesome. She'd know everything and could figure out how to get back to Portland in no time.

"How can I get them to find me? Can I pay you for them or something?"

"Why pay for something you already have. They be part and parcel of you and everyone else. You just haven't figured out how to get hold of 'em yet."

"So, can you tell me how?"

"No."

This wasn't going well.

"Can you show them to me?"

"I'll let you see one of them, if you look into my eyes."

Not quite what she was after, but she'd take it. Molly shifted her gaze from the twitching tapestry and the gypsy's glittering eyes locked onto hers. The world went black and started to spin. Blacker shadows twisted and turned and vanished as new ones swooped in and exploded in tiny multicolored bursts of light. A high-speed gibbering sang in her ears. There was no up nor down, nor front nor back, nor in nor out, nor left nor right, nor now nor then. She was going nowhere fast.

"A mite confusing, ain't it, Dearie?" Madame Rue's voice rasped into her mind like the coarse side of a nail file. "So many memories wanting to be remembered. You must reach for the one you want and only that one. More'n one of these memories in your pretty head at once wouldn't be real good for you."

Shadows of memories flicked past, some felt familiar and some were strange, but one sparkled and gleamed and Molly grabbed for it like a frightened child reaching for safety.

It felt familiar, yet cool and distant.

It was her mother's last memory.

The moment she touched it Molly landed inside her with a jolt, sensing everything her mother felt and did, like an invisible hitchhiker. She and her mother were listening to the drone of air-plane engines and the hiss of air as it slipped over the hull. Molly couldn't remember when she'd felt so peaceful and content, and she relaxed into this alien feeling with a sigh. Was this what it was like to be totally grown up? Judging from the worried, preoccupied looks her parents and teachers usually wore, she doubted it. No, her mother was happy because she was on a working vacation with her husband.

"David, we've got to do something about Molly."

Mother's head was resting on Dad's shoulder and his familiar scent of leather and lime soap triggered a cascade of memories that tore at Molly's heart.

Dad looked up from one of his endless medical journals. "Molly's fine. She's just gained a little weight. Her GPA was 4.0 last time I checked."

Actually, she'd just barely squeaked by with a 2.0 last term. Dad would have been so disappointed and Mother would have been furious.

"She's not! She looks like death warmed over. And all she does is play computer games."

Molly was surprised her mother had noticed. She was hardly ever home and, when she was, she seldom paid any attention to her.

"I've found an adventure camp for her this summer. It will challenge her and get her outside and socializing with other teens."

Noooooo! Mother, I love you. I know I'm fat and ugly and a total disappointment, but I would have done anything—lost weight, cut down on my computer hours—anything—to keep you from sending me away.

Dad was adjusting his already perfect, white silk shirt cuffs. He always did that when he didn't agree with you and was lining up his arguments. "Molly won't like that," he finally said. "If anything, I think we should be spending more time with her, not less."

Yes! Talk her out of it.

The drone of the engines turned to a stutter. Her mother's heart pounded with fear as she searched for the problem. A deafening bang rocked the plane and the starboard engine burst into flames that streaked back from the wing. The cabin exploded into terrified screams that nearly drowned out the captain's voice on the intercom telling everyone to remain calm and stay seated. The plane lurched to the right. Mother screamed and reached for her husband.

The plane rolled into a tight downward spiral.

A cabin attendant who hadn't made it back to her seat slammed against the ceiling and then ricocheted around the cabin like a screaming pinball. Molly watched in horror as passengers were jerked and tossed against their seatbelts like manic jazz dancers.

Her dad managed to get the armrest up and pulled her mother close against him. She buried her face his shoulder and wept in great gasping sobs. "David, I love you so much," Molly's empty, aching heart filled with that love.

The cabin roared with terror and smelled of puke and panic.

Another explosion and bright, electric fear ripped through her.

Quick, searing pain.

Then nothingness.

She floated calm and free in blessed blackness. To her left a blacker blackness began moving toward her. The Shadow. It morphed into a tall figure draped in a long, hooded cape. Stabbing red eyes latched onto her with fierce intensity and she fled screaming through endless space. The Shadow followed. It never got any closer, but it never got any farther away.

A rumble vibrated through the blackness.

What was that? The airplane again? She followed the sound back and back until an irresistible current tugged her into her body.

There was no plane, just Asmodius purring, although it must have been difficult since she was curled around him, clutching him to her chest and shaking with sobs. Tears streamed down her cheeks and onto the cat's black, silky fur. It felt so good to finally just cry. Like every tear was washing away some of the black emptiness that shadowed her every thought and feeling, letting in a touch of light and fresh air.

And then came the memories.

Her dad—dark and handsome in slacks and sport coat, heading out the door to work.

Her mother—dragging burgundy-tipped fingers through her gorgeous mane of flaming red hair and tapping data into an array of computers in her lab.

Walking into the living room and finding her parents making out on the couch.

Her dad—laughing as he tossed her into the air and spun her around.

The sound of surf and the coconut smell of suntan lotion. Shoveling hot sand into a red plastic pail. Her parents sitting on either side of her holding hands.

The smell of damp earth and herbs as she helped Dad weed their tiny garden that always produced an amazing amount of zucchini squash, but never enough tomatoes.

Quiet dinners at home—the chink of tableware, the mouth-watering aroma of fresh baked bread and vegetable soup.

And hundreds more.

They paraded in quick succession through her mind and into her heart.

Finally the last tear oozed out. The cat stirred in her arms and she looked into a pair of reproachful, golden eyes.

"Oops, sorry," she said, releasing him from her death grip.

The big cat stood up, shook, stretched, and began licking himself dry.

"Um, thanks for bringing me back."

No problem. Asmodius concentrated intently on his grooming.

Molly stretched out on the warm grass and let the world seep slowly in.

"Welcome back, Dearie. Nice trip?"

Molly stared up into Madame Rue's gimlet gaze. Trip? It had been a total freak-out. She felt like she'd been put through a shredder. But now she was finally able to not only grieve for the two wonderful people who had been her parents but also face the fact that she had spent her entire sixteen years trying desperately to earn just a fraction of the love that her mother had lavished on her dad.

If only she'd had more time.

But that was none of this madwoman's business.

"It sucked," she replied. "How did you do it?"

"Ah, that be a mystery."

"But it…"

"Enough. I'm done."

"But you never told me how to find my way back."

"Just follow my cloak, Dearie." Madame Rue stood and stepped up into the caravan, which immediately disappeared. All that remained was the shifting, rustling train of her cloak.

"Now that was one scary woman," Molly said, gazing in awe at the spot where the caravan had been. "Where'd you find her?"

The cat began to reply, but a bemused expression came over his face and his tail switched irritably back and forth a few times. *I don't know. It seems like I've always known her. But I do know that we'd better start following this fabric. It may not stay put very long.*

Molly and Asmodius followed the sparkling blue cloth until it began to gurgle and splash around the rocks and sticks in its path, turning into a small stream that flowed along next to the road. She felt The Shadow gliding close behind them and fear spiked through her heart.

But when she turned around, there was nothing there.

3

The Empress

 few miles past Madame Rue's camp, they came upon a house. The first story was built of river rock and the upper story was made of timber and stucco and roofed with thatch. Smoke rose lazily from the river rock chimney and flowers glowed in well-tended beds.

Molly quickened her pace toward the first sign of civilization she'd seen since she'd been dumped into this nightmare. She was exhausted and she hurt all over.

"D' you think I could talk whoever lives there into letting me spend the night?"

I imagine that for a price they'd be glad to have you. This is an inn.

"No, it can't be, it's just a house."

It's not a very big inn, but I doubt they'd have put up that sign if it weren't.

There was, actually, a sign over the door which featured the head and shoulders of a woman. Her hair was the color of ripe wheat, her eyes were violet-blue, her dress was emerald-green, and she wore a crown of twelve silver stars. Under the picture, the artist had printed "The Queen's Inn," although it was unlikely that a queen had ever slept here.

"How much will it cost?"

You can afford it.

"Where did the money in my pack come from—will it replace itself?"

The Webmasters put it there, and it won't replace itself.

OK, this might not be a game, but this part was like WarCraft Universe. You started with a certain amount of money and earned more as you needed it, and you checked in and out of all sorts of strange-looking inns. She'd done this a hundred times; it would be easy.

"I'm gonna go see about a room."

A sensible decision. I hear my dinner rustling and squeaking in the stable. I'll see you in the morning.

Molly opened the inn's heavy oak door and walked into a scene straight out of WarCraft Universe.

Except for the smell.

WarCraft Universe didn't smell.

The place reeked of wood smoke from a fire blazing in a fireplace that was big enough to roast a whole cow. A pot of something simmered over the flames, wafting out aromas of garlic and cooking meat. Although the inn was scrupulously clean, the sharp, earthy smell of spilled ale and unwashed humanity still managed to prevail. As Molly's eyes adjusted to the dimness, she saw that there was an abundance of both these things. A crowd of men occupied the rough wooden tables. All of them wore leggings and tunics of coarse, brown cloth and looked like they'd just come in from a day of working in the fields. The room buzzed with animated, ale-infused conversation, which ceased abruptly the moment everyone caught sight of Molly. They froze, pewter tankards of ale poised midway to their lips, and eyed her with a hungry hostility that creeped her out.

The silence was broken by a chocolate-flavored contralto voice. "And what can I do for you, dahling?"

A statuesque woman was leaning seductively on the bar, her modest cleavage peeking out from under a spotless, white silk under-gown with ruffled sleeves and a lace-up overdress of elegant red brocade. Rhinestones shimmered at her ears and throat. Her hair was long, black and intricately styled. Thick lashes fluttered playfully at Molly.

But wasn't that a five o'clock shadow?

And weren't those shoulders just a little too broad?

And, so, how did "she" get her chest to do that?

Molly pulled her gaze from the mysterious décolletage and looked up into the innkeeper's eyes. One perfectly tweezed eyebrow arched archly at her and ruby red lips formed a mocking smile. "A properly fitted corset is a girl's best friend, don't you think? I'm Blanche Darkness and I run this place. Now, if you're done staring, you can tell me who you are and what you want."

She pouted prettily and fluttered her eyelashes again. If she was surprised to see a twenty-first century, teenage girl in an Elizabethan-era tavern, she didn't show it.

Molly closed her mouth and cleared her throat. "I'd like dinner and a room for the night."

"She'll be needin' some clothes too, no doubt," said one of the men as he leered at Molly.

The others at the table guffawed, but their eyes devoured her greedily.

Molly's skin crawled. She had not had a good day, and the last thing she wanted to do was deal with these jerks. But it didn't look like she was going to get any help from the innkeeper, who was simply watching with detached amusement. So she imagined herself turning into the biggest, meanest WarCraft Universe ogre she could imagine, turned to face her boorish admirers, and jammed her fists onto her hips.

"Leave me alone!"

You'd have thought she'd suddenly sprouted three heads and fangs or something. Their eyes went wide with surprise and one guy dropped his tankard on the flagstone floor. It clanged loudly into the silence.

The man who had spoken was on his feet in an instant. Grabbing the front of her tank top, he pulled her up close to his battered face.

"Who d'ya think yer talkin' to, ya fat slut? I've a mind to beat some respect into that sassy snoot 'o yours." Fumes of ale, onions, and rotten breath turned her stomach.

But before Molly could even think about defending herself, an exquisite, single-edged dagger with a wicked sharp point appeared at the man's throat. Molly and her attacker turned in surprise and looked into a pair of wicked sharp green eyes. Molly looked back at the dagger in horrified fascination. It was a beautifully made thing of gleaming steel that rippled with subtle patterns. Its perfect point drew a deep red bead of blood as it pressed into the stubbly, pimply neck.

Oh the things she could do with that knife.

"Let her go, Wilf—and get out," the innkeeper said in a voice even sharper than her blade.

The man released Molly's top, shoved her away, and slammed out of the inn, snarling curses.

The innkeeper glared at her remaining customers. "Nobody except me beats on anybody at the Queen's Inn. Understand?"

The men mumbled assent, but continued staring at Molly. Molly stared at the knife.

Blanche's red leather shoes tip-taped on the flagstones as she walked behind the bar, tucking the knife back into her belt. "Supper, a room, and breakfast cost seven coppers, and you'll pay me now, just in case it slips your mind in the morning."

Molly paid up and was rewarded with a hollowed-out loaf of bread filled with a ladle full of stew, a polished horn spoon, and one of the ubiquitous tankards of ale. She stumbled over to the only empty table and sat down with her back against the wall. Ignoring the silence and the stares, she choked down some of her dinner, although, for once, she was anything but hungry. The stew was bland but edible, and the bread was brown and coarse. The ale was awful. The words "horse piss" came to mind.

Everyone soon lost interest in her, and the three men at the table next to hers moved on to a more exciting topic.

"Dija hear about those folks wot disappeared down in Tavish County?"

"Yep, an' nearly half a herd a' cattle too. An' they say that the ones wot were left were so crazy with fear that they had ta put 'em down, poor buggers."

There was a moody silence as the men at the table contemplated the fate of the missing people and livestock.

"I was talkin' to my sister and she says that the healer in Piqua—ya know, that liddle town just north of Bontare—she went missin' too. Just yesterday."

"Brigga's bloody blades, that's awful close. Wot's the world commin' to?"

Another silence as they drank to the state of the world.

Molly reached into her pack and pulled out the chalice. *Asmodius can I have some water?*

Immediately the chalice filled with clear, fresh water.

Finally—something had gone right.

Thanks.

You are welcome.

"Beggin' your pardon, miss," a shy voice said.

Molly looked up to see a girl about her age.

"I'm Bonnie Buttercup. I work here. Mind if I sit down?"

"No problem."

Bonnie set herself and her dinner down and began to eat with the avid concentration of the truly hungry. When she had finished every last morsel, she looked over at the rest of Molly's meal. "Aren't you gonna eat that? Can I have it?"

Molly shoved it over.

"Those clothes you've got on look real comfortable." Bonnie said after she'd eaten every last crumb. "Do all the girls wear stuff like that where you come from?"

"Sure."

"And men don't bother you?"

"'Course not. Why should they? They're just clothes."

"Well, they're gonna bother you here. Blanche is worried. The men around here ain't used to seeing young ladies dressed in hardly anything, and they'll think you're no better'n you should be, if you take my meaning. I've got some nice clothes that might fit you an' I need some extra coin. I'll sell 'em to you for a silver piece."

"I'll think about it. Um, how many copper pieces in a silver piece?"

"Ye Gods! It's a lucky thing you stopped here before you got to the city. They'da robbed you blind. There be ten coppers to a silver and ten silvers to a small gold."

Madame Rue had been expensive. She hoped it had been worth it.

"Let's go to my room so I can show you the clothes."

Bonnie had a tiny room off the kitchen. There was a cot and a clothes chest that doubled as a seat. A long green dress with purple slashes in the sleeves and skirt was hanging from one of the hooks by the door. The white chemise meant to go under it was hanging beside it.

"Cool dress." Molly gently ran her fingers over the soft material. "Where will you wear it?"

"The queen's comin' next week. We're the first place she visits on her summer progress."

"What's a progress?"

"Every spring Queen Flora goes around all the twelve counties that make up Damia. That's the progress, see. She sorta gets reacquainted with the land an' everyone again. An' the land gets better an' more beautiful an' the crops grow better an' we get to feelin' better an' happier. Folks come from all over ta see her. It's a weeklong holiday with lots o' music 'n dancing 'n feasting. This year I get ta be one of the group wot carries the county crest up to her so she can bless it."

"You get to meet a queen? Sweet! What's a county crest?"

"It's a shield-like thing with pictures on it. It stands for that county. Our county's County Crue, and we're famous for our produce and forests, so our crest has a horn o' plenty with all sorts o' fruits and vegetables spillin' out of it and an oak tree. When the queen blesses it with a touch, the blessin' goes through the crest and out into the county. A friend's mum got to take the crest up one year an' she said when the queen touches the crest you feel this jolt like lightnin' come up through you and back down into the ground again. An' the folks that take the crest to the queen don't ever get sick for at least a year afterwards."

Yeah, right.

"Now, here's my extra dress," Bonnie said, pulling a full-length blue cotton dress with long sleeves, tie-up bodice, and white under tunic out of the chest. Molly looked at Betsy's trim figure and decided that the dress would be way too tight. And it would be hot and she'd be tripping over the skirt with every other step. And it wouldn't keep her thighs from rubbing together.

"Uh, thanks, Bonnie, but I think I'll pass."

❧

Up in her room, Molly bolted the door and leaned back against the solid wood, but fear and loneliness crept in anyway and wrapped themselves tightly around her. As tears streamed over her cheeks and trickled down into her cleavage, she wished for about the hundredth time that day that her parents were still alive and that she wasn't trapped in this warped version of WarCraft Universe. You never knew when something was going to appear or disappear. Cats were smarter than you were and talked into your brain. And at the blink of a gypsy's eye, dark, precious memories filled your heart and left you shattered. Her exhausted mind began to spin and she collapsed onto the cot...

❧

And woke up running for her life. Black trees loomed out of the murky dimness and reached for her with crooked branches. Their roots snaked out onto the trail making every step a danger. Her breath came in tortured gasps and her legs were lead weights. Asmodius appeared on a branch in front of her.

"You'll never make it, you know," he said as she skidded to a halt.

"Help me!"

The cat stared down at her and faded away, leaving nothing but two golden eyes floating above her. And then those eyes became two red, stabbing pin points of light.

Molly shrieked and bolted away, tripping and stumbling on the uneven ground. As she rounded a bend in the trail she spotted a woman dressed in emerald green and wearing a starry crown. It was the queen—she would protect her. Molly raced toward her, but no matter how fast she ran, she could never catch up.

"Wait! Please!"

The queen looked back, but never stopped. "Not now dear, I have a plane to catch."

"Nooooooo. Don't."

Are you intending to sleep the day away? I've been up for hours and have had one or two naps already. Asmodius' voice startled her awake and she opened her eyes—then squeezed them shut against the sunlight beaming in through the open window. Rotten cat.

"Good for you."

Get your breakfast and let's go.

The smell of frying bacon from the inn's kitchen below wafted in on a warm breeze, making her mouth water and her stomach rumble. And...could it be? She sniffed again.

Yes! They had coffee here.

"In a minute."

Every muscle in her body screamed in agony as she staggered over to a small wooden table with a bowl and pitcher of water on it. Unfortunately, the pain didn't make her nerves tingle with pleasure and relax her into a happy puddle. It just hurt—lots. Yesterday's aches and pains had brought her no joy either. For the first time in months she wasn't craving something sharp to help her face the day.

But some ibuprofen would be nice.

She poured cold water from the pitcher into the basin, rinsed her face, and finger-combed her tangled hair. Grabbing the ugly pack, she gimped down the back stairs to the privy.

I see you ignored Blanche's advice. Asmodius lashed his tail back and forth as Molly hobbled out of The Queen's Inn munching a bacon sandwich.

She paused for a moment in the warm sunshine and allowed herself to contemplate her bizarre situation. If someone had told her yesterday that this morning she would be standing in front of a real, live Elizabethan inn arguing about proper attire with an obnoxious black cat who was probably quite capable of turning her into a mouse and torturing her to death, she would have been sure they were just messing with her.

Then she did the only logical thing. She counter-attacked.

"Why didn't you tell me that the Queen's Inn is run by a drag queen? I thought I was gonna lose it when I saw her stubble."

I thought I'd let you figure it out for yourself. Blanche is pretty much indescribable anyway. Now, why didn't you buy yourself a set of decent clothes? That's why I brought you here.

"Bonnie is at least two sizes smaller than me. The dress would've been a straight-jacket and I would've cooked in it. And besides, I should be able to wear whatever I want."

They don't have sizes here. You're close enough to Bonnie's height that a lace-up bodice dress would have fit just fine. You would have figured that out if you had bothered to try it on.

"Since when do you know so much about women's clothes and how do you know I didn't try it on?"

I am a cat of many talents and you are a foolish girl. Don't come crying to me when we get to Bontare. Queen Flora will certainly not be impressed.

"I'll get to see the queen?"

You will get to meet both Queen Flora and King Alexander. Hopefully they won't kick you out of the palace when they see that outfit.

Like she really cared what they thought of her clothes.

"Bonnie was telling me about the queen. She can't really heal people with just a touch, can she?"

Oh yes. Damia is one of the few kingdoms left in the multiverse where the king and queen still have a mystical bond with the land they rule. As long as they are healthy and happy, their kingdom is healthy and happy. The queen can draw an amazing amount of power from the earth.

"Sweet." But Molly was mentally rolling her eyes. How could you bond with a bunch of dirt? But then, she thought, how could a gypsy and her entire caravan disappear into thin air? "Maybe she'll fix my sore feet. The blisters just popped, I think. I hope it's not too far to Bontare."

We have another ten miles or so.

"You've got to be kidding. I'm not going a step farther. Find me a horse—or something to ride in." She sat down by the side of the road and took off her boots.

The blisters had popped.

You are walking to Bontare. The exercise will do you good, Asmodius said, looking pointedly at the roll of fat around her middle.

"No! My feet hurt."

I'll see you in Bontare, he replied, and stalked off down the road, tail in the air.

Molly glared at the cat's retreating butt and wished she had a BB gun. Muttering and cursing, she opened her pack and took out the extra pair of socks. The ones she had on were dirty and the heels were wet with blister goop. Two pairs of thin, silky socks and two Band-Aids lay in the bottom of the pack. Where had they come from?

"Thank you thank you," she said to no one in particular as she unwrapped the Band-Aids and applied them to the backs of her heels.

You're welcome, a voice replied as the wrappers disappeared with a soft pop.

"Who said that?" Molly looked up in alarm.

There wasn't a soul in sight.

She shivered and went back to her foot first aid. The thin socks were a puzzle, but Molly decided that if she put them on under her boot socks, they might keep her from getting more blisters.

She headed toward Bontare.

Soon she was sticky with sweat and the sun was probably making the freckles scattered across her nose even uglier. But the warmth and movement had eased her screaming muscles a bit and the Band-Aids and thin socks made walking less painful. The upland forest gradually gave way to a broad plain checkered with thriving orchards, meadows, and farms. She passed the occasional small house with a newly-planted kitchen garden. Then a village appeared with a tiny market place, tavern, and houses clustered around an open park-like area with a few artfully placed trees and a pond. A building that reminded Molly vaguely of the small country churches back in Massachusetts stood in the middle of the park.

She hadn't gone more than a few miles before she caught up with Asmodius ambling along the side of the road, and she fell into step beside him. As they approached the city, the villages got larger and closer together. The things that looked like churches were grander and the houses were fancier.

The closer they came to Bontare the more people there were. A few well dressed men on horseback passed them as they hurried toward the city, and they met the occasional roughly dressed farmer walking in the opposite direction.

"Everyone is staring at me."

Of course they're staring, you idiot.

"Can't they just get over it? Nothing's showing and I'm not bothering anyone."

These people are the salt-of-the-earth, but they have very definite ideas about what's decent and what isn't. They look at you and see a young woman walking around half naked and talking to a cat. Trust me, that isn't even close to their idea of decent.

Oh shit! The beast had a point.

You mean these people can't hear cats talking in their heads?

A few can, but the vast majority can't. Just like in your world.

I can't hear them in my world so how come I can hear you?

Because I am a very exceptional cat, and you are an exceptional girl.

Molly almost didn't remember to keep walking and not stop and stare at her companion. No one had ever told her that she was exceptional. Her parents were exceptional, but she had always figured she was just normal. She made good grades and was good at soccer, but not really exceptional.

So what makes me exceptional?

You have a much higher than average amount of magic around you.

How did it get there?

You were born with it.

So there's magic in my world?

There's magic everywhere, it's what binds everything together and makes it tick. Some places have more than others, and this world has more than most.

Magic was real and it was everywhere? For some inexplicable reason this made her heart lift with hope, and she looked around her with new eyes. If Asmodius could see magic in her, then she should be able to see it in him. She stared at her companion, but he looked just as black and solid and cranky as he always did.

Don't look straight at me, look around me and unfocus your eyes.

And there it was. A shimmer, like sparkly heat waves, surrounded Asmodius. As she watched in fascination, they flared out in black and purple flames.

Wow! Way cool! Do I look like that?

No, you look murky red. Now, quit staring at me and try to be inconspicuous. We're almost to Bontare.

Molly looked away from her darkly blazing guide and gasped in wonder. Below her a vast plain surrounded a city that looked like something out of a fairytale. Red tile rooflines marched uphill to a palace of honey-colored stone that glowed in the sunlight. Turrets roofed in the same red tile anchored the corners of the palace and green and gold banners were just visible fluttering from their peaks.

As they drew closer, Molly snorted in disgust. *Ugh! It smells like a sewer. How can the people stand it?*

It smells like a sewer because there are no sewers. Sanitary facilities are something that I haven't been able to convince the king and queen to install. But as far as its citizens are concerned, the excitement, glamour, and convenience more than make up for the odor.

The road had become quite busy and Molly and Asmodius joined the boisterous crowd pouring into the city. It was market day and the streets were packed. Molly's senses reeled with a heady mixture of roaring people, clucking chickens, lowing cattle, carts bumping over cobbles, people shoving and bumping into her, and the stink of sewage and rotting things. But she also smelled the mouthwatering aromas of cooking meat and fresh baked bread and pastries. Molly was always ready to eat.

I'm starving.

The market place is just a few blocks away. You can buy something to eat there.

"C'mere darlin' and gimme a feel!" A grimy, callused hand reached into her tank top and squeezed her nipple.

Pain jolted through her and she stared down at her chest in unbelieving horror. As she grabbed the hand out of her top and shoved its owner away, a man behind her slid his hand up under her shorts. Rage and helpless fear boiled up inside of her as she whirled around and slapped at him blindly. Molly fought her way down the street, desperately knocking aside groping hands and kicking at the shins of anyone who blocked her way. Cruel laughter echoed in her ears.

Asmodius! Where was that stupid cat? Couldn't he see she was in trouble? These people were monsters.

Up here.

Molly looked up and spotted Asmodius gliding over the roof tiles like a black shadow. When he came to a street, he simply leaped over it and landed gracefully on the roof of the opposite house. Unfortunately, looking up meant that she wasn't looking down, and she slipped on something slimy and began to fall into the stinking brownish-green muck that ran down a channel in the center of the street. A man caught her up from behind and began fondling her breasts and crotch. Screaming in outraged horror she jabbed backwards with her elbows and jerked away.

A boney hand grabbed Molly's arm and hauled her around until she found herself looking into a pair of angry eyes that were heavy with makeup and hopelessness. "Just wot d'ya think yer doin'? This is my patch. Go find yer own." Before Molly could swallow her fear and reply, the woman shoved her roughly away. She fell against a well-dressed matron who looked at her in disgust and headed off down the street.

Stupid. Stupid. Why hadn't she listened to Bonnie and Asmodius? She'd been so sure they were just blowing smoke.

Can't you do something? These people are all sex fiends.

They aren't sex fiends. Actually, they think you're a sex fiend. I would like to take this opportunity to remind you that I warned you about this and you ignored me.

Oh, shut up! She pressed on, slapping and kicking at hopeful customers. The market place was gonna be even more crowded.

I'm not hungry. Let's go to the palace.

As you wish. Follow me.

Keeping the shadow on the rooftops in sight, she fought her way uphill through the stinking, grasping crowds. A sick, dirty feeling coiled in her belly.

Molly, have a care for your pack. Bontare is crawling with pickpockets.

A grubby young man bumped into her and caught her off balance. As she reached back for the wall, bringing her pack within his reach, she heard a stifled yelp and turned to see him rubbing his hand and staring at her with huge, frightened brown eyes.

I can't be protecting you all the time. Pay attention.

Just as the youth turned to disappear into the crowd, Molly saw the solution to at least one of her problems and grabbed him by the back of his tunic.

"Stop right now or I'll hurt your other hand even worse."

He stopped. And, looking back at her pitifully, he wiped his runny nose on his sleeve and whined, "Please Miss, lemme go! I'll not dip inta another pocket for as long as I breathe!"

Yeah right.

"Not till you give me your clothes. I'll pay you for them," she replied.

"Wha? I just pinched—er—got these. They're the bestest clothes I ever had!"

"Yeah, they're real nice." Molly dragged him into an empty alley and shielded the entrance as he reluctantly stripped off his new clothes and gave them to her. They weren't much, just a brown cotton tunic and leggings with a plain leather belt, but they were well made and the tunic had pockets. She put a silver piece into the boy's hand and shoved him out into the street. Then she slipped into her new outfit, moved all her coin into the front pocket of the tunic, and shrugged into her pack.

Excellent! You make a fairly convincing young man.

So, was that a compliment or an insult? Molly glared up at the beast and trudged uphill toward the palace. She found that as a roughly-dressed, grubby young man she was suddenly invisible.

❧

The guards bowed and opened the palace gate wide as soon as they saw Asmodius. The big cat strode past them and led Molly through a maze of musty smelling stone corridors dimly lit by an occasional torch and inhabited by busy palace servants. Many twists and turns later, they came out into a large garden.

After the dimness, the garden exploded into Molly's senses like fireworks on the Fourth of July. Lush, green grass and stone-paved paths connected beds of jewel-like flowers of every size and shape. Tall, skinny evergreens towered picturesquely in the background. A stream gurgled and splashed over an artfully placed water-feature and disappeared under the opposite wall. An obviously pregnant woman sat on a stone bench in the center of the garden. She radiated such beauty, peace, and raw power that Molly knew without a trace of doubt that this was Queen Flora, and she was amazed to find herself grinning stupidly and hurrying toward her.

"Greetings, Asmodius. And who have you brought us this time?" The violet eyes smiled as she reached out and took both Molly's hands, then clouded with worry. "Your clients always seem to presage some sort of trouble, and I feel this one is no exception."

If there is trouble ahead, your Majesty, hopefully we shall be able to assist in some small way. Allow me to present Molly Adair. Molly, this is Her Royal Majesty, Queen Flora.

Molly managed to bow clumsily and say, "Pleased to meet you, Your Highness."

"And I am pleased to meet you as well, my dear." Queen Flora rose and touched Molly's cheek. "May the power of this land bring you comfort and healing."

Power surged up out of the earth and into her body. Her aches and pains melted away and her blisters tingled as they healed. The soul-sickening memory of being groped and manhandled all the way through the city faded. It was still there, but the nasty, sharp edges were gone.

Way cool. Bonnie had been right.

Molly gazed up into the queen's gentle eyes in awe. Her mother, in all their sixteen years together, had never looked at her like this. The Queen of Damia, who had only known her a few seconds, actually saw her; actually got who she was. And her radiant smile told Molly in no uncertain terms that the queen knew that she was totally amazing and that she could accomplish great things. It allowed her to entertain the thought that she actually belonged somewhere and had people who loved her.

It gave her hope.

If only she could be sure Queen Flora was right, and if only she could find that amazing Molly; then maybe everything wouldn't seem so pointless. But how was she supposed to do that with a demon cat dragging her all over creation and The Shadow lurking around scaring the piss out of her?

"I know you must be tired," the queen continued, gently squeezing Molly's shoulder. "Perhaps Asmodius will show you to a guestroom where you can freshen up and rest. I was just going to get dressed for the king's reception for his advisers. In fact, you may be interested in attending."

Molly blinked and mentally shook herself back into the now as she realized that some sort of response was required of her.

"Thank you, Your Highness, I'd like that."

And surprise, surprise; she was actually sort of interested in going.

"I will see you there then," the queen said, and turned toward a pair of glass doors that opened into a comfortable sitting room.

4

The Emperor

he feather bed in Molly's room had silk sheets and the deep green comforter was littered with bright satin throw pillows. Hand-knotted carpets in dazzling designs covered the white marble floor and gleaming wooden chests waited to hold her belongings. On the bed lay a gorgeous light blue brocade overdress with a lace-up front and a celery green silk chemise. Matching slippers and a froth of white petticoats completed the outfit. But best of all, two large basins full of steaming hot water and a bar of soap were waiting for her on a marble-topped side table. The queen's palace was nothing like The Queen's Inn.

She stripped off all her clothes and put them by the door to be washed as Asmodius had suggested. Grabbing the washcloth she gazed down at her reflection in one of the basins of water. A filthy, careworn face that she barely recognized stared back at her. She scrubbed herself nearly raw, but she could still feel coarse, cruel hands groping her body in places only a lover should touch. Would she ever feel clean again?

She shuddered and looked around for something she could use as a towel and noticed that where her pack had been there was now a chair, and not just any chair. This was the blue plush chair that had disappeared out from under her, allowing her to fall into this nightmare. Draped across its back was a fluffy white bath towel. The Chair managed to look smug, repentant, and hopeful all at once as it sidled over to her with the towel. For a piece of furniture, this was no mean feat.

Molly was dumb-struck. Here was an obvious co-conspirator, partially responsible for all her problems, meekly offering her a towel. She didn't know whether to kick it or laugh at it. Considering the fact that she was naked and dripping, she settled for just snatching the proffered towel. "You ought to be ashamed of yourself; you helped them send me here. This place is dangerous, you know." Oh geez, now she was talking to the furniture.

The Chair exuded an aura of contrition and condolence.

"I don't suppose you'd take me back to Portland?"

The Chair managed to convey a regretful negative.

As she struggled into her new outfit, she decided that it probably wasn't The Chair's fault she was here. Her bets were still on Estelle.

"Thank you for the Band-Aids, they really helped."

Greetings, Molly! Who are you talking to? Asmodius materialized next to her.

Molly jumped and glared down at him. "Haven't you ever heard of knocking?"

Asmodius looked pointedly at his soft, black paws.

"OK, fine. At least think ahead at me or something before you come slinking into my room."

My apologies. In the future I will announce myself before entering your space. But, I repeat, who were you talking to?

"That Chair."

Asmodius looked at The Chair, which managed to look exactly like a chair.

I see.

"No, you don't see. That Chair is one of the reasons I'm here, and it used to be my backpack." Which made no logical sense at all. Molly looked at The Chair hoping for a bit of support, but it simply chaired back at her.

Ah, but I do see, said Asmodius. He walked around The Chair once, sniffed it, and grinned evilly. Unsheathing his razor sharp claws he began sharpening them vigorously on its upholstery. A wooden leg lashed out and Asmodius deftly avoided it. The Chair scuttled over to the other side of the room. *The Chair and I have a long history. Hello, old friend; up to your old tricks again, I see.*

The Chair turned its upholstered back to them and sulked.

Actually, I'm glad The Chair came along with you. It can be a bit testy at times, but it's quite resourceful and intelligent.

"I still don't trust it," Molly muttered.

Ah, well, I'm sure you two will eventually come to terms. I'm here to escort you to the king's audience chamber.

"Is he as wonderful as the queen?"

He's a good man, but he's a bit gruff and doesn't suffer fools gladly.

"I hope I don't say something stupid then."

So do I. Which reminds me, do you know how to curtsy?

"No."

Then I'll have to teach you, it's not difficult. Put your right foot behind your left foot.

Yes, like that.

Now, keep your back straight, bow your head, and spread your skirts out.

No, don't pull them up—that's a sign of disrespect.

OK, now bend your knees.

No, you're not supposed to lose your balance and stumble. Try it again.

Yes, that's it.

The longer you bend at the knee, the more respect you show, and you don't need to bow your head to anyone except the king or queen. And always curtsy again as the king and queen walk away. Oh, and never turn your back on royalty—there are many reasons for this. And don't speak unless spoken to. And shouldn't you adjust that chemise so it's not so low in the front?

"Oh, Asmodius, you're worse than my dad."

Pain and grief overwhelmed her as she remembered her dad grumpily critiquing her outfits before she went out with her friends. Asmodius and The Chair shimmered into ghostly transparency and she felt herself shimmering right along with them. The room faded.

Shit. This was not a good time for this.

The points on her nails had worn down, but the sting of her fingernails digging into the scabs on her palms snapped the world back into solid shapes. She really needed a knife. Asmodius was staring at her like she was a mouse. What had she been saying? Oh, yeah.

"Um, the neckline is just right. I checked out what the ladies were wearing as we were finding my room. Plunging necklines are apparently all the rage here. And, as you recently pointed out, 'When in Damia, do as the Damians do.'"

Asmodius relaxed. *Just because they go about ready to pop out of their bodices, doesn't mean you have to. But who am I to fly in the face of fashion?*

The Reception Hall was totally amazing and did nothing to calm Molly's jitters. It was a huge, long rectangle with the entryway at one end and two graceful wooden thrones on a raised dais at the other. They reminded Molly of the Danish Modern furniture in their living room back home, but she doubted her parents could have afforded these. Tall arched windows of clear glass that looked out on the palace gardens lined both sides of the chamber, and two rows of deep red stone pillars supported a vaulted stone ceiling and made an aisle down the length of the chamber. Four huge chandeliers filled with twinkling candles reflected off the polished black marble floor. Behind the thrones hung a breathtaking floor-to-ceiling tapestry depicting snow-covered peaks soaring up from a river valley. The two thrones were the only chairs in the room—perhaps a way of ensuring short, efficient meetings.

The hall slowly filled with gorgeously dressed nobles, simply dressed merchants and farmers, and black, white, and brown-robed priests. The conversations she overheard weren't friendly chitchat. They were quick exchanges of information about who supported who on what issue and how they could convince the king that this or that needed doing or funding. Everyone seemed so calm, like they did this every day, and maybe they did, but this was her first time and she felt totally awkward and dorky.

At some invisible signal, everyone lined up in two rows in front of the pillars. The doors at the far end of the room flew open dramatically and the king and queen began to advance down the aisle through the audience hall. A herald emerged and said in an almost conversational tone, which still carried to the far edges of the hushed crowd, "Citizens of Damia, behold and revere Queen Flora and King Alexander II!" The men bowed low and the women curtsied. Good thing she knew how.

Queen Flora wore a court gown of emerald-green satin edged in frothy white lace woven through with tiny ribbons of every color of the rainbow. Her white silk chemise was edged at the neck with pearls and emeralds. She smiled and waved to her subjects and stopped to speak with several of them.

King Alexander stalked beside her, his black knee boots made no sound on the marble floor. Piercing, ice-blue eyes surveyed his subjects over a hawk nose. A graceful iron crown nestled almost invisibly amongst his crisp, black curls; its eight points were each tipped by a golden bead. He was as tan and weather-beaten as any farmer in his kingdom and wore red leather dress armor over a white under tunic and red leggings. A cape of deepest purple was tacked to the shoulders of the armor with disc-shaped golden epaulettes stamped with rams' heads.

The king waited with thinly-veiled impatience as Queen Flora spoke with their subjects. However, when the couple came abreast of Molly, he stopped and turned to her. "Lady Adair, Queen Flora has informed me that you and Asmodius will be staying at the palace for a few days. I would like to take this opportunity to welcome you to Damia and invite you to dine with us and some other members of the court this evening."

Molly's heart pounded as she looked into those fierce, blue eyes and prepared to curtsy. If she screwed this up, he looked perfectly capable of whipping out that sword at his side and executing her on the spot, which, under the circumstances, might be the most merciful thing he could do. Everyone in the entire hall was watching.

She began her curtsy, over balanced, and lurched to one side. Almost before she knew she was falling, the king reached out and steadied her. His grip was like iron, but his eyes twinkled in amusement. Molly's cheeks turned hot.

Just kill me now, she pleaded silently as laughter rippled through the crowd.

He didn't.

She had to continue with this farce. She stood back up and stammered, "I-I'm uh honored to meet you, Your Highness, and I'd love to, um, dine with you this evening."

King Alexander patted her on the shoulder and moved on, his attention already focused on getting the audience started.

Queen Flora smiled at her. "You look lovely, my dear. That gown will be quite suitable for the banquet as well."

Curtsy! growled Asmodius.

Oops, she'd almost blown it again. She curtsied. This time it was perfect, but, of course, hardly anyone was watching.

When the royal couple took their places on the thrones, Asmodius was somehow already there, curled up comfortably on a pillow beside the queen.

Everyone followed the monarchs to the front of the hall and a tall, lean, middle-aged man draped in white robes stepped out from the crowd. Raising his arms, bent at the elbows and palms facing forward, he faced north and called. "Powers of the North, rulers of earth, be with us. Anchor this gathering with your stability and practicality."

Everyone in the hall faced north and said: "Be with us."

The air in the north quadrant of the hall seemed to solidify, and a feeling of safety and peace enveloped the room, followed by the smell of earth and growing things.

The priest faced east:

"Powers of the East, rulers of air, be with us. Bring us your gifts of clear communication and thought."

"Be with us."

A crisp breeze cleared the stuffiness from the hall.

"Powers of the South, rulers of fire, be with us. Bless us with your warmth and inspiration."

"Be with us."

The air in the South shimmered and radiated heat and rejuvenating energy into the gathering.

"Powers of the West, rulers of water, be with us. Infuse us with your gifts of compassion and empathy."

"Be with us."

The smell of cool water flooded the room with joy and peace.

The priest stood with his arms out to his sides, palms up, and called:

"Gods and Goddesses of Damia, we ask that you bless this gathering with your presence and love and guide us with your wisdom."

The hall rippled with power. He touched his right hand to his heart and raised it, palm up. Everyone repeated this gesture. The priest bowed to the king and queen and stepped back into the crowd. Molly was impressed. It was as if some invisible hand had reached in and tweaked the vibes in the room to make them perfect for this event.

The courtiers began their petitions. By the time the priest had returned to his place, one was already standing in front of the king, droning on about something.

Now what am I supposed to do? This is gonna be really boring and everyone will be laughing at me.

No they won't, they're too polite. And from what I've been able to gather from the palace gossip mill, this will be anything but *a boring session. Stand up straight and try to look intelligent. Speak when you are spoken to and pay attention. The king did you a huge service by stopping in the line to speak to you. Everyone will want to meet you since you obviously have his favor—even if you are a klutz. You'll meet the important players in Damia's government.*

Molly had no desire to meet important government officials. As she slunk through the crowd hoping that no one would notice her, the Lord of Roads and Bridges bowed low to his king and asked for money to build a bridge over a river that separated two cities and to pave the main streets in both cities. Other members of the court voiced their opinions about the project and a heated argument ensued.

Unfortunately, as Asmodius had predicted, many people introduced themselves and she got lots of practice curtsying and even stumbled through a few short conversations. And she began to understand how the government of Damia worked. As far as she could tell, the king *was* the government, but the opinions of his advisors and subjects helped him make his decisions. The people in the audience were mostly lords of this or that and high-ranking priests, but there were also a few county prefects here to push for projects and laws that would benefit their people. Merchants and farmers had come to file complaints against other merchants and farmers or to ask a special favor of the king. Some had been here for several weeks, waiting for their turn to speak.

Molly's overstretched nerves felt shifting undercurrents of tension washing through the hall. They focused on two men locked in conversation at the back of the hall. As Molly watched them, she felt a touch on her shoulder. She turned to see a short stocky man in a green and brown satin tunic and leggings and simple, brown boots.

"Allow me to introduce myself, Milady: I'm David Mudd, the Lord of Agriculture. The queen has arranged to have you seated next to my wife and me at the banquet this evening—if that pleases you. My wife, Sylvia, loves meeting new people, and perhaps we can help you through some of the intricacies of court dining."

Dropping a carefully calculated curtsy, she said, "Pleased to meet you. And thank you, I would be honored to sit next to you and your wife."

She was getting tired of being on display.

Lord Mudd smiled and continued, "Those two gentlemen you're watching are Phillip Fuller, Lord Treasurer, and General Wicket. Whenever they put their heads together, it bodes poorly for the farmer. I wonder what they're plotting now."

As Molly and Lord Mudd watched, the two men shook hands and a cloud crossed the sun, filling the hall with dim shadows. She shivered as the general turned and plodded toward the front of the hall.

After the king had made a decision on the bridge issue and several other questions, a young, plainly-dressed man moved toward the throne. Whispers and uneasy stares followed him.

"Your Highness," he said with an awkward bow, "I am the Prefect of Tavish County, and I've come to report a dragon."

Cries of alarm echoed through the hall and Molly remembered the conversation she'd overheard at the inn. Lord Mudd stiffened. "That's impossible," he said.

The king leaned forward. "Has someone actually seen it?"

"No, your highness."

"Then how do you know it's a dragon?"

"Well," he said, shifting from foot to foot, "we had several reports of missing persons and missing livestock. I began inquiries, but found nothing. They'd all disappeared without a trace and for no reason at all. And then," the prefect paused dramatically, "we found a dragon turd."

Cries of disgust and laughter rippled around the room.

The priest who had performed the opening ceremony stepped forward. "What makes you think that's what it is? Dragons are astral beings and therefore invisible in the material realm and not bound by any of its laws. I wasn't aware that dragons defecated."

"I wasn't aware that dragons existed at all," Lord Mudd whispered. "I thought they were just old wives' tales."

"What else could it be, Father? It's black and foul and as big as a haystack—and there are bones sticking out of it—all sorts o' cattle bones, and even a human skull!"

A horrified gasp and then silence.

A nobleman shouted, "Let's send out an army and kill the beast!"

Shouts of agreement. The hall buzzed with excitement.

"I wouldn't advise that, Your Highness," the priest said.

"Why is that, Father?" Was it Molly's imagination, or did King Alexander suddenly look like a boy who had been denied a trip to the beach?

Father Elysius turned to the people in the hall and asked, "Has anyone here seen a dragon?"

No one replied.

"Well I have." He turned back to the king.

"When they do incorporate, dragons are fire-breathing monsters with fangs and claws, just like in children's fairy tales. But you must see one for yourself to realize how mind-numbingly huge and intelligent they are. They move faster than lightning and their scales are so tough that nothing will pierce them. The fire they breathe is hotter than a smith's forge and their tempers are even hotter. If you were lucky, Your Highness, your army would never find the beast, because if it did, the dragon would proceed to destroy every last man and pick its teeth with their broadswords."

Cries of alarm rippled around the hall.

The king leaned forward and glared at the priest. "Then what do you suggest?"

The question dropped into a silent hall.

Seemingly unperturbed by either his angry king or his avid audience, the priest shoved his hands into the ample pockets of his robe and looked skyward.

"That depends upon what sort of dragon it is, Your Highness," he finally said. "Wild dragons steer clear of humans. We only know of them because they are mentioned in several reliable source books. If we are dealing with a wild dragon, it is probably one who has gone mad, in which case there is nothing we can do except pray that whatever is causing its madness will kill it quickly."

The hall exploded with cries of fear and panic.

"If it is a weredragon, which is a dragon that has attached itself to a human," the priest continued after everyone had calmed down, "and the chances are good that it is since they incorporate more frequently than the wild ones, the situation is more hopeful."

"You mean I've got a dragon hangin' around me and don't even know it?" a merchant asked nervously.

"It's possible. Many people are unaware of their dragons. They are selective about whom they choose to live with, and prefer mages because dragons are attracted to magic like iron filings to a lodestone, but many choose to live with non-mages as well—especially wealthy ones, since dragons are also fond of money and jewels and gold. Once a dragon chooses its human, it lives and dies with them through all their deaths and rebirths."

This was news to almost everyone, and dozens of excited conversations sprang up.

"So how can we defeat a weredragon?" the king asked, pulling the discussion back on track.

"We must kill its human—then the dragon will eventually die as well." the priest replied.

Cries of protest.

"That would be murder!" shouted a lawyer.

"Not really. According to Pythonius, the foremost expert on dragons, a weredragon is a mirror of its human's character. If a man is intelligent, his dragon will be more intelligent than other dragons. If a man is evil, his dragon, which is neither good nor bad to begin with, will become evil.

"Now, since weredragons are astral beings, they don't *need* to eat anything. That means this dragon is killing and eating cattle and humans just because it can, which tells us that its human has done the same thing—probably many times over. Killing this person would be just punishment, because he or she is a murderer and a danger to society."

Murmurs of both approval and disagreement swept through the crowd. The king gazed out over the hall, apparently deep in thought. He took off his crown, raked his fingers through his hair, and plopped it back on like it was a baseball cap.

"Father Elysius, I am putting you in charge of investigating this matter. I give you the authority to do whatever it takes to rid us of this beast, up to and including killing its human."

"I am your servant, Your Highness." The priest bowed low and moved to the back of the hall where he began questioning the prefect.

Courtiers and farmers alike were still heatedly discussing the decision as General Wicket approached the throne. He unrolled a map with his beefy hands, hung it on an easel, and placed it so that the king and a good portion of the audience could see it. When he was recognized, the General bowed low and began to speak.

Molly totally missed his introduction because the map grabbed her attention. Finally, a way to figure out where she was going.

Damia and its neighbor, Dalot, formed a long peninsula with the Altaspina Mountains running north south between them. Damia was on the west side of the Altaspinas and Dalot, which included most of the Altaspinas, was on the east. Bordering both Damia and Dalot on the north was a country called Norseland. The Coronas, the mountains Tracy had headed toward, ran east and west across the northern borders of both countries, separating them from Norseland.

Asmodius, is that road that runs next to the river the one we came in on?

Upon hearing the rustle of the map being unrolled and placed on the easel, Asmodius had jerked awake and automatically moved to a stalking crouch. He was gazing at it intently, doing the butt wiggle cats do just before they pounce; but with Molly's question, he sank back on his haunches and blinked sheepishly.

Road? Ah, yes, that would be it.

Molly nodded as she examined the map. The river was called The Selene and the road was The River Road. She followed both south from Bontare and saw how the Selene ran through the center of the entire country before it finally flowed into the sea. Following Madame Rue's cloak would take quite some time.

Pulling her attention back to the hall, she heard General Wicket say; "And, Your Majesty, my sources have been reporting a steady and alarming buildup of armed forces in Dalot over the past year. I suspect they are preparing to invade Damia. Historically, they have chosen to mount their invasions from the south, through The Gap." He pointed to a narrow pass in the southernmost part of the Altaspinas. "If we built a wall blocking The Gap, we would be much safer from invasion."

This proposal was met with jeers and hoots of derision. As the uproar faded away, objections began to be voiced. "And just what are the Dalotians going to do while we're building this wall? Hold ladders for us?" asked a nobleman.

The General replied that the entire Dalotian army was marching north to the Corona Mountains to repel an invasion by the Norselanders, the common enemy of both Damia and Dalot. He also pointed out that the countryside around The Gap was unpopulated. It would be quite some time before the Dalotian government would even be aware that a wall was being built.

"How will we pay for it?" asked a well-dressed merchant.

The stolid military man was out of his element here. He shifted nervously and looked over at the Lord Treasurer.

Philip Fuller glanced impatiently at the General and glided up to the throne. Smoothing his elegant black tunic and his straight black hair into place he replied, "Building a wall will be much cheaper in coin and lives than a war. There is enough in the treasury to begin The Wall and a small tax increase should cover the rest."

As she watched Lord Fuller explain how The Wall would be financed, Molly decided that the guy was a total slime-ball. The air around him flickered a nasty, slippery blue-black. She couldn't understand why everyone was listening to him so politely until she remembered that most of these people couldn't see the magic in their world.

"We may be able to afford it," said a mason, "but The Gap's a mile wide. It would take at least two years to build. I doubt that the Dalotians' war will last that long. They'll be on us like fleas on a dog."

Mutters of agreement rippled around the hall.

Lord Fuller smiled confidently, "Damia has a resource that very few other countries have. If we use it wisely, The Wall should be finished in well under three months."

Exclamations and curiosity.

"What resource?" inquired the Lord of Agriculture.

"I am referring to our very own Queen Flora," Lord Fuller replied. "She possesses the ability to command the earth and keep a labor force in top physical shape. With her help, the quarry stones would practically cut themselves and could be moved as easily as a load of corn. She could triple the strength and stamina of the work force."

Cries of enthusiasm rang through the hall as noblemen, merchants, and farmers alike began to see the possibility of a permanent solution to the threat of the Dalotians. Only the Lord of Agriculture and the queen looked unenthusiastic. But Lord Mudd could offer only one objection.

"Your Majesty, the queen is about to begin her progress. The people and the land are in need of renewal. Your subjects will be disappointed and the crops will suffer."

"Yes, that is a quandary," King Alexander replied. "Is the continuing safety of the kingdom worth a year or two of scarcity? There are a few other flaws in the scheme as well. This affair is much too complex and affects far too many people for us to try to make a decision today. We will have to consider the matter and consult with our advisors. We see that most of you seem to be in favor of building a wall and we will keep that in mind in our deliberations. Next supplicant, please."

Dozens of heated conversations erupted and the hall seethed with tension and excitement as the next petitioner pushed his way forward. Molly noticed that there were at least twice as many people in the hall as when the audience began. Some sort of palace telepathy must have called anyone with a few minutes to spare to come and hear about the dragon and The Wall.

We don't need to stay for any more of the audience. The rest of the supplicants have issues of a personal nature. I suggest we take a quick tour of the palace and have a rest before the banquet. Asmodius had somehow spirited himself through the mass of people in the hall and was waiting for her at the door.

The palace was like a small city and Asmodius knew every corner of it, from the laundry rooms to the gardens and from the attics to the kitchens.

Molly was fascinated by the armory. The walls were hung with swords, knives, maces, and clubs. Dozens of suits of armor hung on forms scattered amongst chests of what she assumed were more weapons. It smelled of dust, oil, and old leather. As she was examining a huge sword with a cutting edge on both sides, Asmodius went into tour guide mode.

That's a broadsword. It's used for hacking. It takes a lot of strength to wield it for any length of time, but it has a long reach and is a very powerful weapon. It's what most soldiers choose to carry into battle. The shorter blade next to it with only one cutting edge and a point is a saber. It's made to be used from horseback. This flimsy one with a sharp point and no cutting edge is an epee. It's used for hand-to-hand fighting without armor. It's what most people think of when they think of a sword.

Molly was drawn to a sword tucked through the belt of a fabulous suit of armor. Its hilt looked just like the one on the sword she had seen at Madame Rue's except that this one had shiny black cords instead of red-brown ones wrapped closely around the hilt, and the head, paws, and tail of a small, silver wolf figurine glared out from under them. It was sheathed in a simple black lacquer scabbard. What would it feel like to hold that sword in her hand? Would it have the same sweet curve to its blade? She reached out to draw the sword from its scabbard.

Molly, don't touch the sword. That armor belonged to King Richard, King Alexander's father.

"Oh, chill out! The guy's dead. He won't mind if I look at his sword." She grabbed the hilt and pulled. The blade glided out of the scabbard. Yes! Just like the sword at Madam Rue's, only up close and in her hand it was even more amazing. Its satiny surface rippled with mind-mazing patterns. The sword was so light it almost floated in her hand and felt like an extension of it. Goosebumps raced up her arm and her heart pounded. She swung it back and forth, delighting in the *whoosh* it made as it sliced through the air. Her palms itched with excitement. This was way cool, even better than WarCraft Universe.

That's called an officers' sword because only a few smiths know the secret of their forging, and the king snaps up every one they make for his officers.

"This sword's lonesome."

How do you know?

"I don't know, I just do. It wants to be used. What would happen if I took it?"

If you stole that sword, even I couldn't save you from the hangman!

—

Back in her room, Molly plunked down in The Chair.

How was the reception?

Molly squeaked in alarm and jumped back up. "You didn't tell me you could talk!" she said, glaring down at her other four legged companion.

I can't.

"You can think at me. Same difference." As her brain wrapped itself around the fact that she was going to be spending a lot of time wandering around a fairy tale country with an obnoxious cat and a talking backpack, hysterical giggles began bubbling up inside her.

So, I repeat, how was the reception? The Chair asked.

"It was awful." Molly groaned and threw herself back into The Chair. The giggles were gone.

Oof! said The Chair.

"I almost fell on my butt when I tried to curtsy for the king, and everyone started laughing. I was so totally embarrassed. And then this dude comes up and says there's a dragon running around killing people, and he lives just south of here, right where we have to go if we follow the river like Madame Rue said.

Oh dear, dear, dear. This is bad, very bad. That must be a very wicked dragon—I've never heard of one actually killing people. I've met a few who loved to scare people, and they can be very hard on their humans, but they never killed anyone. Unfortunately, they're attracted to magic—they crave it. I am made almost completely of magic and Asmodius has more magic in the tip of his tail than you'd find in even the most powerful Damian mage. That scaly bugger will be after us before you can say 'leaping lizards'!

Molly had already worked this much out for herself, and The Chair's gloomy assessment did nothing to improve her outlook. "And that's not all. They're worried that Dalot is going to attack sometime soon and they want to build a wall across this mountain pass to keep them out. I think they should just fight. That's much more exciting than building a stupid wall."

Without warning, the quiet room disappeared abruptly...

And a battle was raging all around her.

Molly shrieked in terror as the clang of broadswords and the screams of the wounded pounded into her like a sledgehammer. Soldiers were using the weapons she had seen in the armory with violent, horrifying results. The sickly-sweet, metallic smell of blood and the choking musk of fear made her gag. Blood was everywhere, making the ground slick and treacherous and turning the men into ghastly, red demons. They fought for their lives with fierce intensity. A youth sat in the midst of it all, holding his intestines in his hands. Gut-wrenching panic gripped Molly as a burly man drew his lips back in a snarl and slashed at her with his broadsword. The man behind her pushed her down into the bloody muck and countered the blow with a bone-shivering clang. A boot heel slammed into her kidney, and as she writhed in agony, a handsome young soldier fell down next to her. He shuddered once as blood gushed out of his mouth and then lay still.

The battlefield faded...

She stood in the middle of a field in late fall. A few skeletal woman and two children dressed in fluttering rags were picking over the field for the remains of the wheat harvest. Every grain they found went immediately into their mouths. Blackened ribs of burnt-out barns and houses littered the background. The utter hopelessness of the scene tore at her heart.

Molly sobbed in relief when she found herself back in her palace bedroom. Maybe The Wall wasn't such a bad idea after all. And then her blood ran cold as she realized the horror of being trapped in a strange country that could erupt in war at any time. She wouldn't stand a chance. She needed to get back to Portland.

"Don't ever do that to me again," she said.

I am sorry. That was cruel. But you needed a reality check. Damia and Dalot have been at war off and on for centuries. Whenever a strong ruler comes to power in either country he has visions of how wealthy and powerful he would be if he could unite Damia's fertile farm and timber land with Dalot's deep, sheltered seaports, wheat fields, and rich iron mines. And, as they say, the rest is history.

Molly's head was whirling as she flopped onto the feather bed for a quick nap before the banquet, but when sleep found her it was troubled. The dead soldier on the battlefield stared up at her with pleading eyes. He opened his mouth and bright red lifeblood gushed out and became two more soldiers who drew their swords and continued the fight. Dragons flew overhead breathing fiery death and destruction and a shadowy figure strode toward her over the dead and dying. Its eyes were red pinpoints of light.

5

The Hierophant

olly gazed in awe at the banquet hall. The place was huge. Where was she supposed to sit? Hundreds of candles in crystal chandeliers gleamed down on white damask tablecloths, sparkling wineglasses, gold-rimmed china, and a rainbow of courtiers dressed in their finest satins and laces. The Hall itself was a confection of intricately carved, creamy white marble hung with huge, jewel-like tapestries depicting events in the lives of various gods and goddesses. Molly figured they were gods and goddesses because they were doing impossible things like turning people into trees, tossing lightning bolts down from the clouds, and walking on water. Rows of small windows that ran just under the high ceiling around three sides of the hall stood open to the mild night air, which was good because she was hot, sweaty, and out of breath. The servant who'd guided her here had been in a hurry. Musicians crammed into a small balcony built over the entryway at the end of the hall played what Molly thought of as mingle-music.

The head table faced the entryway and was flanked by two long lines of tables. Large chairs carved with bas-reliefs of fantastic beasts were placed at the center of the head table for the king and queen. Molly noticed that General Wicket was seated on the right side of the king's chair and the Lord Treasurer was on the left side of the queen's chair.

The Lord of Agriculture with his wife on one arm approached her and held out his other arm. "Allow me to show you to your seat, Lady Adair."

Molly took it gratefully. She felt underdressed, confused, and clumsy.

As they walked toward the head table, Lord Mudd introduced her to his wife, Sylvia, a short, plump, thirty-something woman with blond curls, glowing complexion, and a kind face. She wore an emerald-green satin gown laced over a lavender chemise. The sleeves and sides of the overdress were slashed with deep purple.

"I'm so glad to meet you. My husband tells me you're a traveler from a distant land. You must tell me about where you come from. It is always a treat to hear about strange, far-away places."

They sat at the very end of the head table. It was in an inconspicuous spot that gave her an excellent view of the entire hall.

Greetings, Molly.

A paw patted the toe of her slipper and she peeked under the table to see Asmodius happily devouring the contents of a huge bowl of meat and gravy.

"Hi, Asmodius." *How did you get dinner before everyone else?*

It pays to be nice to the cook. Now keep your feet out of my dish, pay attention to conversation, and don't be surprised when your wine starts turning into grape juice. I have a feeling you'll need your wits about you this evening.

"He turns up in the darndest places," she said to her dinner companions as she sat up.

"He seems to be a particularly intelligent cat," the man to her left observed.

"Oh, he has his moments," muttered Molly, as she turned to face him. With a start, she realized that this was the priest who had performed the opening rite and advised the king about dragons at the reception. He couldn't have been any older than forty-five, but his gentle gray eyes held the wisdom and sadness of a much older man. His head was completely shaved.

"I'm Father Elysius."

"Pleased to meet you, sir, I'm Molly Adair."

"Ah, yes, the queen mentioned you to me. The pleasure is all mine."

Here was someone who could tell her all the stuff she wanted to know about dragons, but Molly realized that dragons were probably the last thing anyone wanted to think about at this fancy banquet. So, remembering her manners, she asked, "Why do the priests wear different colored robes?"

"Damia is a very diverse country with two distinct pantheons and maybe a few others that I don't know about. Each of these pantheons has a priesthood, trained in the rites of its particular gods and goddesses, and each of these priesthoods wears a different color of robe."

"Which pantheon do you serve?" Molly asked.

"Those of us who wear white robes serve king, queen, and country. We are trained to perform the great solar celebrations at the Solstices and Equinoxes. These are events that affect everyone, and so the entire land joins together to celebrate. As the embodiments of the land itself, the king and queen are, in fact, deities. But they are also human and often in need of counsel, so we are trained to give them both practical and spiritual advice. Because our brotherhood extends throughout the country, we provide a backdrop of religious continuity. We also gather information our rulers need to make wise decisions."

"You mean you're spies?"

"Well, not exactly..."

A blast of trumpets interrupted whatever else the priest was about to say. King Alexander and Queen Flora appeared in the doorway behind the head table and glided forward to their seats. The queen was radiant in a gown of emerald green and silver. The king wore his usual red leather dress armor, but his under tunic was of gold cloth. They were spectacularly beautiful.

As soon as they were seated, the banquet began. Efficient servants delivered bowls of steaming, hot broth and an assortment of raw, finely-chopped vegetables to stir in. But no one started eating. Instead, they stood and waited until everyone was served. Father Elysius raised his hands over the food and guests.

"Gods and Goddesses of Damia, come feast with us and share our joy. We ask that you bless this food that we may walk in wisdom and harmony."

He touched his right hand to his heart and then lifted it, palm up, as if offering his love and thankfulness to the universe. The guests repeated the gesture. King Alexander seated Queen Flora, and the feasting began.

The banquet turned out to be a leisurely affair with many courses. The food was a bit strange but it tasted good and each course looked like a piece of art. The guests seemed to be enjoying themselves. But a nervous tension vibrated through the hall. Polite conversations and small talk did nothing to banish the almost palpable specters of the dragon and The Wall squatting in the center of the room.

Father Elysius downed his broth and vegetables with enthusiasm, but only picked at the rich meats and sauces that followed. He was kind enough to show Molly how to remove the head and lift the bones out of a disconcertingly live-looking trout that stared up at her with one accusing eye. After the fish, Molly's jittery stomach refused anything else.

Lord Mudd explained that, by custom, each course at a royal banquet came from one of the twelve counties of Damia. The fish she was having so much trouble with had been caught in a stream flowing off the Altaspinas in Davin County, southeast of Bontare.

As the wine continued to flow, the hall roared with fast talk and laughter. Sylvia was full of information about who was who at court, and Father Elysius entertained her with stories about the gods and goddesses that were portrayed on the tapestries. But the dragon and The Wall still lurked ominously, making every conversation and every laugh forced and brittle.

Molly noticed that General Wicket was speaking to the king, who was nodding his agreement. The Lord Treasurer was speaking urgently to the queen and seemed to be asking her question after question, to which she was nodding. But she looked miserable and leaned as far away from her interrogator as she could.

The final course was being served when a priest in white robes slipped through the door behind the head table and approached the king with his head bowed. When the king acknowledged him he whispered in his ear. King Alexander nodded and the priest backed out the way he had come. Soon the great doors at the foot of the hall opened to admit a tall, imposing man. He carried a simple wooden staff shaped like a shepherd's crook and was dressed in a white, beautifully draped robe. A golden winged disc hung at his breast and he wore a black and white, three tiered, turban-like crown. Each tier was surrounded by small golden balls, and an equal-armed cross nestled at its top. He came to a halt at the exact center of the hall.

"The High Priest of Damia," Father Elysius whispered to Molly.

Where before there had been laughter and revelry, there was now apprehensive silence. All eyes were trained on that still, brooding figure, who held that focus until the room crackled with tension.

Then he raised his staff and said:

"Your Royal Majesties, Lords and Ladies of Damia, the Gods have spoken and as their servant and yours, it is my duty to relay their message. I had a terrible vision during this evening's meditations. There will be a Dalotian invasion. The queen and her unborn child will be in danger."

The silence broke with a snap. Cries of fear and protest echoed off the walls in a thundering roar. The king sat still as a statue, gripping his dinner knife like a dagger. The queen's face turned to stone. The Lord Treasurer's initial expression of surprise turned into a self-satisfied smile as he relaxed back in his chair.

Never underestimate the power of cheap theatrics, growled Asmodius from beneath the table.

King Alexander waited until the uproar had died back and asked, "Are you sure this was a true sending, Your Holiness."

"The vision was clear and unmistakable, Your Highness."

"Father, your message is timely. We will use the rest of the evening to discuss its implications. Thank you."

The High Priest bowed and backed out through the doors.

The hall buzzed with worried conversations. The queen turn to her husband, smiled and touched his hand. This must have been some kind of signal, because he stood and pulled back her chair. She rose gracefully, nodded to her subjects, and left the hall.

Father Elysius, his gentle face frozen into an unreadable mask, turned to Molly and said quietly, "Please excuse me, I am the household priest. I must attend the queen."

Time for us to head out as well. Follow me. Quickly now!

Molly said rushed good byes to her dinner companions and plunged after Asmodius through a side door behind their seats.

She found herself running through a maze of hallways, just barely keeping up with her furry guide. When they came to a dead end, the cat headed for it at a quick trot, and just as Molly was sure he was going to smash into the wall, a door opened. Molly ducked through behind him and it closed at her heels with a quiet snick.

The darkness and silence were absolute. It smelled like she had always imagined the inside of a tomb would smell. Molly's heart raced as she reached out and felt walls behind her and to the left and right. The way lay open in front of her.

Move forward slowly. Be very quiet and don't step on me. I'm right in front of you.

How am I supposed to keep from stepping on you when I can't even see you?

Pretend you are reaching out with sensitive, imaginary fingers and that they are feeling the subtle energies around them. Power will flow where your intention goes.

Yeah, right.

But she didn't have any other options.

She reached out with her mind to the three walls. Sure enough, she could sense their cool, stony presence. Or was it just her imagination? Next she tried for Asmodius, and encountered an unmistakable ball of blazing purple-black intensity. Way cool.

Got it. You're about three feet ahead of me.

Good. Keep your feelers out and let's go.

As they moved through the darkness. Molly was amazed at how easy it was to "see." It was an awesome sensation. A shiver of excitement ran through her. Was this magic? If it was, she wanted to learn more.

She was so busy experimenting with her new talent that her attention lapsed and she stepped on the tip of Asmodius' tail. The big cat just barely stifled a yowl. It came out as a muffled squawk. He whirled around and whapped Molly on the ankle.

"Ow!"

Hush, you imbecile, and watch where you're going!

OK. So, where are we going?

To spy on the queen.

Are you crazy? We should be helping her, not spying on her.

Information is power. We need to know what's happening so we can figure out how to help, who to help, or if we can help at all. Ah, here we are. Look through those two holes and tell me what you see.

Two holes cut through the stone at about her eye level glowed with light. Molly peeked through them and spotted the queen seated on a couch in the room that opened out on her garden. She was rocking back and forth with her arms crossed protectively over her belly. Tears streamed down her deathly pale cheeks. Father Elysius sat on a stool at her feet.

The queen is talking to Father Elysius. She's crying.

Can you hear what they're saying?

Yes.

"Oh Father, I feel so selfish. I don't want to do this. Splitting living rock and moving it from its home is a wrong use for my magic. But I don't want Damia to go to war either. I feel trapped, as if a giant hand were pushing me into a cage. What council can you give me?"

"My Queen, the Gods speak to all of us, not just the high priest. They tell each of us everything we need to know—we just have to be still enough to hear them. They told the High Priest to warn his people of the danger of invasion. Now you must calm your mind and listen for their message to you. What you are hearing now is your own shame and fear, not a message from the Gods. If Your Majesty will permit me, I can help you still your mind so you can pray to the Goddess for guidance."

"Thank you, Father." Putting her hands in her lap and steadying her breath, she closed her eyes and said, "You may proceed."

The priest stood and slowly circled the queen. His hands moved constantly and he sang a soft, humming chant. Rays of light shimmered into being and wove themselves into a complicated pattern around her. Her color returned and her breathing slowed and deepened.

An expectant stillness filled the room.

Father Elysius knelt at her feet and bowed his head.

The light around the queen slowly intensified and the room faded away, leaving the queen and the priest suspended in midair. Molly stifled a gasp and grabbed for the wall in front of her to make sure it was still there. Tendrils of light shot out from the queen's bright aura. They reached down into the earth and shot up into the sky. Soon she was cradled in the midst of a huge tree made up of rainbows of shimmering light. Its roots traveled deep into the earth and its branches reached up to infinity.

Molly gazed at the vision in awe until a strategically applied claw reminded her that she was supposed to be telling Asmodius what was happening.

This is so cool! And she told the cat every marvelous detail of what she'd seen.

If a tree formed around her, Asmodius replied, *she's calling on Dama, the Great Mother. Flora went right to the top—not always the best idea for personal concerns. But Dama will certainly have the big picture, which is ultimately what a queen needs to know.*

Now the tree is collapsing back into the egg of light, Molly continued. *It's just slowly spiraling in on itself and the egg is glowing even brighter... And now the room is back and the egg is starting to get dimmer and dimmer... and now it's gone. The queen's opened her eyes and she's looking around. Oh, Asmodius, she's glowing, just like the egg, and all the worry is gone from her face.*

"I understand what I need to do now," the queen said. "Dama told me that I must be strong and brave, and that the months ahead will be difficult. But she promised me that Damia will remain unconquered and that my baby will be safe."

Ah, the Gods, such helpful buggers! muttered Asmodius.

6

The Lovers

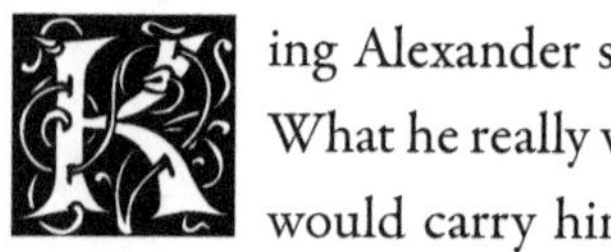ing Alexander strode through the halls of his palace. What he really wanted to do was run, as fast as his feet would carry him, to his wife and make sure she was all right. The High Priest couldn't have had his blasted vision at a worse time. Flora was already worried and his people were frightened and confused. It had taken every ounce of his meager supply of patience to calm them down and direct their energies toward more productive pursuits than jumping up and down and yelling.

He opened the door to the royal suites and plunked his crown down on the hall table beside Flora's. Gods, he was tired. Scrubbing his face with one hand, he crossed to the closed door of Flora's sitting room and knocked. "Flora, may I come in?"

"Alex! Of course."

Flora greeted him with a dazzling smile. Alexander's muscles relaxed and he breathed a sigh of relief. Thank the Gods for Father Elysius.

The priest stepped forward and bowed. "I was just leaving, Your Majesty, I bid you and your wife a good night."

"Thank you, Father. I may as well let you know now; I'm calling a meeting to further discuss The Wall. It will be after breakfast in the Reception Hall. Please attend."

"As you wish, Your Majesty."

After the door closed behind the priest, Alexander swooped to Flora's side and folded her in his arms. "I was so worried when you left the banquet. But look at you—you're radiant!"

Flora laughed a soft, throaty laugh and ran loving fingers through his hair. "Darling, I have something to tell you."

"Hmmm?"

"I spoke with Dama and she told me that I must be strong and that everything will turn out right. So, if you decide to build this Wall, I will do everything I can to help. And listen to this! We're going to have a son! I saw him. He is beautiful."

"Yes!" Alexander gazed adoringly into her eyes. "The first good news I've had all day! My dear one, you've just made it all worthwhile!"

He held her close once more and kissed her very gently...on the corner of her eye...her lips...just under her earlobe...her shoulder...

Molly's heart was doing a rumba and her insides melted.

Gawd, he is so freakin' romantic. Why can't the guys at school act like that?

Asmodius apparently decided that this was a rhetorical question because he offered no explanation. *I doubt that we'll get any more useful information out of those two,* he replied instead.

I don't know, that depends on what you call useful information.

Humph. It's time to give them some privacy, and morning will come all too soon.

The big cat glided into the blackness, leaving Molly with the choice of either following him or being lost in the palace walls.

The next morning found Asmodius and Molly glued to spy holes overlooking the Reception Hall. The heads of the stone masons' guild, the quarrymen's guild, and the teamsters' guild, father Elysius, General Wicket, and Lord Fuller sat at tables in front of the king and queen. The room buzzed with vigorous discussion until King Alexander called the meeting to order and asked Father Elysius to bless the proceedings.

Everyone rose as the good father walked to the center of the hall and faced north. As he had done before at the king's reception, he called in the directions and invited the Gods and Goddesses of Damia to join the assembly and give it their blessings. When he was finished, the hall thrummed with expectation and powerful presences shifted and stirred.

King Alexander rose from his throne and said: "Leaders of Damia, the Gods have spoken. Our land will be invaded and our queen and her unborn child will be in danger. We have two choices. We can muster a huge army and keep it in readiness until the Dalotians begin their invasion, or we can build a wall across The Gap and use the army we have now to defend it and our borders. The question is, can we complete it in time? I have called you here to determine this.

"Your queen has offered to use her powers to help us build The Wall. Without her aid, the task would be impossible. She has offered to demonstrate her powers so that you can factor them into your calculations and deliberations."

With this, Queen Flora rose from her throne to enthusiastic applause. "Leaders of Damia," she began, after it had died down, "as your queen, I have some influence over the earth. Before today, it was my pleasure to use that influence to promote its health and well-being and therefore the health and well-being of all my subjects. However, I have been convinced that my abilities need to be focused in a new way. If you will please observe…"

The audience hall doors were thrown opened to reveal a sturdy wagon large enough to carry a block of stone so massive that it barely fit through the two-story-tall double doors. Twelve strong men dragged it to the center of the hall, and looked thoroughly exhausted by the time they had completed their task.

Queen Flora went to each man in turn and thanked him and touched his heart. They blinked in amazement as all signs of fatigue fell away.

The queen touched the stone and there was a sharp crack as two perpendicular lines appeared on the face of the block toward her audience. A clatter of rock debris from the cuts rained down on the floor. The single large stone had been fractured into four perfectly shaped blocks.

There were cries of astonishment and the stone masons and the quarrymen leaped from their chairs to inspect this miracle.

The queen touched the stone again and asked the twelve men to separate the blocks and set them on the floor. The men looked at her as if she was crazy, but they obeyed.

Murmurs of amazement rippled through the hall as the men found that only two of them were needed to lift each block down from the cart and set it in place. The queen indicated that the men should reassemble them on the wagon. A dumbfounded audience watched as the twelve men obeyed her with ease and whisked the wagon out through the doors.

"Your Majesty, how many blocks can you make in a day?" an engineer asked, breaking the stunned silence.

"As many as you need. The blocks will stay light for about six hours and then slowly return to their natural weight."

A roar of excitement echoed through the hall as everyone began talking at once. The guild leaders began refiguring how long it would take while General Wicket and his aides began refiguring the size of the workforce. The king and queen left, asking to be called back when everyone was done arguing and rethinking.

———

Several hours later, Molly and Asmodius were back at their spy holes watching the head mason approach the thrones.

"Your Majesties," he said, "with our good queen's help and the resources of the kingdom at our disposal, we can build a mile of wall in four months if we split the workforce into two teams, each starting at one end of The Gap and working towards the other."

Lord Fuller stepped forth and announced: "There is enough money in the treasury to begin The Wall and a one-percent raise in taxes over the next three years will pay for it completely."

General Wicket recommended that most of the army be stationed near The Wall. It could be split into two divisions that would alternate between helping with the building and guarding the work-site. He also suggested that the army be in charge of recruiting and provisioning the workforce since those are two things an army is very good at.

Father Elysius informed the gathering that Damian priests who had visited Dalot recently confirmed that most of its army was headed north to defend the country from a Norse invasion. The rest was busy recruiting and training more soldiers. There were small garrisons at each of the passes in the Altaspinas and an encampment watching The Gap.

General Wicket pointed out the necessity for secrecy. The longer it took before the Dalotians found out they were building a wall, the better. If the decision was reached to build The Wall, everyone in the hall must be sworn to secrecy. The recruitment would be for military service. No mention would be made of The Wall. The Dalotian southern encampment must be captured and every effort made to convince the rest of Dalot that it was still guarding The Gap and that all was well.

King Alexander stood and the room went still. His fierce gaze swept the room.

"Leaders of Damia," he said. "We will build The Wall!"

A cheer echoed through the hall.

"I declare Damia to be at war," he continued. "We are now under martial law. No one enters or leaves the palace or city without authorization. The citizens are to be told that we have heard rumors of a Dalotian invasion in the near future and are building up the army. And I swear everyone in this hall to secrecy. Anyone who mentions The Wall to anyone but the people actually involved is guilty of high treason and will be punished accordingly. Father Elysius, please close the gathering."

After Father Elysius had asked for the Gods' blessing and released the quarters, the hall vibrated with a feeling of finality and inevitability. The king looked grim and Queen Flora looked sad and resigned.

Fools! snarled Asmodius, turning away from the spy hole. *Come on, Molly, let's get out of here.*

What's wrong, Asmodius? Molly asked as she ran to catch up. *The Wall sounds like a great idea.*

The whole scheme stinks. What makes them think the Dalotians won't find out? Dalotian spies are as good as Damian spies. And who owns all those quarries and gravel pits? I wouldn't be at all surprised if it just happens to be some of the folks who are pushing this wall idea.

"So maybe you should try to talk them out of it."

Arguing with royalty once they've made up their minds is a thankless task. The best thing we can do is get out of here and leave them to it.

"But we need permission to leave. And anyway we can't go without thanking them. They've been so nice, and I really like them."

The king and queen will understand. They know this isn't your problem. If you leave, it will be one less thing they'll have to worry about.

As they raced through endless corridors, Molly tried another argument.

"But it's late afternoon. It'll be dark soon."

All the more reason to get moving.

"But I want to stay. I was gonna have a hot bath tonight, and that bed is awesome."

With the palace under martial law, you could be conscripted into any number of unpleasant tasks and be killed if you refused. The king and the rest of the court will be too busy to intervene on your behalf.

"But there's a dragon out there, and it'll be after us 'cuz you and The Chair have lots of magic!"

I can shield us so the beast won't notice the magic. You'll be safer on the road than stuck in this madhouse.

Molly gritted her teeth in irritation. She wasn't looking forward to roughing it in that ugly brown tunic and leggings, and she was going to miss the king and queen—especially the queen. However, within the hour she had reluctantly chopped her hair into short, uneven curls, tied a strip of silk sheet around her chest to flatten her breasts, dressed in her traveling clothes, and shrugged into The Chair, which had become a backpack once more. She opened the door to find Asmodius pacing the hall.

Let's be gone!

He led her through a maze of tunnel-like passages. The few people they spotted were servants with more important things to worry about than a poorly-dressed young man headed somewhere in a hurry.

"Ya lazy slut!" a voice ahead of them shrilled.

SMACK

Molly picked up her pace. She came around a corner and found a housekeeper looming over a cringing maid. The girl's eye was already starting to blacken and her lip was bleeding.

"Now yer in fer it!"

SMACK

Molly's heart went out to the cringing girl. She hated feeling helpless—she hated it with a deep, abiding passion. And she hated the bastards who made people feel helpless.

"Smoochin' with a stable-hand when yer otta be sweepin' floors."

SMACK

Blood flew from the girl's cut lip and spattered the wall with crimson violence.

A man walked past the two women with hardly a glance, and another housekeeper hurried after him. Molly couldn't believe her eyes. Why weren't they stopping that horrible woman?

Then she remembered that no one had helped her as she was struggling through the city getting groped. Molten rage boiled through her. In a flash, she was at the girl's side, shoving the house-keeper away.

"Leave her alone!"

The woman glared at her and sputtered in outraged surprise.

Molly turned to the cowering maid. "Run! Get outa here!"

The girl just stood there weaving unsteadily on her feet and staring at Molly with huge, fearful eyes.

"Who are ye?" The housekeeper shouted. She looked at Molly more closely. "Ye don't belong here!"

Her hand flashed out and grabbed the front of Molly's tunic. "Guards! Guards!" she yelled. "Help!"

Molly twisted away and bolted after the retreating cat. All down the hall servants took up the housekeeper's cry and she heard the heavy footfalls and clinking chain mail of soldiers running to help.

The passages went by in a blur. Molly was out of breath and there was a stitch in her side, but she kept running. She had to. The guards were closing in.

The gate was just ahead; but another guard stood at it with his sword drawn.

"Stop! No one leaves the palace. King's orders."

Asmodius slipped around the guard like a shadow, leaving Molly to fend for herself.

"Please sir, they're after me. Ya gotta help!"

"Who?"

"Them!" shouted Molly pointing back down the passage.

The minute the guard looked back, she darted past him and streaked down the road.

There was a roar of anger as her pursuers arrived at the gate. She was just able to hear the words "Spy!" and "Get the horses!"

Once she was out of sight of the palace, it took every ounce of willpower Molly possessed to amble through the busy streets, even though her heart pounded in her chest and urged her to run for it.

She stayed close to the honey colored brick walls, and tried to be inconspicuous. She was grateful that the way out of the city was down-hill. It meant she could tell if she was going the right way, and it gave her a chance to catch her breath.

Well, so much for a nice quiet exit. Asmodius stared balefully down at her from a nearby rooftop. *If you are attempting a clandestine escape from a palace, don't pick fights with the servants. Such a simple concept.* He peered back down the street. *They're coming after you. Act like a street urchin and follow me.*

So how did street urchins act? There wasn't a single one around to observe. She settled for drifting along and peeking in any open doors and shop fronts they passed, even though her heart was thudding and her mouth was dry with fear.

The guards were everywhere, but Asmodius led her on a serpentine route that always kept her one street away from them.

Why didn't that stupid girl run when she had the chance?

Where would she run to? That is the only life she knows. You didn't do her any favors, you know. The housekeeper will just beat her harder now because she lost face.

The rotten animal was correct. Her temper had put them in danger, and for nothing.

They managed to sneak through the town gate by hiding in the back of a homeward bound market wagon. After a few miles it turned off The River Road and they jumped out.

Hurry! Asmodius hissed.

Molly heard faint hoof beats coming their way at a gallop.

In a panic, she turned to follow the fleeing cat and noticed a signpost.

It didn't look like any of the other signposts she'd seen in Damia. In fact, it looked like the street signs back in Concord— two green metal rectangles with white, raised lettering stuck on a metal pole. Except this one looked like it would fade away if you didn't keep an eye on it. Each sign pointed in a different direction. One said 'The Rest of the Journey' and pointed south along The River Road. The other one pointed down an intersecting path. It said 'The Way Back.'

As she stood gasping for breath in the middle of the road, staring at the signpost, the all-too-familiar sensation of disconnectedness, like she was this lonely ghost watching herself muddle through her life, intensified. The breeze died down, the birdsong faded away, and the drone of the crickets in the field hushed to a whisper. The two roads and the signpost became clear and distinct, while Asmodius and the fields faded into the background.

"What happens if I choose The Way Back?"

As if from a great distance, she heard the cat reply: *You will walk down that road, and in a short while, you will find yourself sitting in your room at your grandmother's house once more. You will remember your time here in Damia as a particularly vivid dream.*

Yes! This was her ticket out of this insane asylum. Every muscle in her body melted with relief. "So this is all just a dream?"

It can be if you want it to be.

She took a step toward The Way Back and stopped. Alarm bells like she'd heard on sinking ships in the movies began going off in her brain. Did she really want to go back to Portland and wait for The Shadow to get her? Fear and hopelessness gripped her and she felt herself drifting away. She dug her fingernails into her palms.

The only real choice was to follow the river like Madame Rue had told her.

"Will I ever get back if I decide to keep going?"

Maybe and maybe not. That all depends on you.

"If I do get back, will I still have The Chair?"

Yes.

"So, there *is* magic in my world?"

Yes, of course.

Asmodius gazed intently at Molly and Molly raised her eyes to the sky to think. The light of the setting sun had painted it brilliant red, gold, and purple. A glowing cloud morphed into grubby, Day-Glo-orange high-tops.

Tracy Bliss gradually took shape above them.

He was tattered and twitching and gesturing frantically toward the south.

Her heart pounded and sweat stung her ravaged palms as she turned south on The River Road and started running. The birds began singing, the crickets began cricketing, and the sound of hoof beats drummed in her ears. Asmodius turned and loped after her.

A bit farther along, the cat guided her down a faint path that led toward the river. When she looked back to the road, the path had disappeared. Moments later they lay hidden in the underbrush by the river and listened to the thudding horses' hooves, creaking leather, and clinking chain mail as the palace guards galloped past.

7

The Chariot

he next day dawned bright and sunny and Molly woke with a start to the tickle of whiskers on her nose and two amber eyes gazing into hers. Scrubbing her face with one hand, she reached out with the other to swat the cat away.

Ah, you're awake! Asmodius said, deftly avoiding her hand.

Molly glared at the cat and threw one of her boots at him, which he also avoided.

Eat your breakfast. We need to get going.

Scrambled eggs and sausage appeared on her plate and orange juice filled the chalice. Molly realized she was ravenous and devoured the food. She repacked her pack and followed Asmodius through the underbrush and back onto The River Road.

The countryside south of Bontare was much like the country-side north of it. Rolling forested hills and fertile fields stretched as far as the eye could see. The road meandered gently through them, never straying too far from the straight course of the rapid, young river.

And the road itself was a river of people traveling between Bontare and cities to the south. Well-dressed merchants rode along on well-groomed horses, looking sober and dignified. Placid farmers drove carts full of produce to market. A noblewoman rode by in her carriage, invisible except for her delicate hand flicking impatiently at the curtains. Suspicious-looking characters slipped through the crowd, perhaps searching for an easy pocket to pick. Molly moved her coins to her front pocket and shivered in the warm sunshine as a mob of boisterous, laughing laborers pushed by her making a great, raucous party out of looking for work. All of Damia seemed to be on the road that fine day, and for the most part, Molly was able to observe it all go by like she was watch-ing a movie. But she flinched away when someone came too close. Flashes of faces with laughing, leering mouths and rough, grasp-ing hands flickered through her mind.

A peddler with a full pack and well-worn boots fell in step beside her. "'Ere, young-un, and where are ya headed, all foot loose and fancy free? A boy your age should be home buckin' hay and tendin' the garden."

Molly cringed and almost ran away, but instead she told her-self to stop being such a dork. After all, the man wasn't a monster. He was grimy and ragged, but his twinkly blue eyes were kind and full of curiosity.

"Well, now, I sure didn't mean ta scare ya. But if yer plannin' on doin' much travelin', yer gonna have ta get used ta talkin' ta strangers."

What are you gonna tell him? Think, idiot. You should have had this all figured out.

"Uh, I guess I am a little freaked out. I'm kinda new at this. I'm the youngest kid in our family and they don't really need me, so I thought I'd take the summer and travel around and see what there is to see before I settle down."

"A fine idee, youngun. But watch out. If ye got itchy feet like me, ye may never settle." He laughed sadly and slapped the dust from his tunic. "Ya don't sound like ya come from around here."

"I come from a small village up near the Coronas."

"Ah, never been that far north—not enough trade."

Good. Hopefully that would be true for everyone she met.

A troop of soldiers tramped past at a rapid pace, headed south.

"Stay away from the likes o' them. They're ever'where today. Looks like there's another war a comin' and ya don't want ta be scooped up for sword fodder. I wish ya luck!" He clapped her on the shoulder, quickened his step, and melted into the crowd in search of potential customers.

As the day progressed, Molly moved through all the chatter and laughter like a sleep-walker. She had mostly talked herself out of her fear of crowds, but she was uncomfortable. It felt like there was a glass wall separating her from everyone else. She didn't belong here. The people were nice enough, but they were totally strange. They ate strange food, they talked about strange stuff, and they did strange things. She wished she was home in Massachusetts.

Asmodius kept pace with her, a watchful shadow in the hedgerows.

—

The next morning, Althea sat in her kitchen eating breakfast and looking out at her garden. It was lush and green and bursting with life. A riot of zinnias, begonias, snapdragons, and dahlias flash danced in the sun. There were tomatoes, beans, cucumbers, squash, and corn waiting to be picked, and bushels of weeding to be done.

An elongated shadow glided across the back of the house followed by the shadow maker herself. Judging by the early hour and the purposeful way Estelle strode up to the patio door and let herself in, this was not a social call.

Her friend went to the cupboard over the sink and grabbed a mug. Althea was not at all surprised to see that the celadon mug she chose matched her short, sea green sundress and tennis shoes perfectly. Where had she found sea green tennis shoes? The whole ensemble made her ice blue eyes even more striking. But her face was without its usual accent of tastefully applied make-up, and worry etched the two vertical lines between her eyebrows even deeper. She looked years older.

"Good morning, Althea," Estelle said as she sank down at the table across from her friend and poured herself a mug of English Breakfast tea. Her hand shook slightly.

"Good Morning, Estelle. Did you have a nice walk over here?"

"I suppose." She took a sip of tea and leaned back in her chair. "I hardly slept at all last night. I've got to find out how Molly's doing."

"But you can't. You promised you wouldn't interfere and would stay out of Damia for the whole time Molly was there."

Estelle set her mug down on the table with exaggerated care and leaned toward her friend. "Yes, but you could go and check on her for me."

Althea rubbed her face with both hands and looked at her friend. "You know, my garden is calling me. Jumping around the multiverse is about the last thing I wanted to do today. Can't the Librarian check for you?"

"The snot-brain says it's not Web business, so it can't be bothered. But I need to find out if she's found Asmodius and see how she's doing. If The Chair doesn't get her back here by Wednesday like it's supposed to, I want to know why."

Althea let it out a deep sigh, blowing up the wisps of hair that fell over her forehead. Estelle liked to solve her own problems. The fact that she had actually asked Althea for help spoke volumes about her worry level. "OK, I'll go and check things out for you."

And besides, she was curious too.

"Did you bring a picture of Molly?"

Estelle pulled two snapshots of her granddaughter out of the pocket of her sundress and handed them over.

Althea studied the first photo as she finished her breakfast. A smiling teen gazed back at her. Freckles frolicked over the bridge of her nose and her auburn curls, although tamed for the portrait, looked ready to rebel against the gel and hairspray at any moment.

The two furrows between her gracefully arched eyebrows were just like her grandmother's.

"She's a lovely young lady…"

"That's last year's school picture. Look at the other one. I took it a few days after I met her."

Althea picked up the second photo and gasped. It looked like a mug shot. Empty gray eyes stared defiantly out of a rounder, pastier face. The two furrows had deepened and lengthened, giving her a brooding, dangerous appearance.

"Oh dear."

"And she looked like that even before I told her about David and Angela. Now do you understand?" Estelle began to pour another cup of tea. The pot was empty.

"Drat!"

She pushed herself up from the table, filled the kettle, and set it on the stove to boil. "As you can see," she continued, "she was unhappy even before her parents died. Something awful happened sometime after that first picture that changed her life and she can't or won't say what it was. It's almost as if her soul has given up and she's fighting to just stay alive. I was hoping this trip would help, but things are going bad, I can feel it in my bones."

Althea was still concentrating on Molly's likeness. "How tall is she?"

"She's about my height."

Too bad. A five foot four frame wouldn't carry those extra pounds easily.

"Asmodius is always easy to find, and they should be together," Althea muttered, "But if for some reason they aren't, I think this'll be enough for me to find her. I'll be back down in an hour or so." She took the second picture and headed upstairs.

In her workroom, Althea went to the closet and selected an overdress and chemise appropriate for a Damian merchant's wife. She could go almost anywhere she needed to in this, except the palace. When she went there, she usually dressed as a house-keeper. She slipped into the costume and eased herself down into the comfortable contours of the easy chair in the corner. Althea had bought this house because it sat above three minor ley lines. She had placed the chair precisely above the point where they intersected.

She relaxed and let her spirit sink down into the lines of earth energy and felt their vibrancy and strength fill her. It was possible to jump without their extra boost, but at her age, every little bit helped. She opened her soul to the multiverse and became every-where and nowhere. The feeling was exquisite, but she resisted the temptation to relax and enjoy it. Instead she pictured a point that she knew of in Damia where two ley lines crossed....

and jumped....

...and found herself looking up at the biggest, blackest, meanest looking dragon she had ever seen. Quicker than thought, a tal-oned forehand reached out and grabbed her. Completely sur-rounded by hard, raspy scales, she was just able to peek out over the dragon's "thumb" like a mini action figure in a child's fist. Her heart beat like a trip-hammer and terror paralyzed her.

"WHAT ARE YOU DOING IN DAMIA?" asked the dragon.

Sulphurous smoke drizzled up out of its dinner-plate sized nostrils and menace poured out of it in black waves. She could tell it wasn't a wild dragon because it felt so human, but whomever it belonged to was an evil bastard, and most likely a mage of some sort, because it was bloated with power and had taken on a life of its own. And, judging from the ravenous hunger in its eyes, it had turned into a man-eater. Not good.

Althea tamped down her fear and thanked the Gods that her aging bladder hadn't given way. Never let a dragon see your fear. It will feed on it and grow stronger.

"Whose dragon are you and what are you doing running around terrorizing people? You ought to be ashamed of yourself!"

The nasty little eyes widened in surprise and for a fraction of a second the dragon loosened its mental and physical grip.

It was enough.

Althea snapped into everywhere, reached for the ley lines under her house, and jumped...

—

Althea slumped in her chair and contemplated the fact that if she hadn't had the strong earth link to yank her back, she would have been roasted dragon dinner by now. The morning sun beamed into her workroom, making the Persian carpet glow on the dark oak floor, but it barely warmed her, and the summer breeze wafting into the open window felt cold. With a shuddering gasp, she staggered into the bathroom.

Back in her chair she reached down and let the earth lines replenish her and waited until she quit shaking. What was a man-eating dragon doing rampaging around in Damia? How many people it had killed? She had jumped into it because dragons like to hang out around ley lines when they incorporate—the extra energy helps keep them solid; but she still needed to find out who had turned his dragon into such a monster and what they were up to.

Now she had two things to investigate.

"Oh, bother."

Choosing another site, well away from any ley lines, Althea jumped back to Damia.

—

Half an hour later, the air in the center of the workroom shimmered and an exhausted Althea materialized. She staggered over to the chair and fell into it. Closing her eyes, she allowed herself some quick recharge time and then headed down to report to Estelle. She would rest later

Her friend had a cup of hot, black tea laced with milk and sugar waiting for her, and Althea wrapped both her hands around it, savoring its warmth. The jumps had left her chilled, even on this warm summer day. She had barely taken two gulps of the invigorating brew before Estelle asked; "Did you find her? Is she OK?"

"Oh, yes, I found them both. It was difficult because Asmodius was heavily shielded. They're on The River Road headed south. The obnoxious beast trotted back to me as soon as I caught sight of them. He said to thank you for the client—and I quote,

'Dealing with a surly teen is only a tad more pleasant than getting your tail slammed in a door.' He's not a happy camper."

Estelle's lips twitched upward and her eyes glinted. "It sounds like the old devil is getting a taste of his own medicine. What else did he say?"

"The Webmasters don't allow him to protect his clients from their own mistakes, you know, all he can do is advise and protect her from outside dangers. Unfortunately, she's headstrong and doesn't take advice well. Asmodius says he's already overstepped his limits in that department and won't be able to get away with it again.

"But listen to this. When the Webmasters gave her the choice of coming back or continuing on the journey, she chose to continue. So, it looks like you might have another mage in your family."

Althea was so glad to see Estelle's haggard face light up in a radiant smile and the worry lines ease that she swallowed the "if she makes it back" that had been on the tip of her tongue. She wasn't looking forward to delivering the rest of her message.

"And Damia is officially at war and under martial law. The fighting hasn't started yet, but Asmodius predicts that it will eventually. Damia is going to try to build a wall across The Gap."

"Idiots," muttered Estelle, slapping the tabletop. "Walls never solve anything."

She wasn't smiling anymore.

Althea rubbed both hands wearily over her face and reached out and took her friend's hand. "But that's not all. A mage has turned his dragon evil and it's gone rogue."

"That's unfortunate, but what's that got to do with Molly?"

"From what I was able to sneak out of the beast's malicious, convoluted brain, its human is plotting to take over Damia, and the dragon decided to let him continue with the plan. I don't think the idiot even knows he's not in control anymore. To protect itself and its human, the dragon is trying to keep outside mages from jumping into the kingdom and is eating all the Damian ones he can find. It's even going after people who aren't mages, but have natural talent. I almost got nailed on my first jump."

Estelle gasped. "Oh dear, you should have quit looking the second you found that dragon."

Althea patted her hand and took another gulp of tea. "I wanted to find out about Molly and why that dragon was on the loose. So anyway, it missed Molly when she came in, probably because The Chair is so good at jumping that it didn't cause much of a ripple when they arrived and didn't morph 'til it got to the palace, which is protected."

"Did you tell Asmodius about the dragon?"

"Of course. He's known about it for weeks, and he's still trying to figure out who it belongs to."

"This is terrible! I wish I'd never sent her into this mess." Depositing her mug in the sink and heading for the door she said, "Thanks, I owe you. I'll go away now so you can rest."

⁓

The seventh day on The River Road dawned cloudy and cool. The smells of rain and sea were in the air, blown in by a brisk west wind. The chilly, gray weather matched Molly's mood. Asmodius was dismal company and she felt lonesome and out of place, even though she was surrounded by kind, friendly people. She tried very hard not to think of home and her parents. That only made things worse. Her blisters were back and her body ached from the long days of walking and the fast pace Asmodius set. And so, when a farmer with a load of hay in a covered wagon offered her a ride if she would drive the wagon, she gladly accepted. How difficult could driving a clunky old farm wagon be? Asmodius leaped into the back, curled up, and went to sleep.

"Ah, laddie, I'm glad yer willin' ta help me," the driver said as she climbed onto the wagon bench. I've got ta get this load of hay ta Daraw Market by tomorrow morning and I won't be makin' it 'less I drive right steady through the night. I was up a bit late last night celebratin' gettin' the hay in, and I'm flat out tired. If ya drive Snowflake an' Shadow the rest of the day, I can catch a few winks. Me name's Ben Hurst, wot's yers?" He was a stocky man with a cap of sleek, brown hair and intelligent, hazel eyes. He definitely looked like he could use a good sleep.

"I'm Matty Adair, and actually, I've never driven a wagon before, can you show me how?"

"Sure, it's easy."

She studied the two big, beautiful horses that were harnessed to the wagon. The one on her left was so white it almost hurt her eyes. Energy sparked off him as he danced in his traces. The one on her right was midnight black. He stood still as a statue and radiated a feeling of dignified calm. She looked back at Ben, then down at his empty hands, and then back at the two horses.

"Um, don't you need a pair of reins or something to drive a team of horses?"

Ben smiled at her like she was a prize student who had asked a particularly profound question. "Oh, ya can't be usin' reins an' bridles an' bits on Shadow an' Snowflake. They won't stand fer it!"

"So how do you make them go the way you want?" This was getting weird. She was pretty sure that every other wagon or coach that she'd seen on the road had had reins.

"I use these," he said, holding out his two empty hands that, none the less, seemed to be loosely holding something.

"And, um, what are those?"

"Why, they's lines o' communycation. Here, just take 'em in yer hands and tell those two lugheads wot ya want 'em ta do. 'S easy once ya get the hang of it."

Molly held out her hands and Ben placed a cool, invisible nothingness in each of them. As soon as she had the "lines" in her hands she became aware of the horses. Two opposing temperaments bounced around in her brain.

One said, *Let's go, let's go, let's go!* And she tingled all over with fizzy exuberance.

The other said, *This is a perfectly fine place, and this is a tasty bush I'm eating here.* And she relaxed into calmness and serenity.

Something's happening up ahead. Don't you want to see? All you want to do is eat.

We'll get there eventually. What's the rush?

It might be over by the time we get there and we'll have missed it. Oh, come on, let's go, let's go, let's go! Honestly, you are so lazy.

I'm not lazy. I pull my share. I just don't act like I've got a burr in my butt all the time. And besides, we can't go till Ben's ready.

Yes, we can.

Can't.

Can.

Her thoughts shuttled back and forth until they spun in useless circles. She was beginning to feel nauseous.

"Um, Ben, maybe you'd better take these back. I don't think I can do this. I feel like I'm gonna throw up."

"A' course ya can do it. Ya just have ta get used to it. Them two natter on and on at each other all the time. Problem is, they's both always got a point. It's yer job ta decide what needs doin' and to get 'em both ta do it."

Molly let her mind relax above the dialogue. If her mind started spinning, she simply said to herself, *It doesn't matter. Both horses can be right at the same time.*

And what a difference that made. She felt like she'd just taken off her horrid boob binder and could breathe easy again. Her whole world relaxed and expanded. It felt strangely comfortable, but somehow wickedly adventurous, to just hang with two conflicting ideas and allow them both a place in her mind. One didn't have to be "right" and the other "wrong." She could keep them both. There was a proper time and an improper time for each of them. Since she was the driver, which they did was now her decision.

She turned to Ben and said, "OK, but how do I get them to understand what I want them to do? Do I just say 'Hi, my name is Matty and I'm your driver for the day?'"

Works for me. Hi, my name is Snowflake and this lump over here is Shadow and we're your horses for the day.

Hi, guys, it's time to go forward at a quick walk, please.

See, I told you we were supposed to go.

OK, fine. Let's go.

And the two horses began to pull the wagon on down the road, one reluctantly and one barely able to keep from trotting.

"I did it. I got them to move."

"Tha's fine, laddie. Well done." Ben said and crawled into the back of the wagon, curled up next to Asmodius, and went to sleep.

Just as she was settling into her task, they came upon the commotion that Snowflake had heard. A group of soldiers had stopped a wagon full of produce and pulled it over to the side of the road. One of them was leading a sturdy youth, deathly pale with eyes full of fear, away from it. An older woman, probably his mother, sat on the bench of the wagon, weeping and reaching toward him. Another soldier stood between the mother and son, hand on his sword.

The Captain in charge spotted Molly as she was driving past and stopped the horses by grabbing Snowflake's harness and shouting "Whoa!" The contrary pair stopped immediately and Molly didn't even think about trying to start them up again. The force behind his steady, blue eyes convinced her in no uncertain terms that going on would be a really bad idea.

"Hey, lad," the officer said as he walked back to where Molly was sitting, "How'd ya like to join the army and see a bit of the world?"

Of course she didn't. In fact she couldn't think of a worse idea; but her mind somehow shifted and, to her horror, it suddenly seemed quite obvious that joining the army was inevitable and resisting the idea would be foolish. It took all the willpower she had to say, "Not today, sir, I have to get this load of hay to market."

She felt like an animal in a trap looking up at the hunter and waiting for the bullet.

"Now, isn't that yer Dad I see sleepin' back inside there? He can drive this lot to market and you can come with us." The officer reached up and grabbed her arm. At the touch of his hard, callused hand, fear and anger exploded inside her, but she was unable to resist the force that hauled her down off the wagon.

Before Molly could even begin to protest, she was stumbling down the road with a group of dazed young men surrounded by tough, sword-toting soldiers. Desperation and a sick feeling of violation welled up inside her. She hadn't even fought back. Her raging brain went over all the things she could have done but didn't. But then the youth she had seen taken away from his mother turned to her and sobbed, "Wot'm I gonna do?" and her rage froze into fear.

What was she gonna do?

What would happen if they found out she was a girl?

And would she ever get back if she couldn't follow the river?

"Oh Gods, I don't wanna die, an' wot's me Mum gonna do without me? Dad was killed in the last war; I'm all she's got left." His words tore at her heart. She wished she could tell him that he was just going to build a wall and would probably be home in several months, but she couldn't since no one was supposed to know about The Wall. She reached out to comfort him, but the soldier behind her slapped her hand away. "Buck up and shut yer gob, young'un. Yer in the army now and cryin' about it won't change a thing. It's not a bad life once ya get used to it."

Don't you think that last recruit is a bit young for the army?

And there was Asmodius, strolling along between her and the Captain. She had never been so glad to see anyone in her life.

The officer's eyes glazed over, and then snapped back into focus as he walked over to Molly and punched her playfully on the arm. "On second thought, maybe you're a bit young for the army. I'll be back for you in a year or so! That's a fine lookin' cat you've got there."

Asmodius was also very good at getting people to do what he wanted.

Molly practically ran back to the wagon and its sleeping owner. She climbed up and groped around until she found the invisible lines.

Go. Now! Molly said, almost sobbing with relief.

The two horses pulled the wagon past the new recruits and Molly didn't relax until they had rounded the next bend and were out of sight.

How'd you do that?

If you drive that team of horses much longer, you should be able to figure it out. Keep them moving. We have to get to our turnoff soon. They've started recruiting, and we need to get off the main road.

Why don't you come sit by me and drive the horses then? We'd probably make much better time.

What? I save you from getting drafted and now you want me to do your job for you? I think not. And let me remind you once more, lest you forget, I am a cat. I need plenty of sleep, and I haven't been getting enough lately, thanks to you.

And with that, Asmodius leaped into the back of the wagon and curled up next to Ben.

The wind began piling up an enormous thunderhead over the fields, and everyone on the road seemed intent on getting where they were going as quickly as possible. As the weather worsened and the novelty of a new driver wore off, the horses began to argue with her about everything.

Why should I quit eating and keep moving? I'm hungry. That's a great view out there. Why don't you rest awhile and enjoy it?

Why can't we explore down that lane? It looks interesting. Come on, let's go. And why can't we go faster? We'll never get anywhere like this.

Reasoning with them was useless, and begging and pleading had no effect. The wagon was now at a standstill more often than not.

Shadow was chewing on a bush and ignoring Snowflake, when at last the white whirlwind lost what little patience he had left. Fine, you just stay there and stuff your face. I'm going over here.

He lunged off to the left towards the lane. There was, however, a fatal flaw in his plan. He was harnessed to Shadow, who wasn't going anywhere. But the powerful horse continued to buck and throw himself against his restraint.

The harness was near its breaking point.

Molly was furious. Why wouldn't these stupid horses do what she told them to? That army officer could make people obey, just like that!

Well duh! She told herself, people obey him *because* he's an army officer.

Yeah, but you don't get to be an army officer if you can't get people to do what you tell them to, she replied to herself.

OK, so how does he do it?

Well, for one thing, he acted really sure of himself, like he knew more than you did. Aren't you smarter than those rotten horses?

Of course I am! And I know more. But how do I convince them of that?

Remember what Asmodius said, *Power flows where your intention goes.* Go on; try it—before Snowflake rips the harness apart.

So Molly took her anger and concentrated it into a strong, confident command and sent it down the lines to Shadow and Snowflake.

STOP! NOW!

Shadow and Snowflake froze in mid-chew and mid-buck and stared back at her.

Molly was momentarily stunned as well.

She could do it. Amazing!

You will go forward. You will do this now because I am the driver and you are horses. Period.

With Molly finally in control, the wagon traveled smoothly along the road for an hour or so. But forcing the pair into submission was exhausting work, and the horses were getting mutinous. Both pairs of ears were flattened now and Molly realized that it was only a matter of time before they would finally agree on something. And that something would be to get rid of this driver. How did Ben do it? He and the horses had looked so calm and relaxed.

The wind picked up and turned cold. It was dark as dusk. The road was almost deserted now except for some covered wagons and carriages and a few determined-looking travelers hurrying toward their destinations.

Would her failing energies be enough to control two rebellious horses through a storm? Why couldn't the idiots listen to her and realize that it would be best to just do their job and pull the wagon? They were all in this together, after all.

Of course! That was it.

She gathered her energy one more time and settled it gently but firmly into the horses' minds.

You really want to get to market on time. The sooner you get there, the sooner you can get out of the harness and have your oats. Just cooperate and I'll get you there.

It was much easier after that, which was fortunate, because rain started to pelt the wagon canvas and the wind amped up to a wailing howl. Shadow and Snowflake tossed their heads and danced nervously in their traces.

The thunderhead now took up the entire southern sky. It flickered with light and began to roil ominously. There was a spectacular flash of lightning and a clap of thunder, and the gigantic cloud split in two. With a shattering roar that made the thunder seem like a mumble, a black dragon, limned in writhing, blue-white light, lunged out from between the clouds toward the hay wagon. Its evil eyes were red with rage, and monstrous bat wings fanned out behind it in the stormy twilight. A jagged bolt of lightning snaked from its fang filled mouth and a sharp CRACK exploded between Molly's ears. Asmodius' shield around the wagon flashed into an inverted bowl of blue-white light as it absorbed the lightning, and then faded back to invisibility.

The KA-BOOM of thunder smacked into her chest with rib-shaking force.

Molly screamed, curled into a terrified ball on the wagon seat and dropped the lines.

RUN! screamed Snowflake.

HIDE! shrieked Shadow.

For perhaps the first time in their lives, the two horses acted as a perfect team. They reared up and plowed the lightning-lashed sky with frantic hooves and ran off at a swift gallop, dragging the wildly bouncing wagon behind them.

Molly was thrown backwards into the wagon bed as they lurched forward. Lightning flashed and the rain poured down in wind-driven sheets. During one flash, Molly saw Ben sprawled unconscious. Asmodius sat next to him, his golden eyes blazed.

Get those horses under control. NOW.

The command slammed her into action. She struggled back up onto the pitching bench. The wagon lurched and bucked so violently that Molly was afraid she'd be thrown off. Hanging onto the seat with both hands, she looked out into the roaring madness of the storm. The few horses left on that stretch of road were in a panic and running wild. The frantic shrieks of horses and drivers and the thunder of hooves and wagon wheels filled the seething twilight. The road made a sharp turn a few hundred yards up ahead. At this speed they would miss the turn and plunge into the ditch and through the hedgerow.

The Shadow appeared on the seat beside her, a cold, still swirl of menacing blackness. It was so close—closer than it had ever been before. Fear froze her to the wagon seat and choked away her breath. With strength born of sheer terror, she aimed a single thought at the blackness beside her.

GO AWAY!

The Shadow disappeared.

Whimpering with relief, she groped around with one hand until she found the invisible reins and reached out with her thoughts to find the terrified minds of Shadow and Snowflake. Their distress was so great that for a moment she panicked with them all over again, but she grimly wrestled herself into a calm, clear focus. Into this focus she poured strong, soothing energy and settled it firmly into the horses' minds.

Whoa! You're safe. No need to run.

And miraculously, the two horses slowed and finally stopped—within a few feet of the turn.

Molly drove the wagon well past the turn and onto the edge of the road.

Close your eyes and rest now. Everything is OK.

Shadow and Snowflake relaxed in their harness with a sigh. For once, Snowflake was content to stay just where he was. Molly slumped back on the bench and started to shake. All the terror that she had suppressed while she was getting the horses under control returned in a wave of cold, black nausea.

A paw touched her shoulder.

You did well. I couldn't have done better myself. Now collect yourself. Ben is regaining consciousness.

Ben crawled slowly up from the wagon bed with a puzzled expression on his face. "Must'a whacked myself a good one on the side o' the wagon when the horses spooked, 'cus I blacked out. But fer the life o' me, I can't find a single lump or a cut. S'just a bit sore."

Molly looked over at Asmodius, who blinked.

"I'm glad you're OK. Back by that bend in the road, I saw a wagon in the ditch and I think the carriage behind us went in, too."

"They'll be needin' help then. You stay wi' the horses. I don't want 'em spookin' ag'in." And with that, he jumped down onto the muddy road and disappeared into the driving rain.

Warmed by Asmodius' praise, but still weak and terrified, she drew a shaking breath and asked. "How did that thing find us?"

After the Captain nabbed you, I woke up and realized you were missing. I left the shield up over the wagon and went to find you. I should have shielded myself, but I was in a hurry. So it must have sensed me when I did the mind 'maze on him. The man is a natural magic user, so the dragon had probably been watching him and then zeroed in on me.

"So why hasn't it come after us again?"

Because, if it's anywhere near as exhausted as I am from holding the shield, it's probably recouping. That charge of lightening would have taken a lot out of it. It'll be after us again soon, since it knows we're out here; and it will find us by looking for my shield.

"Oh, lovely, we're gonna be dragon bait. Asmodius, that sucker doesn't kid around. It'll have us roasted and chewed to a pulp in no time." She trembled so violently that the whole wagon shook.

Don't worry, I'll deal with the lizard. Save your strength. I have a feeling you're going to need it. I suggest you get some rest. And with those encouraging words, the mage flowed down into the wagon bed and went back to sleep.

Ben returned awhile later. The driver of the wagon had managed to slow it enough that when it went off the road the horses weren't injured and the wagon was undamaged but stuck. With Ben's help, they had been able to free it by hooking the horses up to the back and pulling it out. The carriage was a total loss. The driver and passengers were all injured and one of the horses was so badly crippled that they had to put him down. The wagon driver volunteered to take everyone back to his village where the healer could treat their injuries.

Ben checked over Shadow and Snowflake and then the wagon. When he was done, he looked up at Molly and said, "That was quite a job ya did gettin' these two lugheads ta slow down. Don' know what I woulda done if they was hurt." Ben's eyes held a haunted expression, and Molly realized that he had been the one who'd put the injured horse out of its misery. "I jus' wanna let ya know how grateful I am to ya fer savin' ma rig."

"No problem." She felt herself blushing.

"Well now, th' rain's let up a bit and I think we should all have a bite o' somethin' an' a rest."

He produced nosebags full of oats for the horses, and there was bread, cheese, and fruit for the humans. Asmodius ate a bit of Molly's cheese. He was too exhausted to hunt.

"I can drive if you still want to sleep," Molly offered.

"I think I'll take ya up on that. I know they'll be in good hands." He crawled back in the wagon bed and went to sleep next to Asmodius.

OK, you two, let's go. Molly put lots of persuasive intent into the message that yes, they really wanted to get moving.

She drove with no problems for a few hours until Asmodius appeared next to her.

That's our turnoff up ahead. Time to say goodbye. He leaped off the wagon and started toward a small trail that led down hill toward the river.

Asmodius, that's nothing but a deer trail.

True. But it is, none the less, our turnoff.

"Ben, time to wake up; I gotta go. Shadow, Snowflake, it's been real."

"You're not goin' in there, are ya?" Ben said as he climbed onto the bench and pointed to the trail Asmodius had taken.

"Yeah. Why?"

He shook his head. "That's the Wildwood. It's full o' strange magics and the trees have a mind o' their own. Sensible folk leave it be."

"It's the way I need to go," Molly said. She handed the "lines" back to Ben, grabbed her pack, and jumped down onto the road.

"Well, if ya gotta, ya gotta, but be careful." He reached down and swatted her gently on the shoulder.

"I will. Thanks for the ride."

8
Strength

he trail twisted and turned and bumped its way down toward the river. It was muddy underfoot and Molly had to watch her step. The dripping, lichen-encrusted alder branches made fantastic patterns against the dim, late-afternoon sky and the forest crawled with silence. The occasional soft rustle in the underbrush and the gurgle of hidden creeks punctuated the eerie stillness. The hair on the back of her neck rose to attention and the spot between her shoulder blades tingled unpleasantly. Something was watching her, but it wasn't The Shadow. That had left as soon as they'd entered the Wildwood. She knew it was gone because she no longer felt its chill heaviness on the edge of her senses. No, this was something else. If she concentrated hard enough she could hear It breathing. And then, after a few minutes, all she could hear was It breathing. It came from everywhere at once. It surrounded her. She kept looking back and off to the sides and up ahead, but nothing stirred in the dripping forest.

"Um, Asmodius?"

Yes?

"Do you hear breathing?"

No.

Asmodius' ears were twice as sharp as hers. Why couldn't he hear it?

"Ben said these woods are haunted or something."

The locals fear this forest, and rightly so. For some reason it's saturated with earth magic. Things get a bit strange in here at times.

"Does earth magic make breathing sounds?"

Not that I know of.

The breathing continued. It wasn't her imagination.

She needed to hear something, anything besides that awful sound, so she asked, "Why didn't you help me stop those horses? You could'a done it in a second."

Because I'm not allowed to protect you from the consequences of your own actions. All I can do is protect you from outside influences like the dragon and getting drafted. You were the one who accepted the ride with that farmer, so anything that happened to you as a result of that was your own problem.

"You mean you didn't make Ben stop?"

No.

"And you didn't make me decide to accept the ride?"

No, although at the time, I thought it was a good idea. I wanted a nap. Look, Molly, I'm just a guide. If I want you to do something, I'll tell you. I will never make *you do anything—even if it's in your own best interests. It is seldom a good thing for anyone to make anybody do anything. And besides, it's one of the Webmaster's rules.*

However, he continued, and Molly was sure she saw Asmodius' tail and ears droop just a little, *I* did *make that officer say I was a fine-looking cat. Pride and power have always been my undoing.*

Molly smiled. "But you are beautiful and powerful. Why have all that power and all those good looks if you can't enjoy them once in awhile?"

An excellent question, and one, I might add, that has been asked by even keener minds than your own. There is nothing wrong with reveling in our assets, even though the things we tend to be proudest of are gifts from the Gods and none of our doing anyway. But when we use those gifts the wrong way, we always wind up paying for it. That officer would never have said I was a fine looking cat. He was definitely a dog person. He loathed cats. I could tell. I made him say I was handsome just because I could. And that, Molly, was abuse of power.

"But that was such a small thing, hardly even worth noticing."

Ah, but the small things add up.

"So there's somebody up there keeping score and pitching down a lightning bolt when we hit thirteen?"

No, of course not. I'm not really sure how it happens, but somehow, we never seem to be able to get away with much of anything.

"Um, Asmodius, are you sure you don't hear something breathing? Something really big?"

I don't hear any breathing.

As evening approached and the air cooled, tendrils of mist started to snake slowly up from the rain wet earth. They looked like lost souls wandering in the wilderness and did nothing to improve the ambiance of the place.

"Er, maybe we should go back up to the main road."

If we do that the dragon will find us. I'm hoping all the magic in this forest will hide my shield.

"But, Asmodius, this place totally creeps me out and you said you could protect us. Let's go back."

Allow me to make a suggestion. The Chair can turn into a warm, dry tent as soon as you put it down. You are tired and hungry and wet, and not in the best frame of mind to make decisions. Things will look different in the morning.

"If I survive until morning! That breather thing is really big, and It wants me." It now sounded like Darth Vader was standing right behind her.

I doubt that it's the dragon that you're hearing, otherwise I would hear it as well, since it's really after me. You should be safe in the tent.

"OK, I'll wait 'til morning, and then we'll go back." And with that she hiked off the path, found a clear, flat place for the tent and set her pack down in the middle of it. The pack sat there for a few moments, then sprouted four feet and took off with surprising speed.

"Shit! Come back here with my stuff!" Molly chased the pack through the underbrush. Wet branches whipped at her face and tree roots sent her stumbling, but she finally chased it down. Only it wasn't a pack anymore, but a large tent. A light glowed inside it and the door was open and welcoming.

Molly sighed with exasperation, took off her wet, muddy boots and crawled inside the tent. "And just what was wrong with the place I picked out?"

Do I hear a "Thank you, I'm so glad to have a warm, dry place to rest in this ghastly forest"? or a "Hello, it's so nice to be talking with you again"? No, all I get are complaints! For your information, the spot you selected was way too close to the trail and I was right on top of an ant hill.

"You might have said something instead of running off like that. I thought I'd lost you."

Indignant silence followed this remark and Molly was sure she heard a contemptuous sniff.

"Oh, all right," she said. "You do make a wonderful tent and I'm sure I'll be safe and sound here for the night. I just wish I wasn't so wet."

No problem. Just hold your boots outside and clap them together to get the mud off and take off your wet clothes and pile everything over here—the corner in front of her lit up briefly—*and I'll have them dry for you by morning.*

"Thanks," Molly said with a bit more humility and appreciation. She proceeded to strip off her wet clothes and slip into her dry tank top and shorts. Cleaning off her boots as well as she could, she piled them and her wet clothes in the designated corner, and rolled out her sleeping bag.

Asmodius appeared at the door, shook himself dry, stepped daintily into the tent, and began his evening ablutions.

Molly lay back on her sleeping bag and watched him. As her tired muscles relaxed and her spinning brain quieted, the breathing started again.

"You still don't hear anything?"

No.

A cold fear began to seep into her bones in spite of the warmth of the tent.

"If you heard breathing that no one else could hear and that wouldn't go away, that would mean the sound was all in your head and that you were going crazy, wouldn't it?"

Just because you hear something that others can't, doesn't mean you're crazy.

"OK, I may not be crazy now, but I'm gonna be if I have to listen to this breathing much longer."

Oh, stop being a drama queen. Your mind is perfectly sound and will stay perfectly sound—breathing or no breathing.

"That's easy for you to say. You don't have to listen to it. And it keeps getting louder. It's like it's just sitting there waiting for me, and when it gets me, it's gonna eat me. You've got to do something, I can't stand this much longer."

You'd be surprised at what you are able to withstand. You're tired and hungry, so why don't I get you some dinner and we'll worry about your nemesis in the morning.

Molly's plate filled with a hearty beef stew and a large chunk of chewy brown bread. She actually managed to eat a little of it.

She crawled into her sleeping bag and Asmodius curled up next to her, pressing his warm, solid bulk into her back. The big cat began to purr and the deep rumble vibrated between her shoulder blades. She slept soundly until morning.

"I think we'd better keep going along this path," Molly said to Asmodius and The Chair as she devoured her breakfast. "I hate this forest, it's creepy, but turning back to the main road would put us all in danger and it probably won't get rid of this breathing in my head. I get the feeling that whatever is doing it is just a bit further down this trail. If I find it, maybe I can get it to stop."

Or it'll eat me.

Molly finished her breakfast, slipped into her dry clothes, and stepped outside the tent. The sun shone sulkily through the gnarly alder branches and ground mist. A few birds muttered into the light dappled gloom. The Chair folded itself into a backpack—neatly repacked with all the gear. She put it on and followed Asmodius through the forest and onto the trail.

The air was muggy and filled with tiny gnats that took great pleasure in tormenting every living thing unfortunate enough to be in their vicinity. Hours passed, and the breathing continued, pressing down on her like a gigantic hand. In spite of the humid heat, she was shaking and covered with a cold sweat.

As they rounded a bend in the path, the source of the breathing became all too apparent. An enormous, black dragon lay curled up asleep. It filled the entire valley formed by the steep, rocky hillsides that flanked the river. Molly shrank back from it in horror. The only way she could slip past it was to sneak under the beast's huge nostrils that were puffing out lung searing gouts of smoke. Its head rested on a forehand armed with wicked claws.

Cruelly sharp fangs as long as broadswords protruded from the monster's upper jaw.

Shit, how do we get around it?

Walk.

What if it wakes up?

Not my problem. It's not my dragon, and it's not the one that's after us.

And with that, he trotted fearlessly around the dragon, and out of sight. The beast didn't even twitch a talon.

There was nothing for Molly to do but follow. If she turned around she would be without a guide and would surely get drafted or eaten by the other dragon. And she'd probably have to listen to this infernal breathing the rest of her life. If she hid and waited until it left, she could be waiting a long, long time. From what she remembered from fairytales, dragons could sleep for hundreds of years.

She tiptoed toward the sleeping hulk. The heat pouring off it was intense; and the sulfurous reek was overpowering. She was just creeping past the dragon's nose, when a scaly hand pinned her foot to the ground with a needle sharp talon.

She hadn't even seen it move.

"Wait just a minute, Molly Adair."

The feminine voice seemed to come from everywhere—even from deep inside her. Cold fear turned her gut to water. She struggled to escape, but the dragon only pushed her talon through Molly's boot and into her foot. Pain lanced up her leg until she held still.

"It's time for us to have a little chat."

The dragon was resting her head on her other forehand, but Molly still had to look up to see into her eyes—and wished she hadn't. They were fierce and totally heartless.

"Y-you can talk," she stammered. "And how do you know my name?"

"I'm a dragon. All dragons talk. In fact, we can speak every language known to humans and several more. And yes, I know your name. In fact I know all about you. For instance, just before your parents left on that last trip, you had a fight with your mother and told her you wished she were dead. Didn't you?"

She gasped. "How could you possibly know that?"

"And you got mad at Glenda Harper and convinced all her friends at school that she was a lesbian. Didn't you?"

Molly was in tears.

"And you are angry with your grandmother. You've decided that not only is it her fault you had to move away from your friends, but it's also somehow her fault that your parents died. You were planning on running away as soon as you got the chance. Weren't you?"

"How do you know all this?" she screamed.

"Ah, that's for you to figure out," said the dragon, shifting to a more comfortable position. Black scales the size of serving platters made dry, rasping noises. The talon, however, continued to pin her foot to the ground. Coughing and sweating in the hot, sulphurous smoke, she felt like a mouse being tortured by a cat.

"And if I can't?"

"Then I eat you."

Raging fury swept through her, completely eclipsing her fear. What right did this oversized lizard have to threaten her? And then the fury was replaced by a steely determination. She'd beat the dragon at her own game.

"How many guesses do I get?"

"Guess."

"Three?"

"Of course."

"How many questions?"

"As many as you like, but if they sound like they could be a guess phrased as a question then they count as a guess."

"OK, first guess. It's obvious, but I have to ask it. You're psychic, right?"

"Wrong. I'm keenly intelligent and intuitive and, yes, very psychic, but even if I wasn't, I would still know all about you. Two guesses left."

Modest, too.

"Have you ever met me before today?"

"Oh, yes, my dear, you might say we've been inseparable."

"But I never knew you were there."

"No, I don't think you were ever aware of me, but recent events have called me to your attention."

Molly thought desperately back to everything Father Elysius had said about dragons, and recalled Asmodius' voice: *It's not* my *dragon.*

"You're my dragon!"

"Of course, that is obvious. I won't even count it as a guess. But what exactly does a dragon become when it attaches itself to a human?"

OK, so it was a part of her, but which part? The dragon knew all her secrets, all the rotten stuff that made her squirm.

Her mother didn't die because she had wished her dead; she knew that, but a part of her still writhed in guilt and self-loathing because of those hateful words.

It had been easy, wicked fun to convince Glenda's homophobic friends that Glenda was a dyke, but Glenda's look of hurt confusion when her friends began snubbing her still haunted Molly.

Her grandmother would have been grief stricken and worried sick if she'd run away, but she was going to do it simply because she had the power to make someone else hurt as much as she was hurting.

So, the dragon knew all this, and she was big and black and scary.

"I know. You're everything that's bad about me. You're like, my shadow side."

The dragon roared, reared up on her hind legs, and spread her wings. Molly was free. She could have run, but she was riveted in place with awe. The dragon was taller than a three-story house. Radiant energy spiraled up and down and around her, making her scales glitter silver and gold and turning her wings into rainbows. But there was no emotion in her eyes, only fierce, bright power.

"Wrong. Look again, Molly Adair. Which part of you am I? You have one more guess."

Power. Molly's quick mind realized that power was really the issue in those incidents the dragon had mentioned. They all represented ways she had tapped into the driving force inside her and put it to use. The most recent time she had used it was when she had willed Shadow and Snowflake to a stop. That had taken a lot of power, and that was what had awakened the dragon.

The dragon came to rest on her forelegs once again.

"You are my power, my strength," Molly said.

"Exactly so. Use me wisely, or I may eat you yet!"

And with a mighty leap, she was airborne. As she spiraled up into the sky, her wings cast a shadow over the entire river valley.

"MY NAME IS RIADA."

There was a flash of light and a clap of thunder, and she was gone.

Sitting in the path in front of her was Asmodius. The sun was clear and bright, a light breeze was blowing, and magic shimmered freely through the forest.

The horrid breathing was gone.

Would you like some lunch? he asked.

Molly threw back her head and laughed hysterically. "I almost get eaten by a huge, fire-breathing dragon and you want to know if I'm hungry? Where were you when I needed you? You deserted me, you rotten animal!"

Now Molly, be fair. I couldn't have helped you, but I did give you all the hints I could. And I am very glad you weren't eaten. Now, I repeat, would you like some lunch?

"I can't eat now! My heart is beating a mile a minute and my stomach is doing flip-flops. I need to walk and calm down."

And so they walked and Molly's heart and stomach slowly began functioning normally. It was still a tentative normal, but normal enough for her curiosity to kick back in.

"Why did the dragon tell me her name? I mean, I didn't ask her for it or anything."

Dragons are careful about who knows their names. They are a close-mouthed bunch in general, but when it comes to their names, they're absolutely neurotic. Your dragon gave you her name because you guessed the answer to her question, and when you beat a dragon at a guessing game, it has to give you its name. They may be neurotic and dangerous, but they play fair. But just because she gave you her name, doesn't mean she wants anyone else to know it.

"Do you know it?"

No. I heard it, but I can't remember it.

"What's the big deal about knowing a dragon's name?"

It gives you the power to summon the dragon any time you want. It has to come, but it doesn't have to be happy about it. I've heard that calling a dragon for trivial reasons can be very bad for your health.

"So, how do I know what's trivial and what isn't?"

You don't.

"Oh, lovely. Well, I guess I won't be summoning my dragon any time soon."

They continued walking in silence. The shadows lengthened and Molly finally said, "Let's stop and eat."

They found a spot well off the trail but right next to the river. Since it was getting late in the day, they set up camp. Molly dropped her pack on a flat, clear space and said "Tent, please," and her pack became a tent once more.

Gives a whole new meaning to the phrase "pitch a tent" doesn't it? Asmodius said. He made her a cheeseburger and a large helping of French fries, filled the chalice with soda, then disappeared into the forest before she had a chance to overcome her surprise and thank him.

The path continued to run by the river and their journey along it was uneventful for the next week or so. They didn't meet a soul, and Molly's days were filled with dappled sunlight and the rush and clatter of the river as it ran impatiently over its rocky bed on its way to the sea. Walking was easy now. She could hike even the roughest parts for hours without tiring, and her tunic and leggings were almost too big for her. Her once pasty skin was tan and glowed with health. A sense of purpose surrounded her. But any thought of the future or of doing anything else but following this safe, comforting path filled her with hopeless dread. Her journey was a luminous tightrope over a dark, endless chasm that contained nothing except The Shadow. If she allowed herself to think about what would happen when she came to the end of it or what would happen if she stepped off it, her palms prickled with sweat and her insides turned to ice water.

And so she learned to concentrate on the now.

Asmodius occasionally kept her company, answering hundreds of questions about The Wild Wood and the magic that ran through it like a living thing. But most of the time he would sprint ahead a mile or so and cat nap until Molly caught up with him and then sprint ahead again. This left Molly to her own devices for most of the time and she got quite a bit of thinking done.

One bright, perfect day when Asmodius seemed to be in a slightly mellower mood than usual, Molly decided it would be a good time to ask him a question that had been rolling around in her head for quite some time.

"Do you know my grandmother?"

Molly wasn't certain, but the big cat's elegant step may have faltered just a touch and the tip of his tail twitched. But he looked straight ahead and continued down the path.

Why do you ask? What difference would it make if I did?

"I know you can't tell me who sent me here, but maybe you could tell me if you know the person that I think sent me— because I'm almost sure it was my grandmother. If you do know her, it would make me feel better; because then she would have been sending me to someone she trusted and thought might be able to help me, which would mean that she didn't do this just to get rid of me."

There was a long silence. Birds sang sweet, liquid songs from the branches above and an otter plopped into the river in search of lunch. And Molly realized that she was holding her breath as she waited for Asmodius' answer.

Yes, Estelle and I know each other well.

She let go of her breath with a soft sigh of relief. Asmodius had stopped in the middle of the path and begun a furious round of face washings. Molly skidded to a stop and plunked down cross-legged in front of him.

"Has she ever mentioned me?"

She has been mentioning you to me constantly ever since you were born. First there were the baby pictures that had to be suitably admired, and then I had to listen to every one of your accomplishments—from your first steps to your latest academic awards. Doting grandmothers can be quite tiresome.

Muscles Molly didn't even know she had relaxed and she felt herself grinning like a fool. Tears prickled the insides of her eyelids. Her grouchy grandma really did love her. Who'd a thunk it?

"Can she do magic like you?"

Of course. She's one of the best. Very few of the mages I know are more skilled.

"And are you one of those?"

The big cat's ears turned into airplane wings.

No.

Molly reached out and touched her egotistical companion's soft paw and said, "Then she must be very powerful. Do you think she would be willing to teach me?"

I think you will have a hard time getting her to stop teaching you.

"Why didn't you tell me all this?"

You didn't ask.

———

A few days later Molly and Asmodius were hiking a section of the path that ran right next to the river. High walls of eroded river bed rose up on both sides of it. An oddly shaped stone lay in the path ahead and, for want of anything better to do, she kicked it.

"Was my dragon really going to eat me if I didn't guess what she was?" The fact that she had a huge, intensely intelligent entity inside of her that was perfectly capable of eating her alive was unsettling to say the least.

Oh yes. But she would have eaten your soul, not your body. You would have become a shell of a human being, a dragon puppet, like the person who belongs to the rogue dragon. And you should bear in mind that if she had really wanted to win, you wouldn't have had a chance in the guessing game. Dragons are wily creatures. Your dragon brought herself to your attention because she wanted to be recognized and used consciously.

They'd caught up with the rock she'd kicked. She knew it was the same rock because it was different from all the other rocks in this forest. It was earthy red and shaped like the arrowheads she'd seen in museums. And it glowed.

She kicked it.

"So I can use her?"

Of course. You are using her and feeding her every time you satisfy a desire or work to achieve a goal—especially when you use magic to do it. That's why dragons are attracted to magic users.

When they caught up with her stone, it was glowing even more brightly.

I wouldn't kick that again if I were you.

"Why? It leaves nice tracers when it moves."

She kicked it again.

The stone veered to the side and hit the high bank that bordered the trail.

It exploded with a deafening KA-POW! All the rocks around it began to glow and tremble.

EGADS! YOU IDIOT! JUMP!

9

The Hermit

olly stood paralyzed with fear as the rocks above her rumbled ominously. They were going to fall any second and there was no way she could outrun them.

She was gonna die.

JUMP! NOW! Asmodius had materialized half a soccer field's length away.

And then she heard his voice from another place and time. *Remember, power flows where your intention goes.*

She reached inside herself for the power that Shadow and Snowflake had taught her to find, concentrated on a spot next to the cat, and willed herself there...

...and became a dizzying swirl in a heartbeat of frigid blackness.

With her next heartbeat Molly found herself standing next to Asmodius, facing a roaring cascade of earth and rocks. Seconds later it was a huge, jumbled pile of debris. She sank down to her knees, waited for her breath to do something besides gasp in terror, and tried not to think about what would have happened if they hadn't jumped.

The only sounds were her rasping breath and the occasional plink as a stone fell down onto its neighbors. No birds twittered, no insects buzzed, and no river splashed because, oh shit, she'd dammed it up.

Now look at what you've done! Asmodius' voice jolted into her whirling brain. *Why can't you ever just do as I say? You could have killed us both.*

Molly shuddered with guilt and misery.

But then, struggling through all the exhaustion and shame came the thought, *You jumped! You can do it!*

Mental air punches—Yes! Yes! Yes!

However, she didn't think this was a good time to mention this to the furious mage, so she just whispered, "I'm sorry."

It's nice that you're sorry, continued the merciless feline, *but sorry doesn't get rid of the dam. The river will flood everything upstream for miles. You must fix things.*

"How?"

That stone you were kicking was a spearhead fashioned by the Unglazy, the Little People of Damia. They infuse everything they create with extra earth prana. Since we are in The Wild Wood, kicking it increased its already high vibration level until it became a tiny bomb, and that pile of rocks it created is loaded with even more earth magic than usual. It will be a simple matter and a good lesson in levitation for you to help each rock and dirt clod back up to rebuild the bank.

Molly stood, put her hands on her hips, and surveyed the devastation. It was gonna take forever, but at least she would be able to correct her mistake—and practice her magic.

"OK, tell me how."

If you can jump, you can move these rocks. Just connect with the rock's energy, tell it you're going to help it go home, and give it a little boost. Like this. A huge boulder from the top of the pile floated up and thunked into its original position. *The stuff in that pile is so heavily infused with earth prana that, if you move one or two rocks at a time, it will only take a tiny bit of mage magic, so we should be safe from the dragon.*

Asmodius curled up and went to sleep.

Molly looked hopelessly at the impromptu dam. The water had reached the top and was beginning to cascade over it. She felt like the woman in the fairy tale who had to spin straw into gold, and wished there was a Rumpelstiltskin somewhere out there who knew how to levitate rocks. But there wasn't. She had to do this herself.

She stared at a fist-sized rock on top of the pile and thought at it as hard as she could, *Hey, rock, get back up where you came from.*

It just sat there.

She tried again and again.

Nothing.

She crumpled down in the path and stared at the slide. Her eyes unfocused and her mind went blank with confusion...and she noticed the earth prana. Every rock glowed with it. She looked back at her rock and tapped into her power; but this time she let it sync up with the magic shimmering around that small chunk of river bank.

She pushed, imagining it back in its original position.

The rock rocketed up and slammed into place.

Asmodius twitched in his sleep.

It was easy after that. She moved rock after rock with gentle shoves.

Then she tried moving two rocks at once.

Easy.

Three?

No problem.

Pure power uncoiled inside of her. It fizzed and bubbled and flooded her heart with ecstasy. She felt Riada spread her wings with joy and ride the magic. Every one of her scales glittered as she breathed it in and then breathed it out. And as her dragon danced, Molly's power increased.

This was so totally awesome.

Entranced by the mage magic coursing through her, she began moving four or five boulders at once and then large sections of the slide. She was almost done when Asmodius screamed into her head,

RUN, NOW, THE DRAGON'S FOUND US!

Shit! The dragon. How could she have forgotten about the freakin' dragon? Fear pounded through her as she raced after Asmodius. They followed the path for a bit and then cut uphill on an animal trail. There was a thunderous roar and an explosion behind them followed by blast of heat.

More angry roars.

They ran until Molly's breath came in gasps and her legs felt like tree stumps.

Hide in the underbrush and hold still. The earth magic will shield us.

They hunkered down inside a clump of stuff that looked like holly.

The dragon was widening its search, flaming chunks of forest and coming closer and closer. The roar of the fire was deafening and the smoke burned her lungs.

A wave of panic gripped her. *I forgot my pack. The Chair's back there!*

She jumped up and ran back down the path, coughing on the roiling clouds of smoke.

Molly, get back here or you're going to be toast! The Chair is perfectly capable of taking care of itself.

If anything happened to The Chair she would never forgive herself.

A low-pitched wail rose up from the forest. It sounded like the air raid sirens in old World War II movies. It sent shivers down her spine and goose bumps swarming up her arms. She stopped and gasped in horror. White wisps were seeping out of every tree and swirling into strangely beautiful ghostlike goblins. As each spirit emerged it threw back its head and added its voice to that awful keening.

She forced her feet to keep moving. The heat was unbearable and every breath seared her lungs. When she saw The Chair pattering down the trail toward her, she sobbed in relief, scooped it up, and hugged it close. "I'm so sorry. I didn't mean to forget you. Are you OK?"

Yes, but I won't be, and neither will you, if you stand here much longer. The wind's picked up and it's blowing the fire our way.

The wailing was now so loud that it nearly drowned out the dragon's roars and the howl of the wind and fire in the trees. Shrugging on the pack, she turned and fled before the advancing storm of flame and smoke. But her feet felt like two rocks, and she could hardly breathe.

The fire was coming closer.

A wall of sizzling magic rushed over them toward the flames. It felt like dense earth magic, but there was an edge of sharpness to it that whispered "mage." The wailing pounded into her head, making it throb with pain. Every step was torture and every breath cut into her lungs like a knife. The heat from the fire seared her skin.

Then, with an angry snort, the dragon flew away. The ghosts slowly disappeared back into the trees—at least the ones that still had trees to return to.

Thank the Gods! The Chair sagged in relief. *Dragons can't stand dryad keening, and I believe Tamerlane just put out the fire.*

Molly collapsed. Collapsing was a good move. The air close to the ground was cooler and fresher. The fire had, indeed, died back, but the forest still smoldered and flared up into the occasional gout of flame. She shook with exhaustion and relief, and her breath came in shuddering gasps.

"Who's Tamerlane?" she asked as soon as she could get a sentence out.

He's a mage friend of Asmodius' that lives a bit farther on in the middle of this forest. I hope he didn't blow his cover putting out that fire. I think Asmodius was headed there....

I was, said Asmodius as he appeared beside them. His mouth was drawn back in a snarl. Rage sparked off him, sending pin pricks of pain over Molly's skin as he turned on her. *I told you to move those rocks one at a time!*

"It was taking forever." She was so not gonna to tell the furious cat that she had stupidly allowed Riada to seduce her into using more mage energy than she needed.

I don't recall that we were in any particular hurry. You might as well have sent out a telegram that said, "Here we are, Mr. Dragon, come and get us!" Get up and start walking. It's late, but we may make it to Tamerlane's place before dark—if it's still there. Hopefully that stinking pile of scales didn't notice the mage magic.

He turned and stalked down a side trail toward the main path.

How could she have been so stupid? Because of her, hundreds of beautiful, magical trees were dead, burnt to a crisp; and their ghosts, The Chair had called them dryads, were without homes. She could see them wandering like lost souls through the living forest. Occasionally, one would melt into a tree. Another dryad must have taken it in. And what if this other mage lost his home because of her carelessness? She shuddered and kept on walking.

A moonless, black night had fallen by the time Molly spotted a light shining high up on the slope above the river. After much casting about and cursing and muttering, they were able to locate the trail that wound its way up to the light, which turned out to be a lamp shining over the door of a small house.

Molly knocked and waited.

Nothing happened.

Knock harder, he's probably asleep.

Molly pounded on the door and this time was rewarded by the thump of feet hitting the floor and a loud snort and several harrumphs.

"Yes, yes, I hear you. You don't have to beat the door down!"

A light came on inside the house and footsteps approached the door. A moment later it flew open and golden light spilled out around a tall, lanky form draped in a long, gray robe.

"Well, where are you? Show yourself!" the figure peered out into the night, squinting in the bright lamplight, which revealed a gaunt, craggy face surrounded by a cloud of snow-white hair and a long, white beard. But it was the eyes that drew her attention. They were a deep, clear blue and glared fiercely into the darkness. They were the sort of eyes that you wouldn't want looking into your heart too closely. Not because you'd be worried that they would judge you harshly, but because you'd be afraid that you might disappoint them somehow.

Lower your sights for once in your life, Tamerlane. We're down here.

"Ah, Asmodius!" exclaimed the mage, making the proper ocular adjustments. "So you were the one that got that dragon all excited. And who is this young man?"

This is Molly Adair, my client. Actually she's the one responsible for the dragon.

"Oh." Molly squirmed through the painful silence that followed until he finally said, "Come in."

He led her into a large room lit by a single lamp. There was wood laid for a fire in the fireplace. Tamerlane glanced over at it and waved his hand.

It burst into flames.

He strode to the back of the room and opened one of two doors. "Here is your room. Get yourself settled and I'll find something for you to eat." He pointed at the candle on the small table by the bed and it flared obediently into life, revealing a small room. A bed and table were its only furnishings until Molly set her pack down. There was a flurry of motion and The Chair appeared, carefully color-coordinated to the room's muted browns and greens. Her belongings sat in a neat pile beside it.

"Ah, you have The Chair. Excellent." He pointed to a pitcher of water sitting next to a washbasin on the table and steam began to rise out of it. "There's hot water and soap, wash up and come have your supper. Asmodius is already out catching his."

Molly dragged herself over to the pitcher and poured its contents into the washbasin. She picked up the soap and scrubbed the grime and soot off her face and hands and dumped the rest of the water over her head and into the basin. When she finished, the water was black.

Then she plunked down in The Chair and said, "OK, who is this guy?"

Here's the short story. He joined the king's army when he was about your age and became a spy for the priests. As payment for six years of outstanding service, the priests sent him to Tesseract Academy. He eventually became the best mage of the lot. After working at his craft for many years, he retired and built this house. He does research and trains the occasional student that the mages send him.

"What's Tesseract Academy?"

A place where they train mages.

—

Tamerlane was nowhere around, but he had laid out dinner for her. It was simple, but after over two weeks of roughing it, eating hot soup and bread from a table was a luxury. As she ate, Molly looked around the house.

Two large multi-paned windows flanked the door and a huge river rock fireplace with a smooth stone hearth took up a good portion of the opposite wall. Fire leaped and crackled on the hearth and small impish figures of pure flame cavorted on the coals. Trivets, pot hangers and a spit indicated that this was where the cooking was done. To the left of the fireplace and along the adjoining wall was the food prep and storage area. There was a polished stone countertop, cupboards, and a sink with a pump. Above the sink was another window. To the right of the fireplace were two doors. The one next to the fireplace probably led to Tamerlane's bedroom behind the fireplace and the other one opened into Molly's smaller room.

The wall opposite the kitchen was lined with books. Most were ancient leather-bound tomes with gold and silver lettering on their spines. Occasionally, one would shimmer and disappear, leaving behind a faint whiff of ozone; or another book would appear with disconcerting suddenness in one of the empty spaces on the shelf. Looking at them for any length of time was unsettling. Two upholstered chairs with matching ottomans sat in front of the bookcases on a fantastically patterned, knotted wool rug. The table between them was piled with books and pipes and papers that shifted lazily in their places like restless sleepers.

The entire house vibrated with magic. But it was an entirely different magic from the magic of The Wild Wood that surrounded and shielded it. This was mage magic—sharp and intoxicating.

As she was taking her dish over to the sink she noticed a sword hanging in its scabbard on the wall between Tamerlane's bedroom and the fireplace. Goosebumps swarmed up her arms and her stomach lurched. It looked just like the sword she'd seen at Madame Rue's and the one in the armory. The hilt was wrapped in a black silk cord, and a gold griffin peeked out from under the wrappings. A simple but elegant iron ring formed the guard that separated the hilt from the scabbard and blade. The scabbard was long and thin and black, and finished to a velvety gloss. Both the hilt and the scabbard had that satisfying, comfortable look of fine equipment that has been used hard and impeccably maintained.

As soon as she finished washing up, she was back in front of the fire staring at the sword. Her hands itched to take it down from the wall, pull it out of its scabbard and examine it; but she knew for certain that touching this sword without Tamerlane's permission would be a bad move.

As she stood there mesmerized, with her hands shoved into her pockets, she realized that she wanted, more than anything else in the world, to learn how to use a sword. The Chair had said that Tamerlane worked with students; maybe he'd be willing to teach her.

At that moment, Tamerlane pushed open the door with his foot and entered with an armload of firewood. Asmodius trailed in behind him looking exhausted but well fed. He jumped up on one of the two upholstered chairs and immediately went to sleep. Molly closed the door while Tamerlane deposited the wood in a box on the hearth, added a few pieces to the fire, sat down in the other chair, and began to fill his pipe

"Where did you get your sword? It looks just like the king's sword in the palace armory."

Tamerlane looked up at her in surprise, but continued futzing with his pipe. "It was given to me by a very powerful lady in payment for services rendered."

Molly waited until the mage had his pipe burning satisfactorily, and then asked, "Would you teach me how to use a sword?"

A spasm of coughing seized him, and the exhaled smoke wreathed his head in a thick haze. "WHAT?!!!"

WHAT?!!! Asmodius levitated up from his snooze and stared at her.

"I said," Molly replied, aghast at their response, "Would you teach me how to use a sword?"

"Why in the multiverse would a young lady like you want to learn sword-craft?" sputtered Tamerlane.

Why indeed? Darkfire, her favorite WarCraft Universe persona, was a sword fighter and so was Xena—swords fascinated her, especially Damian officers' swords. Since her arrival here she'd already seen three of these supposedly rare blades—one floating in front of Madam Rue's tapestry and dripping blood, one tucked in a dead king's belt, and one belonging to a powerful mage. A strong suspicion came bubbling up out of the shadowy depths where dreams and nightmares are born. It whispered that, if she wanted to keep on living, she needed to learn everything she could about swords and sword fighting. But how could she explain this to a pair of irate mages?

"I don't know," she mumbled.

"Well, you need a better reason than that." Tamerlane said, throwing up his hands and glaring at her. "Don't you realize that as soon as you belt on a sword you become a target? You're eventually going to have to either kill or be killed or both. A sword is a subtle and powerful weapon—not a romantic waist decoration! No. I'm not teaching you. Go to bed."

<hr>

A black shadow watched and waited as she fought with a faceless man. He wielded a sword and she had a knife, which he easily swatted out of her hand. He lashed out and cut her arm and followed with two crippling slashes to her legs. As she lay helpless and bleeding, he laughed with pleasure and began slicing away at her. Cut after cut set her body on fire with pain. Just as her tormentor aimed his sword at her heart, he threw back his head and roared a soul-searing roar.

Molly jerked awake. She was trembling and covered with sweat.

Savage roars shook the house and everything reeked of wood smoke.

Her first impulse was to dive back under the covers, but instead she ran in search of Tamerlane. She found him standing under a tree near the front door. Off in the distance, brilliant orange flames leaped and whirled as they devoured the nearby forest, and the rogue dragon danced in their midst. Dark shadows and golden firelight flickered and shimmering dryads streamed out of their trees like living smoke and began their nerve shattering keening, turning the forest into a nightmare of grief and fury. The rogue dragon raked the area with its evil, red eyes, searching for her and Asmodius. Molly's heart thudded in fear. "It's gonna find the house!"

"No, it won't. The property is shielded with earth magic. It looks just like the rest of the forest." Molly could feel the mage summoning waves of The Wild Wood's energy and pushing them toward the blaze, keeping it somewhat in check.

She huddled next to Tamerlane and watched the forest burn. If the beast kept this up, it wouldn't matter whether it found the house or not; they would still go up in flames. But eventually the dryad's wails were too much for it and the dragon gave one last mind-shattering roar and disappeared in a flash of flame. A smoky night breeze chilled her and set her teeth chattering as Tamerlane and the dryads smothered the flames.

"Go to bed," said the mage.

Molly awoke the next morning even more exhausted than she'd been the night before. More sleep was out of the question, however. Her dreams had been full of dodging dragons and getting slashed with a sword. She stumbled out to the kitchen and Tamerlane informed her that she was filthy and looked like something Asmodius had dragged in. "A bath in the river will do you good." He handed her a bar of soap and a towel and gently shoved her out the door.

Bright sunlight dazzled through green leaves that rippled in the warm breeze and the occasional chirp and twitter of a songbird punctuated the sound of the river as it rushed past. The acrid smell of the still smoldering ashes stabbed at her throat and conscience. Instead of heading for the river, she turned and hiked through the trees behind the house and arrived, just a few minutes later, at the burnt-out forest. Smoke drifted up in eerie silence from piles of burnt underbrush, and blackened stumps and tree trunks studded a patch of gloom and death the size of a football field. Molly stared in horror at the damage her stupid, careless mistake had caused. And this was only a small piece of it. Several miles back even more of this beautiful forest lay in smoking ruin.

A deep sadness lay over the charred earth and she could almost hear the forest sobbing. In fact, as she looked around more carefully, she realized it *was* sobbing. Dozens of wispy dryads huddled around the edges of the destruction. Their weeping made every piece of Molly's already broken heart ache.

"I'm so sorry," she whispered to the nearest one.

The tree spirit regarded her solemnly with huge, black, alien eyes and sent a wave of cool, earthy greenness swirling around Molly. "Why should you be sorry? It was the wicked dragon who did this terrible thing."

"Yes, but it was my carelessness that brought it here."

"We know this. And we know that you intended no harm." The dryad's kind words eased the ache in her heart and lifted an almost physical weight from her shoulders. But they weren't enough.

"Yeah, but I still feel terrible. What can I do to help?"

The other spirits had gathered close around her and one said, "You could plant more trees."

Duh! Of course that's what she needed to do. "So where would I get the trees? And I need to know how to plant them."

"We will guide you. Just give us a few more days to mourn our friends and for the ground to cool."

"OK, lemme know when you're ready." She headed down to the river below Tamerlane's house with a much lighter heart.

The river was a bit wider and deeper here. She stripped off her clothes and waded into the cool water. Steeling herself for the shock, she dove in and swam upstream fighting the icy current until her heart was pumping wildly and the blood sang in her veins. As she relaxed and let the river carry her downstream she noticed a sapphire blue pool and swam into it.

The water swirled softly around her like the satiny folds of Madame Rue's cloak and she floated in a time out of time. Her mind cleared and memories began to replay. They flashed before her closed eyes in vivid detail and rearranged themselves into a new pattern.

Everything was the same, but everything was different.

She now knew for certain that her grandmother had sent her on this journey and by doing so, she'd saved her life. She would have died at The Shadow's next appearance. And her life now depended on following the river, even though she didn't have a clue about where it would lead her. And she also knew that the river had brought her to Tamerlane to learn sword-craft. And sure, she'd made some dumb mistakes. But her Dad had always said that making a mistake didn't mean you were stupid or bad—as long as you learned from it, fixed it if you could, and didn't make it again. And she was gonna fix her biggest mistake by planting more trees.

And maybe, if she learned everything she could and worked hard, there was a future out there for her somewhere. Molly floated quietly, savoring her newfound serenity and the cool caress of the water on her skin.

—

Tamerlane sat on a small stool by the fire cooking breakfast. The smell of frying bacon made her stomach rumble. He turned to study her as she walked in the house. "Ah, much better."

The morning sun poured through the front windows, turning the occasional flecks of dust into glitter. It warmed Molly's back as she sat down to eat her morning meal of bacon and fried vegetables.

"Will the dragon come back?"

"I doubt it, but one never knows with dragons," Tamerlane said as he took a sip of his tea. That and a piece of toast were all he was eating for breakfast.

As they were cleaning up, Molly said, "I still need you to teach me how to use a sword."

The mage sighed. "I was afraid of that. However, I need a better reason. 'I don't know' lacks a certain amount of conviction."

Asmodius was lounging on his chair trying to look unconcerned, but Molly could tell by the tilt of his ears that he was listening for her answer.

"My life depends on me learning to use a sword. Not just because I'm going to get attacked, although that might happen, but because it's part of who I'm supposed to be."

"That's a very good reason, but by itself, it's not enough. My answer is still 'No.'"

—

Molly spent the rest of the day learning how to chop firewood and trying to think of another reason why Tamerlane should teach her. By dinnertime she was hot and sweaty and her arms felt like rubber. She went down to her pool for a swim and came back refreshed and ready to eat.

After dinner she said, "I need you to teach me because I want to learn how to fight with a sword so bad I can taste it. Every time I look at your sword, my hands itch, and I break out in a sweat. If you won't teach me, I'll leave and find someone else who will."

Tamerlane smiled. "That is what I was waiting to hear. We'll start your training tomorrow."

No dragons or sword-waving villains disturbed her sleep, and Molly awoke the next morning full of excitement. Instead of putting on her tunic and leggings she decided to wear her shorts and tank top. They would be cooler and give her more freedom of movement.

The clothes hung on her. She pulled out the scoop neck and looked down at herself. The roll of fat around her middle was almost gone. She'd lost a ton of weight without even trying. Cool! Unfortunately, her boobs had shrunk too. But that wasn't all bad. She wouldn't need to wear that awful binder anymore.

Tamerlane had their meal on the table and ready to eat. "I knew you'd be eager to begin, so let us enjoy some fruit and a bit of bread and get started. Have you ever practiced any of the martial arts before? Dance?"

"I took ballet lessons all through grade school, but I got tired of it and quit," Molly said, popping a fresh raspberry into her mouth. "Pink isn't my color and I couldn't stand most of the girls."

"Ah, but at least you've had some dance training. The martial arts are also about moving your body to the right place at the right time. I'm afraid your lessons will be a bit boring at first, just like learning the basic ballet moves was. I will be teaching you the forms. These positions and moves comprise every position and move used in actual sword fighting. Learning to do them perfectly and at lightning speed is the first and most important step in mastering sword-craft. If you can't perform them flawlessly, you will never be anything more than a mediocre fighter and will probably die young. Today you will learn how to breathe, how to stand, and how to take a step."

After breakfast Tamerlane handed her a vaguely sword-shaped hardwood stick and they headed out into the backyard where there was some flat, open space.

"This is the starting position." Tamerlane held his own stick upright and pointing slightly forward in his right hand, placed his right foot flat on the ground pointing toward Molly and his left foot behind and almost at right angles to it. His feet were a shoulder's width apart and his knees were slightly bent. "Try and push me over."

Molly pushed on his shoulder as hard as she could, but he didn't budge. It was like pushing on a boulder.

"You can't do it because I'm grounded and centered. I've collected my energy around a point just below my navel and sent it deep into the earth. To do this, your feet need to be flat on the ground and your knees must be slightly bent. Try it."

Molly imitated the position, but when Tamerlane tapped her shoulder, he knocked her off balance. With practice she was soon able to withstand even a hard shove.

Next came breathing and then forward steps, back steps, and lunges. They seemed simple. But when you had to remember to stay off your toes, put your heel down first and roll the rest of your foot down in front of it, never pick your feet up too far off the ground, keep your knees bent, breathe properly, and stay grounded, the moves weren't as easy as they looked. Tamerlane circled her like a vulture. Occasionally his hand would flick out and give her a tap on the shoulder that would send her sprawling.

Molly was furious and kept yelling at him to cut it out, until she realized what he was doing. He only tapped her when she wasn't grounded or had made a mistake. If she had been doing the step correctly, she wouldn't have fallen. And the taps were actually quite gentle—they were just perfectly placed to take advantage of her imbalance.

By mid-day meal, the taps were coming less often. Molly had managed to stay upright through the last three rounds and was feeling quite proud of herself. By evening meal, she was exhausted and sore all over. Her arm ached from holding up the hardwood stick.

⁓

The next day Molly could barely crawl out of bed. Tamerlane smiled as she hobbled in to the main room for breakfast. "You worked quite a few unused muscles yesterday. Go down to the river for a dip before breakfast and do those stretches I showed you. That should take away some of the stiffness."

When she returned, feeling marginally better, her breakfast was ready. As she snarfed down a plate of fried vegetables, Tamerlane relaxed in the sun and sipped his tea. "You learn quickly. Today I'll teach you the arm and upper torso moves that go with the steps."

Adding these new moves increased the possibility of imbalance, and she spent quite a bit of time sprawled on the ground. To her surprise, Tamerlane called a halt to the practice after only an hour.

"You're too tired and it's causing you to make mistakes that you shouldn't be making. Take the rest of the day off; go for a walk or another swim. Do something that is relaxing but keeps you moving. Midday meal won't be ready for a few hours yet."

She got back just in time for a lunch of spicy lentils, salad greens and a loaf of coarse grained, brown bread that was still warm from the oven. Its rich, earthy smell made her mouth water.

"Where does all this food come from?" Molly asked, helping herself to a large scoop of lentils. "You live out in the middle of nowhere, and the only way to get anywhere from here is to walk."

"When you live alone in the middle of nowhere you learn to do all sorts of things." Tamerlane replied as he began slicing the bread into thick slabs. "I grow the salad greens and herbs in my garden. There are raspberry canes on the west side of the house and fruit trees in the back. I keep six chickens that supply me with eggs. The dried lentils and flour for the bread were part of a weekly food delivery. Fortunately, the next one is tomorrow; otherwise, we'd have had to tighten our belts. The last order wasn't made with a young appetite in mind."

Oh geez, I just walked into this guy's house, demanded to be fed, and hassled him into giving me lessons that would cost a fortune back in Oregon. I am such a toad. She cleared her throat, "Um, it's really cool of you to put me up and feed me and teach me. Thank you. I don't know how I can pay you back."

"You don't need to. You are one of Asmodius' clients; the Webmasters will pay me handsomely. Someone else is footing the bill for this adventure of yours."

"My Grandmother, right? Do you know her?"

"Estelle and I are old friends," he said, ignoring the first question.

So her grandmother definitely hadn't just sent her away. She'd sent her to two amazing people who could teach her magic and sword fighting. How had she known they were the exact things she needed to learn? Molly finished her meal and sat back with a contented sigh.

Tamerlane stretched till his joints cracked, and looked outside. It had begun to drizzle. "I have work to do and there are a few logs in the back yard for you to split. You might want to get started on them before it really starts raining."

He strode over to the bookcases, selected several books, and stacked them on the already crowded side table. When he couldn't find a book, he went to consult a huge tome bound in what looked like black snakeskin that hummed and snorted softly as it snoozed in the middle of its own shelf. Tamerlane opened the book and rifled through its onion skin thin pages until he found what he was looking for. Then he tapped the item twice with his finger. There was a pop from one of the shelves and a book materialized, tucked in among its neighbors. Tamerlane plucked it from the shelf, added it to the top of the stack and sat down to work.

"What did you just do? How'd you get that book to appear?" Molly asked.

"One of my colleagues borrowed that book awhile back and hadn't gotten around to returning it. I needed it. The Librarian," and he indicated the black book, "brought it back for me."

"Can you borrow books too?"

"Any book that's listed in The Librarian," he replied, patting the snakeskin bound volume.

"Awesome! This is almost as good as the Internet," Molly said as she examined the tiny print on the pages of the huge book.

When she came back in carrying a stack of split logs, Tamerlane was cleaning his sword and Asmodius was curled up asleep in his chair, snoring gently. An aura of serenity pervaded the room. A fly buzzed against the front windowpanes looking for the way out.

Molly dumped her armload in the woodbin and went over to look at the sword. Tamerlane wiped the white powder he'd just applied off the gleaming, narrow blade with a soft cloth. She stood in mesmerized silence as her eye followed a line of misty light that undulated and curled down the length of the sword just above its cutting edge. On the upper, blunt edge, its shadowy echo looped and swirled. Underlying it all, the forged steel of the blade rippled in faint patterns. The blade and hilt made a sweet arc and seemed to float in Tamerlane's hands. Molly could have looked at it for hours.

"That is the most beautiful thing I've ever seen, but it looks like it would break in a real fight."

"Yes, it's fragile looking and it only weighs a bit more than a large mug full of tea, but its appearance is deceiving. The way it's forged makes the cutting edge extremely hard and sharp and the rest of the blade soft enough to give slightly so the whole thing doesn't shatter. In the right hands, it can pierce most types of armor and will cut through a bundle of straw like it was a daisy stem. This is the type of sword I am training you to use, and hopefully one will come your way, but they are hard to find. Only a few sword-smiths know the secrets of their making and there is only one smith capable of forging a blade of this quality."

Even Tamerlane was not immune to his sword's fascination. He had stopped cleaning it while he was talking to Molly and was gazing into the patterns in the steel, lost in thought. With a self-conscious cough, he put the sword down on his lap and wiped over the blade with an oiled cloth. Then he sheathed the blade, hung it up by the fireplace, and turned to Molly. "Would you be so kind as to assist me with our supper preparations?"

As they began fixing the meal, Molly asked, "Why do you cook if you can do magic? Why don't you just poof supper onto the table like Asmodius does?"

"Mostly because I enjoy preparing meals, but it also takes much less energy. Conjuring a meal out of nothing is hard work. Asmodius does it for you because he hasn't any alternative. But he hunts his own meals—probably for the same reason I prepare mine. He enjoys it and it takes less energy. The same goes for other chores like chopping wood and gardening. Not only are they useful skills, but they're also good exercise; and it's easier to just do them."

The two of them bustling around the kitchen, banging cupboard doors and chatting woke Asmodius, who leaped down from his chair and glided out the open door.

"Asmodius is sleeping a lot. Is he OK?" Molly asked.

"He's a cat, and an old one at that. He requires at least eighteen hours of sleep a day."

"He didn't sleep that much when we were traveling."

"All the more reason for him to sleep now—he was exhausted when the two of you arrived."

"Well, so was I."

Tamerlane picked up a knife and started chopping carrots. "He was exhausted by the whole trip, not just escaping from the dragon. From what he tells me, you are not one of his easier clients."

Molly felt her face flush. "Why didn't he say something? We could have taken longer breaks or stopped earlier in the day."

"You couldn't have slowed down; you'd never have made it to the cutoff. And he hates to admit weakness. If you know anything about Asmodius, you know that pride is one of his less-endearing traits. I am wondering how many more clients he will be able to guide for the Webmasters."

Molly took a long, appreciative sniff of the pile of herbs she was chopping. "I'll remember that when we start out again. I don't want to wear him out. He's a pain in the butt, but I really like him."

"He seems to feel the same way about you—which is saying something. Asmodius' best friend has always been Asmodius."

They continued their dinner preparations in amicable silence. As Molly hung the iron stew pot over the fire she said, "Tomorrow morning after breakfast, I'm going to start replanting the burnt out forest."

He was beside her in an instant, frowning until his bushy white eyebrows nearly met above his eyes. "What about your practice?" The force of his disapproval was so strong that Molly was tempted to give up the idea. But she pushed back.

Standing up even straighter she said, "I'll only plant for a few hours every day and the rest of the time I'll work with you and do my chores."

"That's insane." Tamerlane began pacing. "The harm's already been done, and the forest will regenerate perfectly well without you. It's what forests do best. You need to spend as much time as possible practicing."

"Yes, I understand that," she said collapsing into one of the kitchen chairs. "But if I plant, the forest will come back quicker."

"What's a few decades to a forest?" Tamerlane threw up his arms in frustration.

"A few decades means a lot to a homeless dryad. And there are dozens of them out there—all because of me. Please. I owe it to them."

Tamerlane leaned back on the counter and scowled at her. "Your heart is too soft, but I will respect your wishes. However, you must wake up an hour earlier to help replace the lost time. Asmodius is already asking me how long your training will take. He says the Webmasters want you back on the trail in two lunar cycles."

"How long is that?"

"Earth's moon goes from full to dark to full again in a bit more than 29 days, and this planet's moon takes 28."

⌒

The next morning, Molly woke early and headed for the garden shed. A dryad was waiting for her, flitting impatiently from tree to tree. "We decided that I should be your guide since I'm best at talking to humans. You will need something to make a hole this big..." She held her long fingered, translucent green hands up to indicate a space the size of a beach ball "...and something to carry enough water to fill it."

Molly found a shovel and three buckets in the shed and filled the buckets at the pump. Remembering her lesson in levitating rocks, she had the dryad spin extra earth magic around them and then added just a touch of mage energy to levitate them, all the time trying not to stare at the spirit's stick-thin limbs, pointy, elfin features and hair that looked like one of her mother's Boston ferns. She sent the buckets floating on ahead and they followed them out to the burnt patch of forest with the shovel.

"The soil and moisture conditions here are favorable, so we will create an oak grove. My sisters and I have found our trees and we are already getting acquainted with them. Bring your hole-maker and follow me to the first ones."

The tree spirit led Molly through some amazing parts of The Wild Wood, but she couldn't really enjoy the scenery because she couldn't take her eyes off her guide. It was like trying to keep up with a laser light cat toy—there one moment and somewhere else the next. Eventually they arrived at their destination and Molly caught her breath in awe. Dozens of oak trees with trunks as wide as the length of her dad's Land Cruiser towered over her, glowing with power in the soft green light that filtered down through leaves held so high above the ground that she could barely see their individual shapes.

Each tree, of course, had its dryad. But there were other dryads scattered among them. And each of them was singing to a tiny oak sapling. When Molly listened with what Asmodius called her "other ears," she could hear the green, vibrant music twining through the grove.

"Those young ones would eventually have died out for want of light and space," her guide said. "But now, because of you, they will have a life."

Molly dug up six of them. It was slow going because the wispy spirits were very picky about where she placed her shovel. They didn't want a single rootlet damaged. Then they spun green sparkles of magic around each sapling's root ball and Molly sent them floating off ahead with a tiny nudge of mage energy. Back at the clearing, each dryad showed her exactly where to plant her tree, making her shift the roots a fraction of an inch one way or the other until they were exactly aligned with the dense network of tiny ley lines that ran through The Wild Wood. She only needed to water them once; after that each spirit would coax just the right amount of water for her tree along the ley lines. If they kept to the same spacing that they used on the first six, Molly figured that she would be planting over a hundred trees, which was just fine. She totally enjoyed being dryad muscle.

⁓

Later that afternoon, Molly was sprawled in The Chair telling it how happy Tamerlane was with her progress.

Would you like to see what the forms will look like after you have truly mastered them?

"Sure."

A moment later she was in a forest clearing with Tamerlane. The Chair's visions were so perfect it was like you were really there—way better than WarCraft Universe. He was standing in starting position, his upraised sword glinting dangerously in the dappled sunlight. He began the first form, and in a series of inhumanly quick moves, he was through it and into the next form. He finished the sequence that took her over half an hour to complete in several minutes.

"That's cute, Chair. Now play it at normal speed, so I can see the forms."

That is normal speed. At least, it's Tamerlane's normal speed.

"I'll never be able to move that fast."

Definitely not by next year, or maybe not even in ten years, but you will eventually be almost that fast—if you continue to practice. You will never have the reach or the strength of most fighters, so you must develop your speed, stamina, strategy, and nerve—otherwise you will be, as they say in the trade, so much dead meat. You can do this, and you must. Tamerlane wouldn't have bothered teaching you if he didn't think you were master swordsman material.

—

For the next several weeks, when she wasn't planting trees, Molly's world revolved around the forms. She even did them in her sleep. Her compact, chunky frame became lean and well muscled. She was exhausted and sore most of the time, but she was content in a way that she had never been before. She chopped wood, weeded the garden, and helped with the meals. And every day she bathed in her enchanted pool.

One morning, after a few rounds of the forms had warmed them up, Tamerlane stepped forward from his teaching position, stood directly in front of her, and tapped her stick with his. "Now I will show you how the forms are used to fight," he said.

And the forms became a series of blocks, parries, lunges, feints, and dodges. It was still a dance, but now she had a partner, and the sharp intensity of their exchanges thrilled her. They started at slow speed and gradually increased their pace with Tamerlane barking out a correction every so often. The most frequent one was, "Get down off your toes!" But the sheer joy of the movement always lifted her back up onto them. The fast paced rhythm of the forms and the clicking sticks were hypnotic. The world collapsed into just the two of them and the dance.

And then she was sprawled on the ground with Tamerlane's stick at her throat.

"You're dead."

All the ecstasy drained out of her, leaving behind emptiness and growing rage.

"Why did you trip me?"

"Because I could. When you are up on your toes you are vulnerable. Those sweeping foot moves in the forms are for tripping, so I used one to trip you. Dueling is not ecstatic dance, you must stay focused and ready to take advantage of any mistakes your opponent makes."

Something inside Molly snapped and anger rushed through her like hot lava. She knocked Tamerlane's stick away from her throat and sprang to her feet. "I am so sick of being focused and balanced. I have worked my butt off for you, old man, and then you knock me down the second I start to enjoy what I've learned. Don't you ever do anything just for the fun of it? I can't do this anymore—I quit!" And she spun on her heel and ran into the house and into her bedroom.

Asmodius was napping on The Chair and blinked sleepily at her as she strode into the room and began throwing her things together.

"Change into a pack, Chair, we're leaving."

Asmodius stretched and yawned. His long, pink tongue curled out between a pair of gleaming white fangs. He settled back down on his haunches and began to clean his paws. *I was wondering when you were going to lose your temper,* he purred. *You do have quite a nasty one, you know. You've been amazingly patient and are actually making excellent progress.*

"I do not have a temper," she howled, kicking a towel across the room. "Tamerlane is impossible. Nothing I do is right and he's mean. Anyone would be pissed off. Come on, Chair, turn into a pack and let's get out of here."

I would love to, my dear, but I can't with this lump of fur and fangs sitting on me. However, it does seem rather a shame to leave right when you're learning something that makes your heart sing.

"Get down, Asmodius, so The Chair can turn."

Asmodius continued licking his front paw and replied, *I think not. I'm quite happy right here.*

Molly tried to shove the big cat off The Chair, but he became very heavy and impossible to move.

Don't push me again or I'll bite you.

Screaming with rage and frustration, she stamped out of the house and slammed the door behind her. What had she been thinking, letting a crazy old man yell at her and poke her with a stick? She wished, for about the gazillionth time, that her parents were still alive and she was back in Concord hanging with her friends. She certainly didn't belong here. As she ran from the house, the now familiar sensation of separating from her surroundings engulfed her. She could barely feel the earth under her pounding feet and the air rasping in and out of her lungs. The slim tree branches hanging over the trail hardly stung as she whipped by them. She was a ghost. Nothing she did here would make the slightest bit of difference and nobody would care if she just disappeared. Empty despair seeped into her bones and even in The Wild Wood she could feel the chill of The Shadow.

Molly skidded to a stop. She'd been here and done this way too many times. It was time for an attitude adjustment.

⌐

A breeze blew up the river cooling Molly's face and ruffling her curls. It set the leaves on the alders whispering and the river murmured and chuckled back. A pair of songbirds chimed in and a squirrel scolded her from the safety of a tree. Molly ignored them all as her pulse gradually slowed and she gazed into the blue depths of her enchanted pool. The water rippled and swirled and called to her in a soft, fluid whisper. Like a sleepwalker, she stripped off her clothes and dove into its waiting caress.

As she floated in the gently swirling water, the empty, achy feeling of separateness eased and she began to see things differently. She remembered the stories Tamerlane had told her about his army training and realized that, by comparison, he was going easy on her. And he *had* warned her to get down off her toes.

She'd ignored him because she'd been too busy tripping out on the dance. If she did that during a fight, she'd be dead. Tamerlane was trying to teach her how to stay alive. And then she remembered the sadness in his eyes when she threw down her stick and quit.

And sword-craft was definitely part of her journey. Not only her life, but her sanity depended on it. With a sigh, Molly swam to shore.

She had some apologizing to do.

—

Tamerlane was sprawled in his chair poring over an ancient-looking book, but he set it aside as Molly came through the open door. His face was expressionless. Nothing was going to make this any easier. Better to just say it and get it over with.

"I'm sorry I got mad and said all those horrible things. I wasn't paying attention and you had every right to trip me. Please let me keep training with you."

His severe gaze softened to a smile. "Your apology is accepted. Believe it or not, I do remember the joy I felt the first time I did the forms as a mock fight, and I remember getting carried away just like you did, and getting a sound drubbing from my opponent. You must always remember, the person you're working with is an opponent not a partner."

—

The morning after her reconnaissance trip into Damia, Althea slipped two freshly baked cinnamon rolls into a bag and headed for Estelle's. She would have taken more, but Max, her housemate, had glared at her when she reached for the third one.

There was no answer to her knock, so she walked in the unlocked door, plunked the bag down on the kitchen table, and wandered around the house calling for her friend.

"Up here," Estelle yelled from her third floor study.

Althea found her gazing into the large mirror that hung on the only wall space that wasn't covered with bookcases or windows. It was a silver scrying mirror shaped like the head of a great horned owl. The owl was exquisitely detailed, down to each shaft and barb of each feather. His saucer-sized obsidian eyes were polished to a glossy finish.

She pulled a chair up next to her friend, sat down, and gazed into the owl's eyes, which immediately merged and displayed a scene of Molly and Tamerlane trying to club each other to death.

Althea grabbed Estelle's arm. "He's going to kill her. That last swipe could have broken her neck." And then, "Yikes, if she hadn't jumped, she wouldn't have any knees left."

Estelle smiled and said, "Although Molly is quite capable of driving even Tamerlane into a killing frenzy, he's not trying to kill her. He's training her in the martial arts."

They watched the lesson for a while and then Althea coaxed her friend down to the sunny kitchen to replenish her energy with a cinnamon roll and oolong tea. As Estelle nibbled at her pastry, she said, "She's good, isn't she?"

"Yes, and she looks marvelous. Seems like you made the right call after all."

Estelle pushed aside the rest of her roll and took a sip of tea. "Now if she can just get home in one piece. She's due back the day after tomorrow."

"Asmodius and The Chair will keep her safe," Althea said, studying her friend with concern. Estelle was a shadow of her former self.

"Hope so. I'm beginning to miss her. And a friend from back east keeps calling. Her cell phone rang and rang until I turned it off. Then she called me and wanted to know where Molly was and why she wasn't answering her phone."

"So what did you tell her?"

"That she's at a grief counseling retreat and had to leave her phone here. I told her she'd be back in a few days."

Althea popped the last of her cinnamon roll into her mouth and chewed thoughtfully. Estelle had actually told Molly's friend the truth.

But what would happen if Molly didn't return?

She deposited her empty plate and cup in the sink and headed for the door. "Take care, Estelle, I have to go."

"Meet me here tomorrow morning?"

"Of course."

A few weeks later, Molly found both Tamerlane and Asmodius seated at the breakfast table. When she finished her meal of bacon, eggs, and oatmeal she looked up to find two somber sets of eyes staring back at her.

"My time's run out, I've taught you all I can for now," Tamerlane said.

Breakfast turned to lead in Molly's stomach. "But I like it here. It feels like home." Even as the words came out of her mouth, she realized that Tamerlane was right. They couldn't go any further in her training until she'd perfected the skills she had. And she'd finished planting all the oak saplings over a week ago. The once ugly patch of destruction glowed with life. She was sure that some of the trees had grown at least a foot since she'd planted them.

It was time to go.

She had a river to follow.

With a sigh, she went to her room, and found that The Chair had packed all her belongings and turned into the ugly leather pack. She shrugged it on and headed back out. Tamerlane was waiting by the door.

"Good bye. I'll miss you." she hugged the old mage and kissed him on the cheek.

"Harrumph," he muttered, gently extricating himself from her grasp and handing over her practice stick. "Keep up your practice—every day, mind you."

10

The Wheel of Fortune

olly kicked at the dusty street and surveyed the town square. A thin, mangy dog skulked into an alley and a few cows grazed on the sparse grass of the commons. It was midmorning. The place should have been jumping. The River Road was deserted too, except for the damn soldiers—they were everywhere. Asmodius had cast a glamour around her that made her look like a scruffy, starving ten-year-old boy, and the soldiers left her alone. Unfortunately, everyone left her alone. The country was at war and no one wanted to deal with another homeless beggar—they barely had enough food for themselves, since the army had requisitioned most of it.

Molly sat down on the curb and Asmodius drifted over and lay down in her shadow. The sun was already hot, and his black fur coat was probably even more uncomfortable than her tunic and leggings. A dingy lace curtain twitched at the window of the house across the street. "They're watching us already. If we're still here this evening, they'll probably run us out of town like they did at the last place."

So let's leave now. This town feels like death warmed over.

Molly totally agreed. The flowers in the pots at the doors and windows were withered and brown from lack of water and weeds grew up through the cracks between the paving stones. The doorsteps of the houses were filthy. A disturbing sign since, according to Asmodius, a Damian household was judged by the state of its doorstep. Most of the shops were closed—no one had any money to buy anything. The bakery behind her was only selling bread, and few people could afford even that.

A well-appointed carriage, pulled by a team of matching black horses, drove into the square and stopped. The driver banged on the roof with the butt of his whip. "Get out, ya lazy slut!"

A young woman stepped out. Black curls cascaded down over her white shoulders, and her perfectly shaped lips sneered as she gave the driver the Damian equivalent of the finger. She moved like a runway model, turning her tattered finery into a gown fit for a queen. The driver cracked his whip, and the carriage lurched forward and thundered away.

"Hey, Boy-o," she called to Molly as she headed for the bakery. "You look like you could do with a bite to eat and I'm rich today. Come share a meal with me. I have a proposition for you."

The woman bought a large loaf of bread and led Molly into a relatively clean back alley. It was shady and cool here and Molly sank down onto the street and pulled some dried fruit and cheese out of her pack to share. The bread was still warm from the oven. They ate in silence until the worst of their hunger was satisfied.

"My name's Amelia, what's yours? And where are you from?"

"Matty. I'm from up north. My parents were killed in an accident."

"Ah, poor tyke. You need someone to take care of you. I have a gentleman friend who likes little boys. He'd be glad to take you in."

Molly's mouth went dry and she stared at the woman in disgust.

"Oh, don't look at me that way. It's not such a bad life, you know. At least it'll keep you alive. I know this man. He's old, and not into any of that exotic stuff, and he's not mean. He just likes a feel and a poke every now and then."

"And how much would you make off this deal?"

Amelia grinned, popped a slice of dried apple into her pretty mouth and chewed appreciatively. "He'd pay me well for you, but it doesn't look like you're interested. You're not desperate enough yet. Let me know when you change your mind. But don't wait too long or you'll lose your looks."

"That is so totally disgusting!" Molly shivered as she realized how fortunate she was. With only a slight twist of fate she could have really been the destitute orphan she was pretending to be, and might even have been grateful for Amelia's offer. Who was she to judge this woman by the way she made her living? But she couldn't help asking, "I can't believe you like screwing dirty old men. Isn't there some other work you could do?"

Amelia rolled her eyes and made a sweeping gesture that took in all of Damia. "Are you blind? The muckity-mucks have decided that it's time for another war. No one has any money to buy anything, so no one is hiring. They came and took my husband a month ago. We'd only been married a few weeks, but he was a journeyman tailor and made enough for us to rent a few rooms. I couldn't find any work and couldn't pay the rent when it came due. The landlord offered to let me stay if he could have a go with me whenever he wanted, but I refused. So he kicked me out and took all our furniture to pay the back rent. Now, here I am, on the street and doing just what I was too proud to do with that pig of a landlord." Her voice broke and huge tears dripped from her eyes. She wiped them away impatiently with the back of her hand.

Molly was horrified. "No one would hire you?"

"The only businesses that are hiring are the wagon maker, the blacksmith, and the tailor my husband worked for. They're really busy making stuff for the army, but that's skilled labor and they didn't want to take the time to train me. None of the farmers would hire me. They assumed I didn't know anything about farms and was lazy and would just be another mouth to feed."

"What about your family?"

Amelia sighed and looked down at her lovely white hands. "My family owns a small estate just north of Bontare. My husband, Thomas, is our steward's son. As kids we were always together—suffering through endless hours of math, history, and literature classes; and playing in the fields and forests.

"When my parents arranged a marriage for me, I realized that I was in love with Thomas and would never be happy with anyone else. I went to him and begged him to marry me, and he said he loved me too, but our parents would never allow it. So we made a plan. Thomas left home and started his apprenticeship here with the tailor. When he became a journeyman, he sent word back to me and I ran away to join him. We were so happy together, and then those bastards came and took him away from me." Her face crumpled into a mask of misery. She picked up a rock and threw it against the wall of the building across the alley. It shattered and left a dent.

"So anyway, I was walking along the street feeling sorry for myself when this swell struts up to me like he was the Gods' gift to the world." Amelia stood and strutted forward a few steps, pretending to wave a handkerchief with one limp-wristed hand. It was such a perfect imitation of some of the nobles Molly had seen at court that she laughed out loud. "'Excuse me, my dear,' he said, 'but I see that you are in need of some assistance, and I have a suggestion that will benefit us both. Come out to my country estate with me for a few days and let me enjoy that luscious body of yours and I will pay you handsomely.' He was old enough to be my father, but I hadn't eaten in two days, so I said, as bold as you please, 'How much?'

"The old goat paid me two silvers and all the food I could eat, and I earned every bit of it. He certainly isn't suffering because of the war and neither are any of my other gentlemen."

She sat down on the curb and took another bite of bread. "I'm doing OK now. I rent a small room and the owner doesn't care if I have the occasional visitor."

"Can't you go back to your family?"

"Impossible! They wouldn't have me. I'm ruined goods. And not only that, I'm pregnant."

Molly could see Amelia's point. Even in her more liberal world, she wondered how forgiving her mother would have been if she'd run away and come home pregnant.

"Is the baby Thomas'?"

"Of course it is! He's only been gone a little over a month."

"Then don't tell them about being a prostitute. Just tell them that you and Thomas were happily married and then he was drafted. You had to come home because you couldn't support yourself and you're carrying his child. From what I've noticed, grandparents always go gaga over their grandchildren."

Even mine! Molly thought, as she grinned at Amelia.

"Anyway," she continued, "If they're halfway reasonable, I bet they'll be so thrilled to see you that they'll forgive you for everything. If not, maybe Thomas' parents would take you in. You'll never know if you don't try."

Amelia looked at Molly in surprise. "My, my, aren't you a wise one? So what happens when Thomas finds out I was a prostitute? He will, you know."

"If he follows you back to your parents' estate, you'll know he's forgiven you. If he can't deal with it, he'll just go somewhere else and start a new life."

Amelia's eyes took on a far away look. Finally she sighed. "That's a great plan you've got there, youngster. I've even thought of it myself. There's still that small problem." She held out her hand and rubbed her fingers against her thumb. "I don't have enough money."

Molly pulled out her last gold piece, and slipped it into the prostitute's extended hand. "You do now."

Amelia's jaw dropped as she stared at the gold piece. "Where did you get this? Why are you giving it to me?"

Molly smiled, shrugged on her pack, and picked up her practice stick. But as she headed out of town her eyes filled with tears and despair flooded her heart. Even a thousand pieces of gold wouldn't pay her way back to her parents and her real life in Concord. The street and houses around her shimmered and began sliding away.

Well, that was certainly a waste of money.

Molly grabbed onto Asmodius' snarky presence in her brain with a gasp of relief.

"Why?"

Prostitutes are infamous liars. They'll tell you any story they think you want to hear. And even if she was telling the truth, what makes you think she'll use that money to go home? She'll probably drink herself silly, buy a fancy new gown, and live like a queen till it runs out in a few days.

Molly could once again feel the cobbles under her feet and hear the clang of the blacksmith's hammer and smell the hot iron in the forge they were passing. "I think she was telling the truth," she said. "She doesn't talk like the people down here. She sounds like the nobles we met in Bontare. And even if she was lying or even if she does waste the money, I'm still glad I gave it to her. I wouldn't have been able to sleep at night knowing she was back there on the streets starving and doing who knows what for creepy old men just because I didn't help her when I could have. At least now she has a chance. Honestly, Asmodius, you are such a cynic!"

Humph!

King Alexander settled back on his throne in the palace Reception Hall and tried to ignore the empty throne beside him. It had been a difficult day, and he'd finally dealt with the last petition. As far as he could tell, no one knew about The Wall, but his people were not happy with the heavy conscription rates, and noblemen from all over Damia were converging on the palace and complaining about the extra taxes and losing so much of their work force right at hay harvest. The country had become prosperous, comfortable, and complacent.

Just as he was about to adjourn the session he noticed a woman pushing her way forward through the crowded room. Fear clutched at his heart as he recognized the only lady-in-waiting that Flora had taken with her to The Wall. He caught her eye and waved her on. When she reached the throne, Alexander stood and addressed his subjects. "Thank you for attending. Your petitions have been noted. Father Elysius, please close the reception."

When the last attendee had left the hall and the great doors were closed, only Alexander, Father Elysius, and the lady-in-waiting remained. What was the blasted woman's name? They all fluttered around Flora like so many exotic birds and he could never keep them straight. "You may speak," he said.

"Your Majesty," the woman said, performing a deep, graceful curtsy, "Queen Flora has dismissed me from her service at The Wall and she insisted that I tell you this in person."

"Why did she dismiss you?"

"She didn't really say." The woman wrung her hands and looked at him fearfully. No, actually, it wasn't fear, it was anguish. This woman hadn't wanted to leave her queen. "We lived very simply and she told me that she didn't need me to help her brush her hair and put on the plain dress she wore every day. But I was able to offer her companionship and she seemed to enjoy my company. Why would she send me away?"

Why indeed? He remembered her now. This was her favorite lady-in-waiting. They'd been together for years. Why would Flora send away her only comfort and company? There was something wrong.

"How was Her Majesty's health? Was she content with her work?"

"Her Majesty was in good health when I left her, and The Wall was ahead of schedule. But she wasn't happy. Using her power to cut into living rock is difficult for her, and seeing her subjects so overworked and miserable was breaking her heart. And she's never said as much, but I can tell that she thoroughly detests Philip Fuller."

—

Dozens of creeks and streams had added their waters to the Selene since Molly and Asmodius had left Tamerlane's house, and the river no longer gurgled and chattered along. It was broader and more dignified, gliding along in a whisper and keeping its own counsel between its sandy shores. The River Road was dusty and deserted and the fields were full of weeds. They passed several hay fields that had gone to seed. The sun blazed down and Asmodius plodded along in Molly's shadow.

And then another shadow fell over both of them—and much of the surrounding countryside.

Before Molly could even look up, a huge, raspy, black hand came out of nowhere, grabbed her, and jerked her skyward. She shrieked in terror as the ground fell away, but stopped abruptly, gasping in horror when she found herself staring into a pair of evil, red eyes. The air was so thick with smoke and sulfurous fumes that her lungs burned and her eyes watered. The rogue dragon was mind-numbingly huge. Waves of wickedness poured off it and smashed into her, leaving her stunned.

"Well, well. I thought I'd fried you two back in that ghastly forest. What good fortune that I just happened along this road and found you. My human doesn't like other mages, so I eat them. They're quite tasty. The magic sizzling around them gives them a nice tang."

Who is your human, you stinking, overgrown lizard? Asmodius demanded from the beast's other hand. The feel of his voice in her head gave her courage.

"Nasty, aren't we?" replied the dragon, scorching them with his hot, foul breath. "Why in the multiverse would I tell you that?"

Molly squirmed desperately against the dragon's hard, scaly grip. Anything, even falling three stories, would be better than looking into those insanely cruel eyes. The dragon grinned with pleasure and squeezed her, sending her breath out with a whoosh. Her whole body pulsed with agony and panic gripped her as she struggled to breathe. The beast watched her with interest. Just as she was about to pass out, it loosened its grip and smoky air surged back into her tortured lungs. The effect was excruciating and the cough that followed almost made her faint. "A live mage is much tastier than a dead one," it said, licking its scaly chops.

Oh freakin' fine, she was a mage now. Just in time to be a dragon snack. Tears streamed down her cheeks.

The beast opened its jaws ever so slowly, revealing broadsword-sized fangs that dripped with venom. Molly shrieked in terror as its gray, forked tongue snaked toward her.

A geyser of flame shot into the dragon's mouth.

Molly felt the evil wyrm's grip release.

JUMP! Asmodius' command slammed into her brain.

Molly was much better at jumping now. She'd been practicing in The Wild Wood with Asmodius. Reaching out with her mind, Molly located a ley line, "grabbed" it, and followed it out to a point just at the edge of her vision. She focused on that point, and jumped.

Howls of pain and fury shook the countryside.

One more jump.

Asmodius materialized way ahead and to her left at the edge of a distant forest.

She jumped toward him.

Into the forest. Quickly. No more jumping.

Molly ran after Asmodius, tripping and scrambling along the faint suggestion of a trail. When the big cat collapsed in front of her, Molly almost fell over him. She was so exhausted after two jumps that she was ready to join him, but she scooped him up and kept running. After what seemed like forever, she staggered to a halt, crawled under a thicket and dragged the limp cat in with her.

Asmodius lay still as death on the leaf litter. Molly stroked his silky fur and sobbed bitterly.

He's not dead, you know.

Molly jumped in alarm and then groaned in relief when she realized it was The Chair.

"Is he gonna be OK?"

Maybe, maybe not. He's recharging. If he collapsed before he was totally exhausted, he'll survive; if not, his heart will stop beating and he'll die.

"But he can't die!"

Why not?

She looked down at Asmodius in panic. She hadn't thought her parents would die either. She took the limp cat into her arms and held him with a gentle fierceness. "'Cuz I won't let him."

All the rest of that day and well into the night Molly held her friend and tried to instill some of the forest's vibrant energy into him. She wished they were back in The Wild Wood. This would have been much easier. But as the night pulled them farther into its cold darkness, Asmodius' breathing slowed almost to nonexistence and his body began to cool. Oh Gods, she was gonna lose him.

Gods! Of course.

They were mighty forces—at least in this universe.

OK, the Mother Goddess. What was her name again?

"Dama! Please! I need some help here. Please don't let Asmodius die." Oh geez, that was so lame. Why would someone like Dama listen to her? But she'd listened to Queen Flora, hadn't she?

Molly held her friend close and continued to plead with the Goddess.

Asmodius took a full breath and stirred in her arms. His body warmed up to cat temperature, and Molly sighed with relief. He was gonna make it. There was a rustle in the thicket and a small, gray mouse, scurried past the quiet girl and her patient. Quicker than thought, she reached for the practice stick on top of her pack and clubbed it dead.

"Thank you, thank you, thank you," Molly whispered to Dama, the mouse, and the multiverse. She pulled her sleeping bag out of her pack, wrapped it around herself and Asmodius, laid the mouse next to him, and collapsed into oblivion.

—

Molly woke to loud crunchings and purrings. She opened her eyes to dappled sunshine and Asmodius devouring the mouse.

Thank you for hunting. I was starving.

Molly gazed at him in stupefied wonder.

Why are you looking at me like that? This is for me, isn't it?

"Of course it is, you rotten animal. Oh, Asmodius, I was so afraid you were gonna die."

Not a chance. It was touch and go there for awhile, but I made it.

Molly sat up and regarded the egotistical beast fondly as he finished his gory breakfast.

"We're gonna stay right here for a few days so you can rest and get your strength back. You're no use to me if you're weak as a kitten."

Humph, said Asmodius.

Several miles farther on the forest thinned and the trail broadened to a path which led them into a clearing with a tiny house and a well-tended garden. Heartrending sobs spilled out of the house as Molly and Asmodius approached the open door.

When her eyes had adjusted to the gloom, she saw two figures on the floor. A boy of about ten years or so crouched beside a nearly naked woman who lay ominously still. He was rocking on his heels and crying bitterly, but stopped and looked up in terror as Molly's shadow fell into the room.

"It's OK. I won't hurt you," she said, stepping into the house so the boy could see her. "Why don't you come outside and tell me what happened."

"Who're you?" he asked. "I never seen you around here afore."

"My name's Matty, and I'm from up north. I heard you crying and stopped to see if you were OK. What's your name?" Molly asked, but her attention was riveted on the woman's body. She lay staring at the ceiling arms and legs splayed out like a discarded ragdoll. Her face was battered and bloody and she was covered with scratches and bite marks. Her throat was bruised and her tongue protruded stiffly from her mouth. Molly felt faint and there was a buzzing sound inside her head. She had to get the kid away from that awful corpse.

To her relief, the boy reached up and took her outstretched hand. She led him out of the house and over to a garden bench. "I'm Jackie," he said as he sat down, "an' that's me mum back there." Fresh tears fell and he started rocking again. Molly took him in her arms and rocked him gently.

A long time later, he took a deep shuddering breath and wiped his runny nose with his arm. "I was out gettin' wood," he said, pointing to a scatter of small logs and sticks at the edge of the clearing, "when I seen this soldier come slinkin' out a' the house like a thief. He were tall an' thin an' his hair looked like moldy hay. Mum was at market sellin' our veggies. He musta' followed her back." His face took on a haunted expression. "Wot kinda monster would do that?"

Molly had no answer. She hugged him again and said, "We need to report this. Do you know where the soldiers stay?"

He nodded against her chest, leaving a trail of slime on her tunic, and stood up. "They're camped just outside a' town."

—

By the time Molly, Asmodius, and Jackie reached town the market was over. A few stragglers were taking down stalls, but for the most part the place was deserted. Jackie led her to the edge of town where a unit of soldiers was camped. Molly spotted the captain coming out of a large tent and started toward him, but stopped when Jackie grabbed her arm and hissed, "That's him!" He was looking past the officer to a man sitting on the ground cleaning a sword. He matched Jackie's description perfectly. "Captain!" he shouted and sprinted over to the burly officer. "That man killed me Mum!"

Every head in the camp looked up and every gaze followed the boy's pointing finger.

The captain scowled. "Come over here, Zeek. What have ya got to say for yourself?"

The soldier got up and strolled over to them. His dishwater-brown eyes were wide and innocent. "I'm sorry your Mum's dead, boy, but I didn't kill her."

The officer turned to Jackie. "Did you actually see this man kill your Mum?"

"No, sir."

"Then how do you know he killed her?"

" I seen him come sneakin' out of our house and run away. When I went in, me mum was dead."

"Were there any other witnesses?"

"No, sir."

"Well, then it's your word against his. There's no way to prove it one way or the other. I can't punish a man for that. I'm sorry, son."

Molly looked up at Zeek, who smiled a thin-lipped smile, spat, and went back to his cleaning. Jackie turned and ran back into town. She and Asmodius followed him to a temple.

It was the largest one in town. Its massive stone pillars were painted in geometric patterns of mossy greens, blacks, buttery yellows, and blood reds. Inside, at the very back of the room, stood a larger-than-life statue of a woman seated on a throne and holding her arms out in welcome. Her face was kind and gentle. Offerings of food were piled up on a large altar at her feet. This had to be Dama, the merciful Goddess who had comforted Queen Flora and spared Asmodius' life. Molly reached into her pack, took out a silver coin and placed it on the altar.

"Thank you," Molly whispered.

Jackie hadn't come to make an offering or give thanks. He found a priestess and arranged for his mother's body to be brought to the temple, blessed, and buried. Then he marched over to a smaller temple across the square. This one was built of red and black stone and had a spare, simple dignity. Asmodius told her it belonged to Mardoc, the god of war. Inside, Jackie strode to the altar in front of the statue of a powerful warrior and placed two coppers next to the red flame that burned there like a baleful eye. Molly and Asmodius stood several paces behind him.

"You owe me a life, Mardoc." Jackie's voice rang through the temple. "One a' your soldiers killed me mum. His name's Zeek. I want 'im dead." He drew his knife, cut his finger, and dabbed the blood on the altar next to the coppers. It barely showed on the red stone, but Molly was able to make out several other similar smudges.

—

Mercifully, Dama's priestesses had Jackie's mother's body wrapped in a white shroud and were carrying her out the door when they arrived back at his house. The priestess at the head of the group approached Jackie and touched him gently on the shoulder. "We are so sorry for your loss. Tess was a good woman. I'll miss her." Guiding them into the house, she continued. "Dama sends you today's offerings." The table was piled with food—and a single silver coin. The taint of death was gone, and the room smelled faintly of incense.

After the priestesses left, Molly gathered some of the food from the table and led Jackie out to the garden bench. "Here, sit down and try to eat something." She offered him a handful of nuts and something that looked like a plum and plopped down beside him. He ate the nuts, nibbled at the fruit, and then slouched back on the bench and stared dumbly into the distance. Molly and Asmodius sat with him and dozed through what was left of the afternoon. That evening they had a bit more to eat and Molly asked, "What will you do now?"

"The soldiers came and took me dad a month ago and now Mum's gone. We don't own this house, so there's nuthin' left for me here. I got an aunt an' uncle in the next town south an' I'm gonna go live with them. Mum's death rites are tomorrow. I'll leave when they're done."

"Would you like some company on the way to your aunt and uncle's house?"

"Yeah, thanks."

As she drifted off to sleep in the little house, she grieved for Jackie. The Wall had seemed like such a good idea back in Bontare. Did the people who had favored it understand all the sadness and misery it would cause? Did they care? None of them were going hungry and none of their fathers had been snagged to work on The Wall.

And then she wondered if she and Asmodius would be doing Jackie any favors by traveling with him. After all, there was a dragon hunting them and they would be easy to spot on The River Road.

11

Justice

olly stood next to Jackie at his mother's gravesite and gritted her teeth. They called it a death rite here, but the whole ordeal reminded her of her parents' memorial service eight months earlier. Eight months? It seemed like just yesterday. And here were the priests saying all the same useless crap about her being in a better place and the same weepy neighbors who said all this wonderful stuff that only broke your heart all over again. And the same empty feeling of despair curling around her heart. Fortunately it was over quickly. She didn't know if she could have stood it much longer.

A woman walked up to Jackie and hugged him. "I'm so sorry, hon. Tess was one o' me favorite folks. I hope they catch the monster wot done 'er in." She held him at arm's length and asked, "Do you have a place to live?"

"Aye, Mistress Livey, I'm leavin' fer me Aunt Carla n' Uncle Seth's down in Clyo soon as I get packed."

She smoothed his hair back and put a silver piece in his hand. "Jenny couldn't come, she had veggies ta pick fer market. Stop by an' see her afore ya leave. Good luck ta ya, darlin.'" She kissed him on the forehead and turned away with a sob.

Jackie wiped tears away with the back of his hand and looked over the deserted gravesite. "C'mon, let's go see Jenny. Mistress Livey was me mum's best friend, an' Jenny's like a big sister ta me."

—

They arrived at a small, neat house and garden in a sunny clearing that was the twin of Jackie's place. An overturned market basket and smashed vegetables littered the yard and garden. Fear gripped Molly's stomach, and she stopped Jackie as he headed for the door.

"Wait here," she whispered, "and don't come in 'til I call you." Jackie's eyes went wide, but he nodded.

Molly grabbed her practice stick, strode silently up to the open door, and looked in. A frantic young woman was struggling against a man who was choking her with one hand and ripping her tunic off with the other. Molly's mind filled with terrifying memories of coarse hands groping her as she struggled through the streets of Bontare. Fury thundered through her and the strength of ten men flowed into her as Riada awoke and uncoiled. Molly roared and leaped across the room. The rapist pushed away the battered, half-naked young woman and turned to face his attacker.

It was Zeek.

His eyes were not wide and innocent now; they smoldered with lust and rage as he grabbed the stick out of Molly's hand. "Leave me alone, ya little swine!" he snarled and swung it at her.

Molly ducked and felt the draft from the stick as it thrummed over her head. She punched her attacker in the crotch. He screamed and bent over, dropping the stick. Molly grabbed it and aimed a blow at his head. He managed to duck and pulled a knife out of his boot. Molly jumped back from the blade as he thrust it toward her heart. Before he could recover, she bashed his other arm. The bone snapped. Howling in pain, the killer lashed out, and Molly felt a quick pinch and a tug along her ribcage. The lunge left him open and Molly smacked his head on her backswing. It didn't seem like a hard blow, Tamerlane would have knocked it aside easily. But the killer's head burst open and bright red blood and gray brains spattered the scrupulously clean floor and wall, and drenched the front of her tunic.

Molly's fury drained away as quickly as it had come, leaving her weak and shaking. She looked down to see her bloody tunic cut open and tons of her own blood pouring out of her side. Bitter sharp pain chose that moment to slice through her ribcage and she collapsed in a heap and stared in horror at the gory mass of blood, brain, and bone that had once been a man's head.

An iridescent green fly was already buzzing around it.

She shivered as Riada stretched contentedly inside her and curled up. She had just used her power to brutally kill a man. How much longer would it be before her dragon reached out and devoured her soul? Or would The Shadow get her first? It was much closer now. In fact, if she squinted just so, she could see it standing right beside her. Nausea overwhelmed her and she retched up her lunch, each spasm shooting white-hot jolts of pain through her side.

Molly squeezed her eyes shut and gasped. When she opened them, Jackie was staring at her in horror. He had his arms around Jenny and they were crouched as far away from her as possible. She looked into Jenny's blackened eyes and saw pain and terror fighting a losing battle with numbness. Blood ran from her split lip and there were two thumbprint-sized bruises on her throat. The girl had covered herself with her shredded tunic. Molly gestured lamely at the dead soldier and mess. "Uh, sorry."

"It were Mardoc!" Jackie stood up and tugged Jenny to her feet. "He grabbed ahold a' ya and took the bastard's life like I asked him to!"

Molly wasn't so sure. It felt to her like all the pent up rage at the loss of her parents, at being forced from her home, and at everyone who had hurt her or made her feel used, terrified, and helpless had finally come howling out to claim justice.

"I gotta go get the priests," Jackie continued, edging toward the door and dragging Jenny with him. "That soldier's dead 'cuz I asked Mardoc fer his life. I gotta make sure his priests come get him. He belongs ta Mardoc now and I wouldn't wanna be in his boots fer nuthin.'" As they stepped over the threshold, Jackie stared grimly back at the remains of his mother's murderer, swiped tears from his eyes, and said, "I'm glad he's dead, but I sure ain't as glad as I thought I'd be."

12

The Hanged Man

hat same evening King Alexander II paced restlessly in the top room of the tallest tower in his palace. The dragon was still at large, terrorizing the countryside, and Father Elysius continued his search for its human. Flora's lady-in-waiting and his agent's reports about The Wall were troubling. The work was progressing nicely, but the living conditions were deplorable and the workers were treated cruelly. And that agent, his best and brightest, hadn't sent his weekly report. Things weren't right. He needed more information, and he needed it now.

He continued pacing. His crown hung from a knob on the back of the desk chair, his tunic was unbuttoned, and he had raked his hands through his hair so many times that it stuck out in spikes. Every once in awhile he touched the tiny silver whistle that he always wore on a chain around his neck and rubbed the inside of his left wrist.

Finally he growled and strode out the open doors and onto the balcony. The setting sun glowed over the red tile roofs of Bontare, burnishing them with gold. Fertile, green fields stretched as far as the eye could see, and the river Selene sparkled through them; but Alexander barely noticed the beauties of his kingdom. He put the silver whistle to his mouth and blew. There was no sound, but the air in front of him shimmered and two enormous ravens appeared. They were Hither and Yon, the magical birds of Mardoc, who fly throughout the multiverse every day and, at the end of every day, bring back the news of all its comings and goings. They hung fierce and silent, suspended on outspread wings, until the king motioned them into the room. Two sets of black wings flicked, and they glided through the doors and onto the desk. Obsidian eyes tracked him as he sat down.

"I need information."

The birds went still.

Alexander pulled his knife out of his boot and rested his left hand, palm up on the desk in front of his guests. A livid scar ran across his wrist.

One question used up; two left.

He made a freely bleeding cut just below it. Hither and Yon dipped their beaks into the wound and supped until their eyes gleamed as red as the blood on which they feasted and their jet-black bodies glowed with magic.

Their eyes locked onto his and Alexander shuddered as he felt them flicking ruthlessly through his mind and heart. They scrutinized all his hopes and fears, his strengths and weaknesses, his victories and failures until they understood exactly what he needed them to find out. They would have answers for him by morning.

The king felt them release his mind, and as he sank back into his chair, they sprang into the air and vanished. He breathed deeply as sweat evaporated and cooled his face and the light-headedness of shock receded. Fishing a fairly clean handkerchief out of his pocket, he mopped up the puddle of blood on the desk, and bound up his wrist. When he stopped shaking, Alexander went down to his evening meal.

—

Dawn found the king pacing in the tower room once more. He jumped when the ravens materialized with a sharp pop. Cursing silently, he turned to greet his guests, who had already settled on the desk. Alexander sat down and they locked eyes.

Phillip Fuller is a traitor. Hither's voice rasped and croaked into his brain like a slowly descending, rusty drawbridge. *His goal is to kill you, the queen, and your unborn son, invade Dalot, and rule both countries. To achieve his ends, he needs a very full purse and the Damian army under his control—hence The Wall. He owns all the gravel pits and quarries that provide the materials for it and he's blackmailed General Wicket into helping him control the army. It seems the good general was stealing from the officer's fund.*

Your Lord Treasurer is now the wealthiest, most powerful man in your kingdom.

He controls your army, has killed the agents you sent to watch him, and has taken your queen.

Yon's slightly higher voice clicked and rattled into his aching head. *But Fuller is unaware that the king of Dalot has already defeated the Norse and is headed south. He has captured and killed most of your agents in Dalot and all of Fuller's.*

He knows about The Wall.

King Louis III is on his way to destroy it and invade Damia.

Shaking with rage, Alexander clutched the arms of his chair as the ravens poured detail after painful detail into his head. "Thank you," he said, after the litany of bad news ended, "You have done your job well, and now I must do mine."

With a look that might very well have been relief, the ravens sprang into the air and vanished.

And so, despite all his efforts, the High Priest's prophecy had come true. Damia was being invaded and his beloved queen and unborn child were in mortal danger. Alexander sank into his chair and waited until his fury calmed. He had a kingdom to save. And, thanks to Hither and Yon, he just might be able to succeed.

He drew up a detailed course of action—a little surprise for Lord Fuller and General Wicket. Fortunately, it would take the Dalotian army another several weeks to get into position. There would be just enough time, Gods willing.

He spent the next few hours writing orders and organizing the kingdom's affairs, so it would continue to function smoothly, as a well maintained household should in its master's absence.

His plans complete, he sprinted down the tower steps to begin his race with time.

"The bastards!" he snarled. "I'll have their heads!"

The morning sun cast a thousand sparkles over the River Selene, and a soft breeze made the trees murmur and sigh. The river snaked quietly through the flat land, occasionally lapping the shore to remind you it was there. Molly trudged beside Asmodius in sick silence as ghastly freeze frames of the brutal killing played over and over in her head.

Mistress Livey had asked Jackie to stay with her and Jenny, and Molly was satisfied that he would be well cared for. Mardoc's priests had tended her wound and they'd left town the next morning. She wasn't really welcome there; people eyed her warily and kept their distance.

They were on a small side trail that snaked through the broad band of poplars bordering the river. It was pleasantly cool in the shade, and they were making good time. As they rounded a bend, Asmodius stopped and sniffed the air.

We need to get off this part of the trail. There are trees with long vines that grab you by the ankle and lift you up to hang until you die and then devour you—truly nasty things. We'll take this side trail and go around them. It will only be a few miles out of our way.

"It doesn't look like it's been used in years. I'd be tripping over tree roots and getting scratched up by brambles. And there are probably snakes in there. I hate snakes. Can't we just jump past the trees? How far do they go?" She walked a little farther ahead and peered down the main trail.

Molly! Come back! You're way....

With blinding quickness, a vine snaked out, snagged Molly's ankle, and hauled her up to the top of its tree.

...too close.

"Shit!"

She was suspended upside down by her right ankle near the top of a huge tree. There was a stab of pain as the knife wound reopened and blood started trickling toward her armpit. The air was shadowy still and warmer than it should have been. A nauseating smell slammed into her senses. Breathing through her mouth didn't help; the reek was so strong she could taste it. Gagging and retching, Molly wriggled and jerked, trying to free her ankle. The movement caused the vine to tighten its grip and rotate her a quarter turn, putting her face to face with the source of the stench. Her heart stopped and then tried to lunge out of her chest. Her bladder contracted and warm pee soaked her tunic and ran down her body and into her face and hair. She screamed and screamed until she couldn't scream anymore.

A grinning skull partially covered by shreds of skin and tufts of brown hair hung right in front of her. Birds had pecked the eyes out and brains oozed from the sockets. Iridescent green flies buzzed furiously around it. The snake-like vine that suspended the body by its ankle had grown in a tight spiral around its leg and over its hips and torso. Tiny rootlets grew off it and into the corpse, forming a living mesh that covered it from chin to toe.

"ASMODIUS! HELP! GET ME DOWN FROM HERE!"

I'm sorry, Molly, but I can't. Those trees are magical entities and have strong shields. The one that has you has just...er...eaten and its shield is particularly strong. I can't get through it. Believe me, I've already tried.

"Then how do I get down?"

I don't know. The Chair informs me that the trees feed on fear and they use that fear to maintain their grip.

"Oh great, all I have to do is stop being afraid and I'll get dropped on my head."

That would seem to be your best option.

Molly went still as the horror of her situation sank in. She shivered as a soft summer breeze blew over her soaked tunic and chilled her to the bone. It would take several miserable days for her to die of thirst, unless the tree started eating her right away. In that case, she would die a bit more quickly as the tree rootlets pierced her skin and sucked the life out of her.

She was almost relieved to feel her grasp on sanity loosening and wild delirium beginning to take over. If she let go and went shrieking into madness, maybe dying wouldn't be so painful. And then she decided that because she was thinking about going mad, she probably wasn't. And maybe she deserved to die. Molly cringed with self-loathing as the memory of her uncontrollable rage and its gory results haunted her for at least the hundredth time. What kind of monster was she turning into?

One that still really wanted to live.

"Asmodius, please, can't you think of something else?"

I've given you all the information we have.

"Then I'm gonna die. Don't leave until I'm dead, OK?"

Molly, you're not anywhere near dead yet. You're smart and strong and you have much more magical ability than that tree. I can't do this for you because I'm not up there and I can't feel how the tree reacts to your escape attempts. But you can. Use your talents. You have no idea how bad I would feel if you died.

"Not near as bad as me," Molly muttered. But the cat's encouragement and faith in her abilities worked its own magic and she calmed down and began to think.

If she could just stop being afraid, then the tree would release her. Of course, she would fall—but it would be a quick, clean death. And if she didn't die, Asmodius could probably heal her.

So, how to stop being afraid?

Maybe if she told herself she wasn't afraid enough times, she would believe it.

And so she began reciting, *I'm not afraid, I'm not afraid, I'm not afraid…*

What felt like hours passed and nothing happened because she was still afraid. And the sun had only moved a tad toward the west.

Then hours really did pass as she hung in terror on the tree and waited to die. Her pulse pounded desperately in her ears as she felt the vine growing slowly around her ankle, making it scream in agony. The reek of death and the droning buzz of the flies were a constant reminder of her fate.

Finally she told herself sternly: This is stupid. I can't just hang around up here. Maybe if I told it to let go and put all my energy into it, like I did with Shadow and Snowflake…

She gathered up a great burst of energy and threw it at the tree along with the command, *LET ME DOWN!*

The result was immediate and frightening. The vine tightened its grip and grew around her leg another two inches. So it wasn't just fear the thing fed on, it was any emotion.

Panic gripped her again. It started in her bowels and washed out over the rest of her body, bathing it in a drenching sweat. Her heart raced and her breath came in quick, short gasps. And sure enough, she felt the vine grow a bit more, which sent another jolt of fear through her that made the first seem like a sadistic caress. The vine grew. It was almost up to her knee. Hope scurried furtively away, leaving her cringing and helpless.

And then, like a dash of not-so-sweet reason, Asmodius called up. *Come on Molly, quit messing around up there and get yourself down. You really don't want to be up there all night.*

"I'm not 'messing around'—I'd like to see you do better."

I wouldn't have been caught up there in the first place; and if you'd just done what I suggested, you wouldn't be either.

All of her fear suddenly coalesced into one white-hot knot of anger. How dare he! He was supposed to be guiding her and helping her, and instead he was sitting down there being snarky. She was so angry she didn't even panic as the vine grew another inch.

She closed her eyes and clutched that anger to herself like a talisman, focusing it just below her navel. It gave her strength. She hung still for a few minutes, allowing her breath to slow down. Her anger vanished and the vine stopped growing.

She had rotated and her gruesome companion was no longer in view.

The air shimmered Day-Glo-orange and solidified into a canvas high-top. A leg and then the rest of a body materialized below it.

Tracy Bliss floated upside-down in front of her.

Her mirror image.

His clothes were still filthy and ripped to shreds, but his face was serene and he no longer twitched like a meth addict. Strangely enough, the sight of him gave Molly comfort and hope.

He smiled, winked at her, and vanished.

Yes! She could figure this out. She was gonna make it.

She took a deep centering breath. In her head she could hear Tamerlane saying, "Ground and center."

But how do you ground when you're hanging upside down?

You can't. But you can still center. I need to accept my situation. And that means accepting the fact that I really am just hanging around.

OK, ungrounded, but centered. Now what? Relax?

Pay attention to your breath, Tamerlane was always telling her that—breathe in for five counts, pause, breathe out for five counts, pause, and continue...

And then her nose itched, and she scratched it.

More breaths...

Everything itched. She scratched all over.

More breaths...

And then her mind accelerated into overdrive as it presented thought after thought—little gems that it was sure Molly wanted to think about *right now*. One thought after another came creeping and slithering out. It was amazing how many there were. She couldn't stop them, but maybe if she just noticed each one and let it go without all the trauma and drama, maybe she could keep the vine from growing. Maybe, eventually, it would let go.

So she hung, observing her thoughts. No sooner had she let go of one, than another was there to take its place. But the vine wasn't growing anymore.

And then, slowly, like a hooked fish, her mind quit its thrashing and settled down.

More breaths...

She saw her practice stick lying where she'd dropped it on the trail—The Chair had already scurried out of the tree's reach. A dark stain shadowed one end of it. The river had washed the bloodstains out of her tunic, but no amount of scrubbing would remove the soldier's blood from her stick. The sight of it made her nauseous. But it also reminded her of Tamerlane's sword and the way the firelight gleamed off its impossibly complex, swirling finish. She imagined holding it by its black hilt and feeling its perfect balance. Gods! Even though she had just killed a man, she would still give anything to own a sword like that. The vine grew.

More breaths......

The view was awesome. Looking down the trail one way she could see where she had been and looking the other way she could see what lay ahead. She was suspended in a still and perfect balance between past and future. Present in this one perfect moment. Way cool. She needed to be present in each moment. Thinking about the past and anticipating the future caused emotions that fed the tree. Maybe this would work.

More breaths................

She noticed that she was now looking at her gruesome neighbor's foot, or what she could see of it, and not his head. The fine webbing of rootlets around it was drying out and disintegrating. As she watched, the vine lengthened. The tree was done feeding. There was no more nourishment to be gained from this particular tidbit. But why didn't it just drop it? Ever so slowly, the vine lowered the corpse to the ground, unwound itself, and slithered back into the shrubbery to await its next victim. What had once been a living breathing human being collapsed into a heap of fine dust that was already scattering in the breeze. She realized, with a surge of relief that it would probably do the same thing to her if she could refrain from feeding it. The vine grew another fraction of an inch.

More breaths...

And the vine lengthened. She was going to make it! The vine stopped.

Time passed.

She was almost to the ground, and the sun was setting.

"Not so fast, Molly Adair," said a voice.

13

Death

t was the sort of voice that tap-danced up your spine, froze the inside of your heart, and then slithered away, leaving you to wonder where it had come from and if it had ever really been there at all. It filled you with painful yearning, while it set your teeth chattering and lifted the small hairs straight out from the nape of your neck. It was like no voice Molly had ever heard before and she sincerely hoped she would never hear it again.

She gasped in terror; and the vine snapped her back up to the top of the tree. As she swayed back and forth, a hooded, black cloaked figure glided toward her out of the branches. It was The Shadow, and she was, as always, impressed by how black that cloak was. It was the sort of black that sucked the daylight right out of your eyes, the breath right out of your lungs, and the hope right out of your heart. A gleaming white skull grinned down at her from the depths of the hood. Two red points of light beamed out of its eye sockets, latched onto her soul, and invited it out to play in the infinite, starry sky that lay behind them.

So beautiful, and so compelling.

She reached toward those eyes and slid out of her body. A thrill shivered through her as she felt herself become as light and sinuous as smoke curling off a stick of incense. And, like smoke, she began to expand and dance toward the universe behind those empty sockets.

And then she noticed with horror that her body had begun shutting down. Someone was walking around inside it turning off the heat, electricity, and water. She had to go back, or she would be totally dead. With strength born of desperation she jerked her gaze away from those two awful pools of infinity and breathed in great gulps of cool evening air. She wriggled her fingers and toes, shook her head, and slapped herself back into herself. She was alive!

But for how long? Death—and she had no doubts that this was Death—was still there, patient as the grave, waiting for her sad, empty soul.

Maybe if I ignore it, it'll go away.

"Not a chance. We have things to discuss." The voice whispered through her like dead leaves on the wind and chilled her to the marrow.

"Am I gonna die?"

"Oh yes, my dear, most certainly. But not necessarily now, and maybe not for some time to come."

"Then what did you want to talk to me about?"

"I wanted to show you this." A skeleton hand appeared out of the cloak. It held an hourglass about the size of a coffee mug. The sand had all dropped to the bottom half, but when Death inverted the hourglass it stayed stuck in a lump and refused to run back down into the empty half.

"What's that?" A sick feeling churned in the pit of her stomach.

"It's your time, of course. As you can see, it has run out."

"Then why aren't I dead?"

"Because you are one of those people who has managed to escape death. You were supposed to be on that plane with your mother and father."

Molly felt like someone had hit her in the stomach with her practice stick. As she struggled for breath, things started moving into place like players on a soccer field lining up to start a match. The Nightmare wasn't just about her parents. She had been dreaming about her own death as well. A part of her had understood she was going to die very soon and was scared shitless.

No wonder she felt half dead.

She was.

If only she had gone to the conference with her parents, maybe she could have done something to save them. Or she could have died with them and spared herself this awful guilt and grief that overshadowed any joy that life had given her since.

"The point is, you're not supposed to be alive." The voice was cold as banished hope.

"Then why don't you just kill me?"

"I don't kill people. You folks do an excellent job of that all by yourselves. I just make sure that the soul separates from the body and moves on to the next phase. Whether it stays there or not isn't really my problem. Some souls do insist on returning for various reasons.

"The thread in the tapestry of the multiverse that was your life ends in all the universes with that plane crash. Since then, your actions and their consequences have begun to weave a new thread into the tapestry. If that thread continues in its present pattern, you are destined to become a talented warrior mage and will be responsible for ending many lives. The guilt you feel now will be magnified many times over. Eventually its burden will become so unbearable that the only way to keep what sanity you have left will be to let go of your sense of right and wrong. You will become an empty shell of a human being. A merciless killing machine."

The awful voice stopped, and Molly sobbed with relief. But as the implications of what it had said began to sink in, her relief gave way to a sense of bleak hopelessness. Her soul was dark and heavy with guilt and Riada, the fierce, shining dragon within her, was stirring—just waiting for a chance to gobble it up.

"There must be something I can do."

"There are several things, but I can only offer you one."

"And what would that be?" Molly asked, but she knew the answer.

"Allow yourself to die."

Yup, that was it.

"And then, perhaps you won't."

"What!?"

"If the life you've started after your parent's death has enough meaning and purpose and promise, the multiverse won't take it away. You will continue to live."

"And if it doesn't?"

"You will die, of course."

"But if I don't die, will I be happy again? Will I be OK with killing people and stop feeling guilty?"

"There are no guarantees."

"Will it hurt?"

"What? Not feeling guilty?"

"No! Dying."

"There will be no pain. Just look into my eyes and let go."

"It would probably be easier if someone would shoot me. I don't know if I can just let myself die."

"You may have as many tries as you like."

"Oh gee, thanks," Molly muttered. "So, why are you helping me? Why not just let me keep on living my crumby life?"

"I'm helping you because the multiverse has enough problems without a highly trained, remorseless killer traipsing through it—I am busy enough already."

"I see," she replied, although she didn't. Not at all. The concept of Death as a helper and healer was totally weird.

"I have to think about this."

"I will wait."

And so she hung between Death and dying and considered her options. There were, of course, only two: Continue trying to avoid Death and live a life that would become more miserable and more destructive with each passing year; or accept reality and allow herself to die and hope she wouldn't. She tried to convince herself that she really didn't need to die, that she could turn herself around and everything would be OK; but deep down she knew that Death's prediction was correct. Like a relentless video, her mind played out her last gruesome killing and then she began to imagine doing it over and over and over again. And probably most of the people she'd kill would have people who loved them—mothers, fathers, sisters, brothers, wives, children—people who depended on them, people who would grieve for them just like she was grieving for her mother and father. And the pain and agony that those deaths caused would echo down through generation after generation. The thought left her speechless with horror.

Tears streamed down over her forehead and into her hair.

No, not an easy choice, but an obvious one.

"I choose to die."

"A wise decision."

With a shudder, she looked up into the remorseless eyes of Death and felt herself being drawn out of her body and into those two dark wells.

She watched in panic as the light that was her life force burned to dimness and began to flicker out. The twin demons of fear and doubt gnawed at her. She had no idea how long she hung suspended in terror between life and death, the known and the unknown, matter and spirit; but she finally let go.

Her body called to her like a lost child.

If she went back now she might be able to save herself. A part of her longed to do just that, but the Molly Adair who had two gifted parents, lived in a beautiful home in Concord, Massachusetts, played soccer like a pro, maintained a four point average at Concord Academy, and loved to hang out at the mall with her friends—that Molly danced out beyond the eyes of Death with joy and relief, dragging the other Molly behind her.

And then there was light. The kind of light that was so bright and beautiful that when you looked at it you weren't quite sure what color it really was. It was red, orange, yellow, green, blue, indigo, and purple; it was all the colors at once—the whitest white imaginable. It formed a swirling tunnel and pulled her in. At the end of the tunnel Molly saw two radiant beings. Her heart filled with joy, and she flew into her parents' outstretched arms.

The next morning Althea sat with Estelle in her study once more, and gazed into the owl's obsidian eyes. As soon as the picture came into focus, they gasped in horror.

"Dear Gods!" Estelle shrieked. "What in the multiverse is she doing in a corpse tree? How could Asmodius have let this happen? I'll wring the wretched beast's neck."

"Hush, Estelle," Althea said, shaking her gently. "With that dragon on the loose, Asmodius has done an amazing job of keeping her alive this long. Your granddaughter seems to be about as easy to control as a hurricane. Give the poor cat a break."

They watched in tense silence as the vine crept around Molly's leg and then as she began to yo-yo slowly up and down.

"This is torture," Estelle said, gritting her teeth and squeezing Althea's arm.

"Think how Molly feels," Althea replied, shifting her friend's grip to a less tender spot. "She's a brave and clever young lady, though. Look, she's figured out how to get the tree to let her down. She's going to make it."

Molly was almost to the ground when her eyes snapped open. Their look of abject terror would haunt Althea to her dying day. The vine snapped up to the top of the tree. Molly hung there and seemed to be talking to someone. And then she was still.

Much later, the two mages watched in stunned disbelief as the vine lowered her to the ground. Her practice stick levitated over to lie across her chest. She rose in the air like a magician's lovely assistant and floated over to lie just off the trail beside Asmodius.

Althea had never seen the inscrutable cat look so miserable.

Estelle dissolved into tears and the owl's eyes went black.

Little by little and piece by piece Molly became aware of her body. The first sense to kick in was smell—the fresh, earthy aroma of a forest awakening to a new day. And then the raucous morning chorus of hundreds of birds lifted her heart with their ecstasy and the gentle glow of sunrise beamed warm comfort through her closed eyelids.

She was back.

And for the first time in many months, the world felt lush and warm and welcoming.

But was she still Molly Adair?

An inspection of all her body parts was painful but reassuring. The knife wound had healed completely. Her memory came flooding back in clear, crisp detail, and as far as she could tell, those details were accurate. Her life in Concord was a pleasant, distant memory that no longer had any meaning in this life. Her heart still hurt when she thought of her parents and she knew she would miss them terribly all the rest of her life; but she had, at last, let them go. The Shadow was gone from her heart, and her body was relaxed and at peace with itself.

Death waited nearby, holding her hourglass. The sand was flowing freely from the top to the bottom.

"Thank you," she said.

"You are welcome," it replied, and vanished in a shroud of gray mist.

And wonder of wonders, Death's voice was sweet.

—

Molly wiggled her fingers and toes, stretched, opened her eyes— and looked up into two golden eyes that sparkled with joy.

YOU'RE ALIVE!

"Yes, thank the Gods—and you and my grandmother," she said, sitting up with a groan. Even though her body was complaining bitterly, all she could do was look at Asmodius and grin. "I can't remember much, but I don't think I had a lot of choice about living or dying. I wasn't gonna come back; I was with Mother and Dad and it was wonderful; but these two silver threads attached to my bellybutton kept tugging on me. You were pulling on the end of one of them and Grandmother was on the other. And then I remembered that I still had stuff to do here, so I let them bring me back."

She hugged the big cat and kissed him on the top of his head. "It's great to be back. Thank you."

Humph, said Asmodius.

The Chair unbuckled itself to reveal the chalice. *Welcome back, Molly. Are you thirsty?*

She drank the first chaliceful with slow pleasure and held it out for more. She poured the second and third over her head. Her leg that the tree had claimed screamed with pain, and she removed her boot and massaged it. And then she just sat and enjoyed the soft morning air, and her friends' presence, and the amazing realization that Asmodius and her grandmother loved her enough to pull her back from Death itself. Sometime later she slipped on her boot and held out the chalice for a refill, which she drank in small grateful sips.

More silence as she stared out into the forest. "You were right," she finally said, "it would have been easier to take the side trail. But, you know, sometimes the easy way isn't the best way."

And sometimes it is. Shall we take the easy way this time?

Molly limped over and proceeded to bushwhack her way down the side trail with her practice stick. The tangle only lasted about thirty steps. After that the trail was clear.

Molly glared down at Asmodius. "You knew this path was gonna open up. Why didn't you tell me?"

You didn't ask.

14

Temperance

Fire and Water

olly and Asmodius headed down The River Road the next morning at a brisk pace, and the river slid silently along beside them. Molly moved easily, savoring the warmth of the sun, the touch of the breeze on her skin, and the peace in her soul. But she felt like a blank computer screen. Death had erased so much of her. Who was she now? Tamerlane had told her that if she worked hard she could become a warrior mage. But what exactly was that? Was that really what she wanted to be? The soldier's ghost still haunted her. If she became a warrior mage, she was pretty sure that she would kill again—probably many times. Would she be able to deal with that? Her new self could see that killing Zeek hadn't been all bad. In fact, she was beginning to see

it as sort of a good thing. He would never rape and kill another woman again. So, if the good out-weighed the bad, did that make killing OK? Somehow she didn't think so. But how was she supposed to decide which times were OK and which ones weren't?

Another week or so and we'll arrive at the delta of the River Selene which empties into the Cycladian Sea, Asmodius said, interrupting the flood of questions running through her brain.

She was almost there and the thought didn't throw her into a panic like it used to. She was actually looking forward to it, because she could start filling up that blank computer screen. She did, however, have one concern. "What happens if I can't figure out how to get back to Portland by then? Am I stuck here?"

Molly never got an answer because the woods suddenly echoed with a volley of clangs. They hurried to investigate and soon came upon a three-sided shed nestled in a curve of the riverbank. Inside the shed the single golden eye of a furnace glowed. An anvil and a vise sat on a sturdy table to one side of it and a trough of water sparkled on the other. A workbench with a grinding wheel ran the length of the wall next to the table.

But the real eye-catcher was the smith. This was definitely not your ordinary, run-of-the-mill blacksmith. As Molly approached, her heart began to pound and her skin tingled with the power radiating out from her.

The woman was immersed in her work and seemed not to notice them as she beat a red-hot chunk of iron into shape with a large hammer. Her body gleamed with sweat in the golden light of the furnace. The muscles of her arms rippled with each stroke and the veins in her forearms stood out like cords. A white bandanna pulled golden curls off her face and neck. She wore a loose, sleeveless shirt that had once been white, a leather bib apron, leggings, and boots.

She thrust the chunk of iron into the furnace with long-handled tongs and connected bellows to the gears of the water wheel that turned beside the smithy. The bellows blew the fire to a yellow-hot heat and made the furnace roar in an earnest, whispery way. When the metal glowed red, she pulled it out and started beating on it again. She repeated this process several more times and then plunged it into the water trough.

The finished product was a large nail. But this was no ordinary nail. It was a work of art. Its proportions and shape were perfect—it was the quintessential nail. Even if you had no earthly use for a nail, you would still want this one, just so you could look at it and touch it and know true nailness.

Molly was still staring at it in awe when a gruff voice asked, "And just what brings you folks to my smithy?"

She looked over at the woman and raised her eyebrows in surprise. Cranky old Asmodius had actually leaped up on the table and was purring away while the smith scratched around his ears and under his chin. She had asked Asmodius this question, not Molly.

This is Molly Adair, a client. Asmodius replied between ecstatic purrs. We were following the river and heard your hammering and here we are. Molly, this is Brigga, one of the few goddesses who actually works for a living.

Oh geeze. A freakin' goddess. Now what was she supposed to do?

Curtsy, said Asmodius, *As low as you possibly can.*

Molly bowed her head and curtsied till her butt nearly touched the ground.

"No one comes to my forge unless they need something from me." Steel blue eyes unwrapped her, took her apart and put her back together again in one glance. "Now what would a wee might of a girl like yourself need from a smith?" Brigga's generous mouth twitched up into a grin, and Molly realized that the Goddess already knew the answer.

Unfortunately, *she* didn't. Desperately searching for a clue, Molly looked around the smithy and her gaze locked onto the sword hanging unsheathed next to its scabbard on the wall behind Brigga. It was the same marvelous sort of blade that she'd seen at Madame Rue's, and in the armory at the palace, and at Tamerlane's. But this sword was different. She could feel its presence, and it stole her breath away. When she could speak again, she blurted, "I want that sword!"

Both Asmodius and the Goddess stared at her in astonishment. Asmodius actually cringed and Molly's heart thudded in fear. She couldn't believe she'd had the audacity to demand that the Goddess give her what was obviously the Goddess's own sword. Didn't people get struck by lightning or something for an offense like that?

But Brigga tossed back her head and laughed a laugh that echoed joyfully through the forest. "Well you cannae have it! It be mine. You'd have to kill me to get it, and I dinnae think you're quite up to that yet. But I will make you a sword almost like it."

Molly's jaw dropped. Had she heard right?

"You will?"

"Aye."

She couldn't believe her luck.

As if he had read her mind, Asmodius' voice whispered in her brain, *There's a catch. Brigga wouldn't make a sword like that for anybody without asking a very high price. Find out what it is before you agree to anything. The Gods are sly devils.*

I'll be careful.

But all she could think of was the promised sword.

She turned to Brigga, who had been listening in on their conversation. "Um, Tamerlane, my teacher, has a sword like yours. Did you make it?"

"Indeed I did. I owed him a favor and repaid it with a sword."

Molly imagined it had been a pretty big favor. "So what will my sword cost me?"

"Before I tell you the price, I want you to understand what it is you'll be paying for." She lifted her sword down from the wall and handed it to Molly.

The sword was feather light and perfectly balanced, and the hilt molded itself to her grip and became an extension of her arm. On one side of the hilt a swan's head and wings peeked out from under its dove-gray silk cord wrapping. Marvelous patterns swirled and shifted in the steel, pulling her into the depths of the blade. But, unlike Tamerlane's sword, this one sang to her. It caught her up in its silver sharp intensity, trilling sweet, fierce songs of the blood it had tasted and the victories it had won. It was alive with magic! Molly could feel it tingling in her head and hand. She examined the bright shimmer around the blade more closely. A thin strand of it led straight to Brigga.

The Goddess held out her hand and the sword appeared in it and Molly was left staring at her own empty hands. "Would my sword do that?"

"Aye."

A feeling very close to lust welled up inside Molly. "What do you want?"

"I want you, Molly Adair, for the rest of your life. If I make you this sword, you'll become my agent, someone who will carry out my wishes in the multiverse—especially in your world."

Her heart cried out, *Yes! I'm yours. Just make me the sword*, but she remembered Asmodius' warning.

"So, what sort of stuff would I have to do?"

Brigga turned and hung the sword in its place and leaned back against the workbench. "People usually call on me for protection and inspiration and your job would be to make sure the folks that I promise to protect and inspire get protected and inspired. Much of the time, I be able to pull the right strings myself, but once in a while I have a case that requires a wee bit more finesse."

"How would I do that?"

"I'd leave that up to your imagination."

Molly stared longingly at the sword. "Would I have to kill anyone?"

Brigga looked at the ceiling. "Maybe in self defense or to protect someone."

In other words, Yes.

"Would this be a full time job?"

"Nay, you'll have time for your studies and a bit of your own life. The more you know, the more valuable you be."

Tearing her gaze away from the blade she asked, "What if I refuse to do a job you give me?"

"Then you'll have voided our contract. Your sword will turn back into a chunk of steel."

Ah there's the catch. If I accept her offer, I'll never be able to refuse her anything.

"So, if I use my sword when I'm not working for you, will it still do all the same stuff?"

"Yes and no. It will respond as if it was a part of you, but my energy will nae be there to help you."

"So if I'm working for you, you'll help me fight?"

"Aye, most definitely. When you fight for me, the sword will channel not only your intelligence, but mine as well."

"Is there anything else I should know?" She could still feel Brigga's sword tingling in her hand. It was a fabulous weapon and her body ached with the desire to possess one like it.

"The process of forging you and the blade together be quite intricate and powerful and oh so painful. The terrible forces of the magic may kill you or break you beyond repair," said the Goddess, watching her closely.

Molly ran both hands through her hair. Death and pain she could deal with, but the thought of becoming a cripple or a vegetable terrified her. "I gotta think about this, OK?"

"Take all the time you want, lass, I'm not going anywhere for awhile." She picked up another chunk of iron, thrust it into the flames, and started the bellows.

Molly headed downstream, shrugged off her pack, and set it on the riverbank. Her belongings immediately appeared in a neat stack and a bright red canvas beach chair shaded by a large blue and white striped umbrella sprouted up next to them.

"That's cute."

One tries to adapt to the milieu.

"Except that I don't think anyone in Damia has ever seen a canvas beach chair, let alone a big gaudy umbrella like that." Molly laughed at the thought of Queen Flora lounging in The Chair.

That's not my problem. Are you going to sit down or not?

"Of course I am; how could I resist?" She flopped down, pulled off her boots and wiggled her toes in the warm sand, reveling in her newfound ability to relax and enjoy the moment. Picking up the chalice from her stack of belongings she asked Asmodius to please fill it with orange juice.

I'm sleeping, or at least I was before you woke me. There's a perfectly good river with perfectly drinkable water right beside you—or at least it will be drinkable once you put it in the chalice. Get your own drink and quit bothering me.

Molly sighed, waded out into the river, and dipped the chalice into the sparkling water. She was so thirsty that she drank it all and refilled it. By the time she got back to The Chair, the water had turned to orange juice.

"Thanks, Asmodius, you're a sweetheart."

No reply.

"OK, Chair, tell me all you know about Brigga."

Ah, Brigga. She's one of my favorites. The only Damian or Dalotian goddess that's more beloved than Brigga is Dama. Brigga is a warrior goddess, but she's also the goddess of smithcraft, medicine, healing, fire, inspiration, poetry, wells, and the protector of pregnant women. She is one of the few Gods that still incarnates into human form and talks to people. Gods don't like to do this because they must leave behind almost all of their power. What you're seeing is only a tiny part of the Goddess. Your mind would shatter and you'd burn to a crisp if you were confronted with the entire being we call Brigga.

"Are all the Gods that powerful? What are they, anyway?"

No one knows. They are vast, and they can be everywhere at once. But they have their limits and are shaped from the same life force that shapes and permeates everything in the multiverse and connects us all. The same stuff that you and I are made of.

Molly shoved her feet deeper in the sand and took a sip of juice. "So why would something that big and that powerful care about us? Doesn't she have anything better to do?"

Who knows? Probably only the Gods, and they aren't telling. All I know for sure about the Gods is that they exist and they are unimaginably powerful. What they are, where they come from, and what their intentions are toward humanity is anybody's guess. Listening to someone talk about the Gods tells you more about that person than about the Gods.

Molly finished her juice and scooted her chair farther into the shade of the umbrella. "OK, let's look at this another way. You say people love Brigga, so she must have a history of helping them and at least making them think she cares. Does she keep her promises?"

Yes, Brigga is a very people-friendly goddess, and she does keep her promises. But, if you look at the stories of the Gods in your own universe, you will find that people who make deals with them usually come to realize they've gotten themselves into a lot more trouble than they bargained for.

She drained the chalice, shoved her feet deeper into the sand and lifted them out, watching the stream of grains flow back onto the riverbank. These were not the answers she had been hoping for, but they hadn't convinced her to turn down Brigga's offer.

A soft paw touched her bare foot and she looked down to see Asmodius.

You look comfortable, but you don't look very happy. Why?

"Because I've just decided to sell my soul for a sword."

Don't do that. The price is way too high. Even if you survive, you will be a slave, bound to the sword and to Brigga. And the Gods are not easy on their champions—especially the warrior Gods. You will condemn yourself to one painful death after another—because she can keep bringing you back if she chooses.

This was a possibility she hadn't thought of. Asmodius saw her hesitation and added the clincher. *Perhaps I can convince King Alexander to give you an officer's sword.*

Asmodius was right, of course. He always was, dammit. An officer's sword was a fine blade and would kill people just as dead as the one Brigga would make for her. But she didn't want that sword, she wanted one made for her by Brigga, and her desire for that particular sword had nothing to do with killing.

So if it wasn't about killing what *was* it about?

The answer came in a flash, and in the blaze of that flash, her life fell into place.

"I have to have that sword because I'm supposed to be Brigga's agent; and Brigga's agent needs a magic sword and needs to know how to use it. That's the reason the multiverse spared my life not just once, but twice."

Hmmm. Asmodius purred irritably. He began an intense round of ablutions and Molly began the dance of the forms, imagining what it would be like to do them holding her own fabulous sword instead of her practice stick and what it would be like to serve a goddess.

—

Molly's stomach was in knots when she presented herself at the forge the next morning.

Brigga looked up and wiped the sweat off her forehead with the back of her arm. "And just what have you decided then, lass?"

"I've decided to accept your offer. If you make me a sword like yours and bind it to me, I agree to work for you for the rest of my life."

Brigga grinned triumphantly, "Ah, you could nae resist the sword, eh?"

"No, my Lady, I couldn't."

Brigga took Molly's hand in hers and shook it, sending invigorating jolts of energy ricocheting through her body. "We have a deal then!" the Goddess said. "After I finish these nails I will begin forging your blade."

"Who are they for? Can't they get their own nails?"

"Aye, they can, but these be very special nails for a bonny young lordling. This forge sits on the edge of his lands, which be rich and bountiful and well placed for trade. His neighbor covets them and has managed to find a mage willing to call up a demon to attack the lordling's manor and kill him and his family in their beds. But if he does as I tell him, and has a new front door made for his manor house with these nails, he and his wife and wee ones will be safe. The demon will go to bash in the front door—do not ask me why, but they always go for the front door—and the moment he touches it, the magic in the nails will blow him to smithereens!"

Molly observed the wolfish grin on the Goddess's face and vowed not to get on her bad side.

—

The next day, after the young nobleman arrived at the forge and received his nails and his instructions, Brigga picked up a piece of rusty cable about a foot long and an inch in diameter.

"We'll be starting your sword today."

Fear shot through Molly, but she was so not gonna let Brigga see it. This goddess wouldn't want a coward for a champion, would she? So Molly tried to look calm and collected and said, "You're not gonna make it out of that, are you?"

"Ah, but I am," Brigga replied, making a few elegant slashes and lunges with it. "This be the perfect material for a blade. I taught the Little People of the Altispinas—at least the ones willing to lay hands on bitter-cold iron—where to find the purest ore and how to smelt it into fantastically shaped blooms of shining iron. The Little People sell it to smiths in Bontare, who heat it in furnaces that blast it with great breaths of air and turn it into steel fit to make blades for Gods and Heroes."

The story claimed Molly's attention and calmed her nerves.

"But to make a sword, the steel must first be folded over upon itself many times and welded at each fold," the Goddess continued. "It be much easier to weld the strands of a length of steel cable and shape that into a sword. But alas, steel cables did not exist in Damia. So I found a steelworker who was bright with intelligence and energy and gave him the knowledge of drawing steel out into wire and twisting those wires into cable. He made a fortune. In payment for this knowledge, I made him promise that every year he and his descendants after him would produce fifty feet of steel cable of this diameter made from the pure Altaspina iron. And every year at my festival at Lambing Time, they coil it 'round my altar."

Remembering her conversation with The Chair, Molly asked, "If you hadn't wanted special steel for your swords, would you have shown the Little People where the iron ore was and would you have taught that steelworker how to make cable?"

Brigga smiled the smile of a mischievous child caught in a small deception. "Well, probably not. I'd never have thought to do it." She handed Molly the length of cable and turned to start the bellows blowing into the already glowing hot furnace. Molly stared into the flames and prayed that she would survive. And that if she did survive, that she would be sane and healthy. "Now, to wed this sword to your body and soul, some part of you must be forged into it. Blood works best." Brigga set the cable on the anvil, pulled her knife from its sheath at her waist, and motioned for Molly to come stand beside her.

Off in the distance a pack of wild dogs howled in unison and began the steady baying and barking that meant they were running down their supper.

Molly's heart thudded with fear as she took her place beside the Goddess. Brigga held Molly's right hand in hers and rested them both on the cable. Power from the Goddess surged through her, extracted a bit of Mollyness, and flowed out into the piece of cable, which proceeded to shimmer in a most uncable-like way. Every speck of dirt and rust jumped off it like rats abandoning ship.

Molly could hear the individual yelps of the dogs as they crashed through the underbrush.

"We must cut your wrist."

Molly held out her arm. She had cut herself so many times that she had no fear as the Goddess drew her knife across her skin. But now the pain brought neither release nor relief. It was just pain. She was, however, intensely aware of the power in the bright, red blood that welled up out of the shallow cut, fell onto the glowing cable, and sank down into the myriad twists and turns of steel wire. Brigga touched the cut and it was gone, leaving no trace.

The baying crescendoed into an almost earsplitting din as Asmodius streaked into the clearing and leaped onto the railing. His yellow eyes glinted wildly and his mouth was pulled back in a snarl, exposing murderous looking fangs. His fur was puffed out and his tail was a bottlebrush, making his already imposing black bulk frighteningly huge. He could easily have passed for the demon that was his namesake. Glancing back at the dogs as they entered the clearing, he gave a yowl that sent them into a frenzy of anger. They slammed into the barrier of power that protected the forge. Snarling and snapping and throwing themselves against it, they couldn't pass, but they wouldn't leave.

Asmodius leaped to the rafters as Brigga turned to the dogs.

"Away with you! Be gone, be gone," she commanded. The dogs immediately slunk away with their tails between their legs. She glared up at Asmodius, who stared back at her from his perch with wide, innocent eyes.

Molly turned her attention back to the shimmering length of cable. Brigga fixed a pair of tongs to one end it and Molly braced herself as the Goddess thrust it into the heart of the furnace.

Hot, searing pain lanced through her and she screamed a scream that could never be loud enough to stop her agony. She writhed in torment until she realized that resisting the force of the magic and fire only made the pain worse. She relaxed and opened herself to it and the pain subsided, leaving only the awareness of intense heat and power rippling around her and sinking into every pore. It flowed along the paths of her muscles, nerves, and sinews. It filled her heart and poured like lava into her veins. Anything that blocked it was burned away, leaving behind a feeling of lightness and freedom.

She floated and swirled along hundreds of luminous, shimmering strands of steel. She could hear each of them singing its own silver song as she glided from one to the other.

And then she felt anger—white-hot, seething anger. Where was it coming from? She searched herself and could find no trace of it. Was there someone else trapped with her in this world of fire and steel? She searched for the Other and found Brigga.

Frothing and fuming, the Goddess was trying to escape from the confines of the cable, but she seemed to be bound there as firmly as Molly. She threw her energy against its confining boundaries, making the space echo with loud booms and bangs. "A thousand curses on that evil animal," she snarled, walloping the unyielding barrier one last time. Sensing Molly's presence, she turned her anger toward her and screamed, "Did you know what he was planning? Tell me, did you?"

Shock and terror reduced Molly's reply to a whisper. "No. What has he done?"

As quickly as it had thundered in, Brigga's rage flowed out of her. "Ah, Wee One, forgive me. The wretched beast would never hae told you for fear you'd give him away. He must love you dearly or he would na hae done what he did."

"What did he do?"

"Asmodius be a very clever mage—sometimes too clever for his own good. He knew that I would bind you to the sword with your own blood and he also knew that this would make you my slave. It seems that he didn'a want that for you. I would guess that he tried to talk you out of letting me make you a sword?"

"Yeah, he did."

"Aye, well, when he jumped into the rafters he must hae cut me with a claw so quick and sharp that I didn'a notice and dropped a bit of my blood onto the cable with yours. Now, like you, a small part of me be bound here. The magic was set in the furnace; it canna be undone. As we forge its fibers together, our spirits will be intertwined within the blade. I will never be able to use you as I had planned because now I be unable to command you to do anything that is nae ultimately in your best interest. Our wills are forged together in this blade. And so, you see, he has done you a great favor. And the clever beastie knows that I know that you be fond of him and that you need him to guide you through Damia and so he be safe from me for a bit. But I will have my revenge. No one crosses the will of a goddess and comes away unscathed!"

Molly was horrified. Asmodius had given her a precious gift, and now he was going to suffer for it. "Oh Lady, please! He did it for me. Let me take the blame."

"Nae, Lass. Now, to work. We have a blade to forge."

Brigga turned to the cable that glowed in the heart of the furnace. She pulled it out, sprinkled it with a white powder from a tray on the floor, and plunged it back into the furnace. The powder melted to buttery softness, and bubbled and sank into the grooves of the cable. Molly could feel its soothing protection enveloping her.

Brigga laid the cable on the anvil and lifted the heavy hammer high above her head. At the first strike, the hardened glaze shattered and skittered off the glowing cable. The blow sent shock waves ricocheting cruelly through Molly and she gasped in pain. The Goddess turned to her and from the set of her jaw, Molly could tell that she'd felt it too.

"That be the first of thousands, my brave one. Relax into them and they willnae be so bad," she said and took her second strike.

Again the shock, and she could feel the steel strands being pushed closer together, cradling her spirit. Several more blows and she could feel the presence of the Goddess, herself. Molly and Brigga and the steel were all being forged together by the relentless force of the hammer. And then came a feeling of hardening and resisting. Back into the fire. Brigga repeated the process over and over again.

By furnace fire and by hammer's force, the three of them were being forged into something new and different. Molly was intensely aware of being a part of that thing, yet she could no longer tell where she left off and the other two began. As the steel was shaped and lengthened, she felt her spine lengthening and strengthening. She felt aches and itches and energy explosions as muscles and nerves were coaxed into more efficient positions by the relentless force of the forge

Molly writhed on the floor of the forge for what seemed like an eternity as the Goddess plunged them in and out of the raging inferno of the furnace and beat them into a new shape. If she relaxed into the pain and didn't try to block the surges of blazing hot power and the hammer's brutal force, the agony was bearable and she could float above it. But it took tremendous will and concentration. Eventually the blows stopped and the heat cooled and she lay in the delicious, pain-free stillness and watched Brigga clean up the forge. She could tell from the slant of the sun through the trees that it was late afternoon. When all the tools were in their place and the floor was swept as clean as a dirt floor can get, the Goddess reached down and raised Molly to her feet and held her close, which was a good thing because there was no way she could stand by herself. Together they gazed at the long, gray rectangle of steel that contained a part of each of them.

"Ah, lass, you were very brave and very strong. Not many mortals would have survived this day. Asmodius and Tamerlane prepared you well."

"They knew this was gonna happen?"

"'Course not! They be tricksy mages, but even they can na predict the acts of a goddess! Nay, they saw talent in you and, not being able to leave well enough alone, they decided not to let it go to waste and taught you what they could. And if you hadna learned what they taught you and learned it well, you wouldna have been fit for this blade."

The next morning dawned rainy and cool. As Molly clutched her length of steel and ate breakfast, Brigga lit the furnace. The charcoal blazed up immediately—it would not have dared do otherwise—and Brigga turned from it and asked, "Did you sleep well and dream sweet dreams?"

"I slept like a log and don't remember dreaming about anything," Molly said through a mouthful of bacon and greens sandwich.

"A pity. I hear tell, from those who should know, that the dreams of mortals give insight into the soul and hints of possible futures. If you have a dream, it pays to remember it."

Molly thought of all the dreams she'd had recently and shuddered.

"But we have work to do!" Brigga continued, gently prying the steel from Molly's reluctant hand.

—

After what seemed like forever, Brigga laid down her hammer. The agony of blazing heat and brutal force ceased and Molly relaxed with a sob of relief. The Goddess picked up the steel, ran her eyes over it and sighted down its length. It looked like a dull, blurry, blunt version of her own blade, only shorter.

Brigga turned to her and crooned happily. "Ah, 'tis a sweet blade. And now we let it relax, soften and come to center after the beating it has taken. T'will be a happier blade and much easier to fine shape and sharpen."

"Relax? Swords get tense?"

"Oh, Aye."

After a brief check in with the steel and her own body, Molly had to agree.

"And so we heat all of it to yellow-hot heat and let it reset itself. Close the shutters, it must be dark enough to read the temperature." As Molly struggled to her feet and darkened the forge, the Goddess piled yet more charcoal in the furnace and the bellows blew the coals to bright yellow. Fierce heat consumed her once more as Brigga began passing the blade through the flames, heating the entire length evenly. The girl and the goddess sweat rivers as they watched the blade turn from cherry red to orange to yellow. Brigga pulled the glowing blade out of the furnace and tested it with a magnet. "It doesnae stick, 'Tis done." She set it edge up next to the furnace to cool slowly. Molly collapsed cross-legged on the floor beside it and reveled in the feeling of relaxed suspension that they shared. Brigga closed the furnace, swept out the forge, and disappeared without another word to disturb Molly's trance-like torpor.

It was sunny and hot the next morning. Molly ate her bread and cheese and watched Brigga grind the dull gray scale from the surface of the blade in a fountain of sparks.

"Did you dream sweet dreams?"

"I dreamed. Not sure what it was, but I don't think it was sweet."

"Well, that be progress. Perhaps tomorrow you will remember a dream. Today I will finish the grinding and filing and shaping and you must rest."

The next morning dawned clear and bright. Brigga was busy in the forge and the smell of frying bacon wafted down to the snoozing Molly. Her belly gurgled and she sat up and stretched. But her breakfast was nowhere to be found and neither was her sword.

"I thought that might wake you," the Goddess laughed. "Just look at yourself, all covered with dirt. You have nae washed in days, an' I'd be willin' to bet your mouth tastes like a midden heap. Go to the river and bathe. Your blade awakens today and ye must prepare yourself to greet it. There'll be a bacon and greens sandwich for you when you get back."

"Where's my sword?" Panic began snaking through her.

"Behind you, lass."

Molly turned and saw that her blade was still clamped in the vise that had held it while Brigga did the fine grinding. But now tiny brown stripes ran up both sides of the blade perpendicular to its cutting edge and an intricate design of some sort had been painted on both sides along the opposite edge. Closer inspection revealed two pairs of profiles, face to face, with long wavy tresses.

"My lady! That's us. It's fabulous. But why did you paint the blade?"

"That isna paint, it be clay, the stuff of Mother Earth herself. You see this blade hasna been born yet. It has only been shaped. Its metal be soft and it wouldna stand up in a fight. It must be heated again, but this time, we do not cool it gently. We quench it in the cool waters of the Selene." She pointed to the long wooden trough full of sparkling water next to the furnace. "The shock makes the steel crystallize and become strong and hard, and spirit enters the blade."

"So what's the clay for?"

Brigga gazed fondly at her creation. "Steel quenched in water be brittle and shatters easily. The clay protects the parts of the blade it covers and keeps them from getting quite so hot in the fire and from cooling quite so fast in the water. The parts of the blade covered by clay be softer and more supple and give way under force so the blade doesnae shatter."

She turned, put her fists on her hips, and looked sternly at Molly. "Now away with you. And no you can nae take your blade with you, you'll spoil the clay."

—

When she returned, Brigga had set her meal out as promised and was bringing the furnace up to heat. As Molly tucked into her sandwich, the Goddess asked, "Did you dream last night?"

"I did, My Lady. I dreamed I was up in the air looking down on The Wall and it turned into this horrible snakey monster and I started falling down into its mouth."

Brigga grinned. "Excellent!"

Molly didn't think it was at all excellent; but she figured it would be safer not to argue with a goddess, so she asked, "But what does it mean?"

"Ah lass, you must interpret your dreams yourself. The important thing is to remember them, and you will be prepared when they manifest in your life."

Molly contemplated her dream as she munched on her morning meal. She wasn't looking forward to having it manifest. As soon as she finished eating, they closed the shutters and the inside of the forge became dark with shadows. The bellows were working full blast, and the furnace roared its peculiar, muffled roar.

Brigga fixed tongs to the tang, the end of the blade that would fit into the hilt. "Are you ready, lass?"

Molly's heart was pounding with excitement; the best she could manage was a whispered, "Yes."

Brigga thrust the clay-enshrouded blade into the yellow-hot furnace and began passing it through the flames, heating it evenly. Once again, Molly felt the searing heat of the furnace race along every nerve, muscle, and vein, dissecting them out into glowing hot lines of agony. But as she relaxed and let go, the pain faded and her body floated blissfully as the molecules of the blade fell out of their strict metallic order and danced luxuriously alone and free. No worries, nowhere to be, nowhere to go.

There was a soft tapping as Brigga touched a magnet to the glowing blade. She struggled out of her reverie as Brigga said, "It be ready now! Brace yourself." and plunged the blade into the water. There was a quickly smothered hiss.

Molly stiffened and caught her breath as the cool water jerked the blade and her spirit into intricate crystalline lattices of steely symmetry.

And time stood still.

She became simply herself again. She was still connected to Brigga and the blade, but no longer a part of them. Molly and her blade had become two separate beings.

And they were both weapons.

Molly gasped as she felt the triumphant, innocent joy of her blade's self-awareness. There was a soft chink and then a snick from the blade. When Brigga drew it from the water, they found a small slash carved neat as you please into the tang—the part of the blade that would fit into the hilt. It looked as if a point had been thrust into it and then flicked upward to the right.

"Its name is Flick," Molly said, and collapsed as the agony and stress of the past few days flowed out of her. Her whole body felt like jelly. Just lifting her hand was nearly impossible. But she gazed about in awe as her world clicked into sharp new focus. There was a clean, pure intensity in her that hadn't been there before and a deep awareness of where she stood in time and space. She knew that after some rest she would be able to move with blinding quickness and brutal strength. But right now the cool earth of the forge felt marvelous, and she relaxed into it gratefully.

Brigga ran Flick through the furnace once more, heating it evenly but not nearly so hot as before. Then she laid the blade edge up beside Molly to cool and come into balance.

Molly was doing that as well. The forge, the forest, and the Goddess hadn't changed a bit, but they felt unfamiliar and vaguely frightening. She was the one who had changed, and she needed this time to come into new balance with the world around her. To let go once again of her old self and figure out where and how this new Molly fit in. There was no logic to it. She closed her eyes as her mind began the mysterious process of relearning itself.

Hours later Molly hadn't moved and made no response when Brigga took up her now cooled blade and began the polishing process. Brigga checked and rechecked every angle, plane, and curve. When she was satisfied, she stamped her mark and Molly's initials above Flick's mark.

—

The aroma of grilling meat curled seductively into her brain and Molly awoke with her mouth watering and her stomach clenched in hunger. It was dark and a sliver of moon rode soft clouds high above the trees. She stood and stretched and every joint in her body cracked.

"Aye, you needed that rest," Brigga said. "Now go bathe and refresh yourself. Your supper is ready."

—

As Molly was finishing her grilled meat—she was afraid to ask what kind it was—and vegetables, she heard a shuffling of feet and looked up. Three armed men were standing in the middle of the smithy. In a flash, Molly grabbed her meat knife, jumped up from the workbench, and stood ready to fight, knife low and close in front.

For a long moment they all froze. The men were clothed only in blue tattoos, suntans, and brown loincloths. Like the obsidian tips of their spears, their black eyes glinted with a sly intelligence. And every one of them was even shorter than she was.

Earth and Air

The one in the middle smiled a smile that went around his face three times. "Very good, young one. But not good enough! If you were our enemy, you would be dead."

Molly stared at the trio in horror and confusion. She was just beginning to come to grips with her new reality and the last thing she needed were these three nightmares.

"Welcome to my forge, gentlemen," Brigga said. "I see you have already taught your first teaching. Molly, you must close your mouth and put down the knife."

Molly complied, but she never took her eyes from the visitors. "How'd you do that? You appeared like magic."

The three smiled gleefully.

"Molly, this be Feather, Tor, and Ripple. At least that be what their names mean in our speak. Their people have lived in this land since before recorded history. They be Unglazy, the Little People, an' they know all there is to know about seeing without being seen an' moving without being heard. They will teach you what they can of their skills and fit your blade out into a sword."

The Unglazy turned toward Brigga and bowed in unison, touching their foreheads.

"It is a privilege and a pleasure to be in your presence once again, Great Ladee," said Feather. "Now where is the young one's blade?"

Brigga laughed. "To the point, as always. You only love me for my blades!"

Feather's eyes twinkled as he replied, "That is not so, Great Ladee. The Unglazy love you for your beauty, kindness, and generosity—but you do make bee-you-teeful blades."

"An' this one be no exception," Brigga said as she handed Feather her latest creation.

Feather bowed low once more as he accepted the blade from her hands, holding it by the tang. Ripple and Tor gathered round and they began their examination.

Although Molly didn't like these strange men handling her new blade, she held her breath as she waited for their verdict.

The three ceased muttering and fussing, and Feather looked at Brigga in amazement. "This is fabulous, Great Ladee. You have poured your soul into this one!"

"That be for certain."

He looked up at her and raised one eyebrow. The three craftsmen turned their attention back to the blade and became very still. "Ah, yes, we see now. And the young one also. This is, indeed, quite a piece of work! I will be honored to polish it for you."

"I will make the hilt, Little Ladee," Ripple said. "Have you given any thought to what you would like?"

Brigga reached back for her own sword and pointed to the hilt. "Ripple makes these fittings here." She pointed at two delicately made rings, one just under the sword guard, where the blade slid into the scabbard; one just above the guard, where it met the handle; and at a cap at the top of the handle. "He also does the sword guard, the handle and wrappings, and the charm that goes under them. When he be done, Flick will be a finished sword."

Molly reached for her blade and Feather handed it over. She studied it for a moment and said, "I'd like the wrappings to be auburn colored, like my hair; and a black cat for the charm."

Brigga frowned, but couldn't keep the corners of her mouth from curling into a grin. She turned to Ripple and said, "That would be Asmodius."

Ripple hissed, but his eyes danced with amusement. "Ah, that devil. Yes, I will carve him out of ebony and use yellow topaz for his evil eyes. Now, what about the guard?"

Brigga pointed to the wall of the forge. It was covered with dozens of wrought iron rounds, ovals, and rectangles about four inches across. "Those be sword guards. Do you see one you like?"

Molly decided on a simple round pattern for the guard and asked Tor to make an auburn-colored lacquer scabbard to match the hilt wrappings.

"Well, that be done." Brigga said briskly. "You'd best be off now if you're going to make it back to your forge and get any sleep tonight. Safe journeys, Molly Adair. My love goes with you." She hugged Molly and saluted the Unglazy.

The Goddess and her forge shimmered out of sight.

A feeling of panic swept over Molly. First her parents, then Tamerlane, and now Brigga. "Don't leave!" she cried, holding her arms out to where Brigga had been.

"As long as you have that blade, I will always be with you. Now get on with it, I have work for you, but you can nae do it without a bit more training." The Goddess's voice came from everywhere and nowhere.

Molly stifled a sob and turned to face the three strangers. "I'll get my stuff."

Tor touched her arm gently. "You will need this. He held out a long strip of leather and reached for the blade. Molly handed it over and watched him wrap it securely and strap it on her back.

The Chair scuttled forward, all packed and ready to go.

"Thanks," Molly said as she shrugged on the pack and arranged her new blade so it didn't dig into her back.

Not a problem.

"Where's Asmodius?"

I'm behind you.

Molly spun around. The cat was a menacing shadow anchored by two gleaming yellow eyes. Not a comforting sight. But Molly knelt in front of him and reached out and touched his paws with her hands. "Thank you, my friend, you gave me back my life. But Brigga won't forget. You're in danger. I owe you—big time."

Asmodius shifted and pulled his paws out from under her fingers. Then he reached out and patted her hand. *You owe me noth-*

ing. You have a several hours' journey to The Unglazys' forge and workshop. I'll meet you there eventually. Your new teachers are perfectly capable of keeping you safe. They work with earth magic, so the dragon won't notice them. Now move, they are a restless folk and don't like to be kept waiting.

Molly grinned as the big cat melted back into the shadows.

The Unglazy set off down the trail, walking with long, mile-eating strides, and Feather began her instruction. "When we arrive at our workplace, we will all rest and then our work will begin. Ours will be to complete your sword, and yours will be to come upon at least one of us and tap him on the shoulder before he notices you. Only then will you receive your sword. We will teach you about moving quietly and masking your presence tonight, so notice carefully."

"But it's my sword. I won't give it to you if you're not gonna give it back!"

"A gentle reminder, Leetle Ladee: that is not a sword you have there, it is a blade and as such, it is useless to you. And what is most important, you will not be worthy to be the Great Ladee's warrior and to carry this blade without the skills we have to teach you. We will do it our way or not at all."

The three stopped and waited for her reply.

Molly threw up her hands in defeat. "OK! We'll do it your way." What could be so hard about sneaking up on one of them and tapping him on the shoulder?

That night, they taught her about moving silently and invisibly.

"Become like a mist," Ripple said. "Flow softly over the ground, disturbing nothing," Feather added "It is a state of mind. You must will yourself into it."

Tor disappeared from in front of her and reappeared at her side. "Hide your power and keep your feelings close in, but be totally aware of everything around you."

The rest of the night, they praised her lavishly the few times she accomplished these goals and laughed and called her "Eleephant Girl" when she failed. Molly was ready to strangle them by the time they reached their workplace, but she was too tired to make the effort. She rolled her sleeping bag out in a corner of the forge, which looked almost exactly like Brigga's, and slept until late the next morning.

When she awoke, her blade was gone!

They'd just strolled in and snatched it.

They'd also left bread and cheese and fruit. She heard voices and movement in the workshop next door. This would be a perfect time to sneak in and tap one of them.

She tiptoed toward the workshop. Before she got to within twenty feet of the building, she heard Feather say, "Ah, here she comes. I am surprised. She is not even trying to move silently. Now would have been her big chance!"

Mortified, Molly stepped into the workshop and greeted the grinning Unglazy. Feather was kneeling on the floor at the back of the room in front of a large window that opened out into the cool, green forest. A bucket of water and an array of polishing stones lay within easy reach. But her attention went immediately to Flick. Her blade was humming happily as Feather moved a stone over its surface. The blade trilled a joyous, silvery greeting, and a jolt of relief ran through her. Flick was safe, and happy, and in capable hands.

Feather looked up at her. "Flick is good company. It doesn't have many stories yet, except the one of its birth, but it is a good listener. It loves stories, and I have plenty to tell!"

Molly smiled and Ripple motioned her over to his workbench. "Come and see how a sword hilt fits together."

Two ring-shaped fittings, a cap, a peg, and a tube wrapped in red silk cords around a golden dragon charm lay on the workbench. There was also a sword guard with two swirling dragons. Ripple picked up the tube and pushed the cap into the top of it and one of the rings into the bottom. They fit perfectly. He lifted a beautifully finished blade down off the wall with a soft cloth, and slid the second ring down the tang to where it met the blade. "This fitting holds the sword in the scabbard." He picked up the sword guard and slid it down the tang and onto the fitting, and slid the gleaming red tube and fittings down on top of the sword guard. He pegged it all in place through holes in the tube and in the tang. "And poof! You have a sword." What had, just moments ago, been a litter of stuff on a workbench, was now a fabulous sword hilt.

Ripple handed the finished sword to Molly, making sure she held the blade with the cloth.

She gazed at the weapon in awe. "Who's it for?"

"King Alexander ordered it several months ago and we have just finished it, which is lucky because we hear he will be down this way soon and we can give it to him. Tor! Where is the scabbard?"

"It is right here; don't get your breech cloth in a twist!" Tor came over from his bench carrying a black, flattened, lacquer tube. He took the sword from Molly and slid it into the open end. There was a whispery, shushing sound as the blade slid in, ending with a soft snick as the ring under the sword guard slipped into the scabbard.

Ripple tied an intricately woven black mesh belt around Molly's waist and Tor slid the scabbard between the belt and her body so that the edge of the blade pointed up. A black lacquer nub protruding from the outside of the scabbard caught on the belt and held the scabbard in place. They showed Molly how to reach across her body with her right hand (palm facing out, fingers up), grasp the hilt, and anchor the scabbard with her left hand. When she drew the sword, it came out correctly oriented and ready to slash down or across.

The firm pressure of the sword and its scabbard felt good at her waist, and she felt a wisp of sadness as Ripple pulled them from her belt. "You may keep the belt. I am sure the king has plenty of his own. Now, we have work to do. The Ladee wants your sword complete and you back on the path by the end of the week. Go practice being invisible. It is a skill you will need very soon, I am thinking."

She wandered back to the forge and ate her breakfast. How could she practice being invisible when there was no one to tell her if she was invisible?

When in doubt, ask The Chair.

Picking up her pack, she headed for the river. As she went, she outlined her problem.

That's easy, it said, after it had assumed its beach-chair-with-umbrella persona. *I'll tell you when you've managed to blend in with your surroundings enough to be totally overlooked.*

Molly sat down in The Chair and recalled her lessons of the night before. The first thing she had to do was slip into the same frame of mind as when she escaped from the Corpse Tree. She calmed the mental chatter that set her apart from the rest of the world and opened herself to her surroundings. She became the soft, silver wind rustling in the trees and the patient forest, shimmering with emerald light and bustling with hundreds of creatures going all their hundreds of ways. She was everywhere and nowhere, and she worked on convincing everything around her that she wasn't really here.

The sun made its way across the sky and into afternoon before The Chair informed her that, if someone were to walk past, they wouldn't see her unless they were looking for her and knew ahead of time she would be sitting right in that particular spot.

Hanging on to the feel of invisibility, she got up from The Chair and began to slip as silently as she could through the forest. By the end of the afternoon, she had managed to sneak up on a squirrel, who scolded her for her efforts—loudly, and for a long time without stopping.

This was so flipping cool! It opened up a whole world of possibilities.

She practiced hard for the next few days and got really good at sneaking up on small forest creatures. Because she was so excited, she couldn't resist the occasional "Aha!" or "Gotcha!" when she succeeded, so most potential victims soon left the area. She also tried several times, unsuccessfully, to tap one of the Unglazy.

On the fifth day, as she sat cross-legged under a tree near the trail being invisible and enjoying the feel of being everywhere at once, Tor and Ripple came ambling down the trail behind her. They were having a heated discussion about the fittings on her sword. This was her chance!

They were coming closer.

They were even with the tree.

They were past the tree, still in hot debate.

Molly rose soundlessly to her feet, and glided up behind them. She tapped each one on the shoulder. For a moment they stood like stones, and then they spun around with huge grins on their faces and jumped up and down yelling, "You did it! You did it!" Molly let out a whoop of joy and began her own victory dance.

After they settled down, Ripple announced, "Now we have another challenge for you." He reached into a fold in his loincloth and took out a rock about the size of a walnut and handed it to her. "You must keep this with you at all times."

That seemed easy enough. She put it in her tunic pocket. The two Unglazy patted her on the back and congratulated her one more time and then headed off again in the direction they'd been going. Ecstatic at her success, she danced down the trail toward The Chair. Hanging on to a rock would be simple compared to what she had just done.

Wait a minute, her pocket was empty. They'd pinched it just like that and she hadn't felt a thing.

She turned and ran back down the trail toward the Unglazy. As she approached, they turned and smiled at her. Ripple was juggling three rocks. Around and around they sped, so fast they became a gray blur. And then the pattern changed. Two rocks went up and when they came down, the third went up.

"Would one of these happen to be yours?"

"I don't know, I can't see them."

"Ah, but you can feel them. And you should especially be able to feel *your* rock."

"Oh, come on, a rock's a rock." They were messing with her, but Molly managed to hold on to her temper. She reached out quick as a flash and snagged two of the rocks out of the air. Fortunately one of them looked like hers. She handed the other one back to Ripple and stamped angrily back to her camp.

The rest of the day did not improve her temper. The Unglazy always seemed to have a reason to be near her and she spent her time chasing her rock from Ripple to Tor to Feather and back to Ripple.

When she awoke the next morning, not only the rock, but her sleeping bag, the rest of her belongings, and even The Chair had vanished. She'd never worried about being robbed when she traveled with Asmodius, but he wasn't going to be with her all the time, was he? As she sat chilled and alone in the forge listening to the river whisper past and the birds tune up for their morning chorus, she realized how important this lesson was. It wasn't about hanging on to a rock; it wasn't even about hanging on to her stuff; it was about paying attention, being present. It was sort of like being invisible, except her attention also needed to be turned in toward herself and the stuff close to her.

She picked up a rock and reached into it with her mind. It did have a certain rockish feel and a solid, slow-moving spirit of its own. She picked up another rock and inspected it. Sure enough, there was that same feel, but it was different from the first rock. Her rock would be different as well. So if she was present with it, she would know if anyone even touched it. In fact, if she was truly present and in the moment, she would feel it the instant anyone came close.

OK, just let them try to take that stupid rock away.

She found Ripple and Tor sitting outside the workshop eating breakfast. Tor handed over the rock and pointed to her traitorous pack. It was exuding conflicting waves of self-righteousness (I did for your own good), and apology (I'm really sorry, they made me do it). Molly glared at it and slid the rock into her pocket. She snatched an apple and some bread and cheese and sat down to eat.

Before she started, however, she turned her attention toward her rock and searched for its spirit.

Yup, there it was. This one wasn't nearly as slow moving as the first two, and it hummed a deep stone song. She sat back to enjoy her breakfast and listen to the rock. Molly finished with her bread and cheese and started in on the apple. She had actually forgotten that she was supposed to be protecting her rock, but she sensed Ripple's fingers the moment they closed around the rock because the rock's voice changed. She grabbed his hand just as he pulled it out of her pocket.

"Ah! So you have been listening to the rock. Very good!" He patted it fondly and tucked it away. "Now, enough of this. We finish your sword today and I must get busy."

By noon the sword was complete. The three Unglazy stood in a row in front of their workshop smiling as Feather handed Molly her sword.

Am I not bee-you-teeful?

Molly grinned. "Of course you are, silly. We've been telling you that all week. You're the most beautiful sword in the multiverse."

Flick trilled a bright, silver riff of contentment.

Feather gave Molly a gleaming hardwood box full of soft cleaning clothes, vials of oil, powder, and a soft brush, and showed her how to clean and oil her blade.

And then there was nothing left to do but slide Flick into her belt, shoulder her pack and bid Feather, Ripple, and Tor good bye.

She was surprised at how hard it was.

15

The Devil

olly's new awareness made walking in the forest an adventure in itself. She sensed a host of small dramas and traumas unfolding right under her nose. The mice and squirrels were particularly alarmed just now. Death was stalking past them, and they were frozen in terror in their hidey-holes praying that they would live to see another sunrise. This particular death was a black shadow with golden eyes, and it was coming near.

Molly turned to greet Asmodius as he glided silently onto the trail behind her. His eyes widened slightly. *It seems those squirrelly Unglazy have managed to teach you something after all. Well done.*

"Those guys are awesome!" Molly exclaimed, feeling heat flush into her cheeks at what, from Asmodius, was lavish praise. She began recounting her week. The big cat listened patiently, asking a question here and there, until Molly ran out of story.

So, show me this sword that you have given so much to possess.

In a single fluid motion, she drew Flick from its scabbard, and sat down in the trail cross-legged in front of Asmodius so he could examine it. Asmodius studied the blade carefully and sniffed up and down its length. The sleek fur along the ridge of his back lifted straight up, his mouth opened slightly, and his whiskers lay flat against his face.

This is, indeed, a treasure. Brigga has kept her end of the bargain admirably. The hilt charm is especially fine. Ripple does have a way with wood. He touched the ebony cat with his paw and its topaz eyes glinted even more wickedly.

There was a silver shimmer of joy from Flick. *Oh Molly! I can see. It's not all just shadows anymore. But when I don't want to see outside, I don't have to, I just close my eyes. Like this.* And the eyes on the charm closed.

Asmodius sat back on his haunches. *Guard each other well. Would you like me to put the glamour back so people will see a ten-year-old street urchin with a knife instead of a young woman with a fabulous sword?*

Molly tore herself away from listening to Flick's ecstasies on how wonderful it was to see long enough to thank Asmodius and to say yes, the glamour would be a good idea.

Now, the river delta is about a few weeks' hike from here. Shall we begin?

Molly jumped to her feet and headed after the retreating cat. She was getting anxious to return to Portland.

—

Several days later Molly and Asmodius were headed down The River Road at a mile-eating jog. The weather was muggy and Molly began to feel uneasy. At first, she figured it was just the close, hot air, but as she stilled her mind and allowed her awareness to travel out, she found something toward the southeast that filled her with dread.

"What's over there?" she asked, stopping suddenly and pointing.

The Wall.

"No. It can't be."

Asmodius' ears flattened back against his head. *But it is. I went there while you were with the Little People. It's a terrible place. Reminds me of a prison colony.*

"But Queen Flora loves her people, she would never treat them like prisoners. Something must have happened to her."

Yes, I've managed to make that leap of logic, and I've also managed the next step in the progression. If the queen is in trouble, it's probably a very big sort of trouble, and whoever or whatever is causing this trouble is very powerful and very nasty. We need to stay as far away from The Wall as possible.

Molly stared down at her companion in angry confusion. Here was a skilled magician who had the guts to fight fire breathing dragons and go up against a goddess. How could he be afraid of helping Queen Flora?

"That's not logic, that's an excuse, and you know it." She jammed her fists into her waist. "What are you scared of?"

Asmodius sat back on his haunches and began an intense bout of face washings. He even did behind his ears. When he'd finished, he turned to Molly, who was now sitting cross-legged in front of him.

I am afraid because I have seen The Wall. It is a monstrous, evil thing that slithers over the earth, sucking the life out of all it touches and leaving fear and hopeless desolation in its wake. But that's not why I'm against going there. In case you haven't noticed, let me remind you that you've nearly died several times on this trek. We're almost to the end and I want to get you back in one piece. Not only because I've become quite fond of you, but also because Estelle will roast me alive if I don't. How about this—I promise that once you are safe and sound in Portland, I will go help Queen Flora.

Molly's heart did a joyful pitty-pat. She knew Asmodius loved her, but it was wonderful to hear him say it.

Now quit grinning at me and let's get you home.

And that was so exactly what she wanted to do. Not only was she ready to be home, but Asmodius' description of The Wall had reminded her of the awful dream she'd had at Brigga's forge. Asmodius was right, she didn't want to go there. And by now she was well aware that it was always safer and wiser to take Asmodius' advice. But Queen Flora had a special place in her heart. She was the first person to truly believe in her, and the gentle monarch's unconditional faith had given her the courage to continue her journey. She owed her big time; and there was no way she was gonna just walk on by and do nothing to help her.

"No," said Molly, "We're going to The Wall."

Oh let's not and say we did. That place is a hell hole.

"We're going. It's time for your morning nap and you're tired. Things will look better when you wake up."

I'm fine.

"Whether you take your nap or not, I'm still going to The Wall."

Drat.

The cat leaped up onto Molly's pack and The Chair broadened and lengthened to accommodate his bulk. As he curled up and went to sleep, Molly set out at a more sedate pace, looking for a trail cutting off to the southeast.

—

When Asmodius woke up a few hours later Molly was heading toward The Wall. The well-traveled road led straight uphill, and the poplars and alders of the river valley were giving way to somber, brooding evergreens.

"So tell me something about The Wall besides 'It's god-awful and you don't want to go there.'" Molly was moving at a fast trot again and Asmodius was a shadow beside her.

There are two camps, one at each end of The Wall. They are building it from both ends to meet in the middle. Each camp is divided into ten units composed of ten large tents that have their own mess tent, cook fires, and laundry. The whole thing is surrounded by a wire mesh fence and guarded by regular patrols. It's unclear whether they're trying to keep the enemy out or the workers in. They're nearly finished—an amazing achievement. Too bad it's so ugly.

For the rest of the day, they moved in companionable silence. Toward late afternoon, she noticed that the sun didn't seem quite as bright as it should have been and the few birds that were singing went about it in a halfhearted manner. When she let her awareness range out over the forest, she could feel skittishness in the small animals.

Let's find a clearing off the trail and make camp. The Wall is about an hour hike from here, and it just gets worse, Asmodius said.

Portland, Oregon

Althea headed up Alameda Street toward Estelle's house. It was a perfect warm, sunny August morning, but she wasn't appreciating its joys.

She was trying to decide what to do about Estelle.

She knew from experience how long the grieving process takes, and she was wondering if her friend would survive to the end of hers. When Estelle had finally accepted that Molly was dead, Althea had watched the powerful mage's petite form crumple in on itself and a black shadow wrap around her heart. This was the stuff that coronaries were made of, and Estelle lived alone.

When she arrived at the house, the front door was standing open.

"I'm in here," Estelle called.

Althea followed the sharp, sweet tang of just-squeezed oranges and found her puttering around the kitchen. Estelle grinned and gestured toward a pitcher of orange juice, a bottle of champagne, and two wine glasses sitting on the table. "Let's celebrate!"

Althea eyed her friend uneasily. Had the grief been too much? Had she gone mad?

Estelle popped the cork on the champagne, and proceeded to make mimosas. She handed a glass of champagne and orange juice to her wide-eyed friend and plopped down across the table from her. Beaming with joy, she took a big gulp of her drink and said, "Molly's alive!"

"That's impossible."

"I know, but it's true. Asmodius never sent her body back to me, so this morning I looked to see what was going on, and I saw the two of them trotting through a forest."

"Are you sure it was Molly?" Althea reached for her mimosa.

"At first I wasn't. Her face is all planes and angles and her eyes aren't just gray anymore, they're steel gray. In fact, steely pretty much describes her. She reminds me of a wrestler I used to date in college. I wouldn't want to be in her way when she goes after something. But, yes, it's Molly. Which means, it's still possible that The Chair will bring her back in an hour or so as we'd planned."

Althea sank back in her chair and downed her drink. Estelle poured her another one.

This was going to be some story.

She hoped Molly would make it back so she could hear it.

❧

The next day was cloudy. A misty drizzle followed Molly and Asmodius, brushing clammy fingers over Molly's face and down the neck of her tunic. They never returned to the road. Instead, they followed faint animal paths through the deepest part of the forest.

The smell was the first thing that hit them—a growing stench of wood smoke, garbage, horse manure, and sewage. Not a bird sang and not a single animal stirred the undergrowth. Any edible creatures had either been killed for the stew pots or had left long ago. Gloom and hopelessness swirled through the trees.

They walked through this dismal no-man's land for quite awhile before they reached a wide vista of stumps and dead branches that overlooked two long, gray snakes wending their way across The Gap. They had reached The Wall.

Tall as a three-story house with four-story watchtowers set at quarter mile intervals, The Wall was made of two parallel walls of quarry stone blocks about two sidewalk widths apart. The space between the watchtowers was filled with gravel and formed a walkway between them. A city of tents skirted the towers at each end. They were gray too, and so was the fence that surrounded them. The smoke curling up from hundreds of cook fires was gray. And all the workers were gray. Their uniforms were gray, and, even at the end of a beautiful summer, their skin was gray.

A fine grit of rock dust covered everything and hung in the air like a restless phantom. It was deathly still. There was no laughter, no chatter and no singing, only the muffled sounds of work in progress.

Molly stood transfixed with loathing. The wind breathed an especially noxious breath of pit toilets up the hill. A wave of nausea shuddered through her and a cold sweat chilled her from head to toe. "You're right; it's awful," she said. "I really, really don't want to go down there."

Then don't. Let's head for the delta.

"I don't want to, but I need to. You can stay here; just turn my clothes gray, please."

She began a stealthy approach, blending into her surroundings, and Asmodius followed. He was gray too. They found a place where the ground dipped, leaving a space at the bottom of the fence. There wasn't a soul in sight, so they slithered under it, coating themselves all over with gray dust. They were now a perfect match for their surroundings. Molly reached out and became the encampment. It felt like swimming in sewage, but she could move about freely and no one noticed her.

The hunger and despair of the workers and the sadness of the earth beneath them made her itch to find whoever was responsible and give him a good shaking. Or worse. Most of the units were filthy and the midday meal cooking in their kitchens didn't look fit for pigs. But one or two units were clean and neat. Bits of colored cloth hung from the tent poles, relieving the mind-numbing gray. These cooks had the same meager ingredients to work with as everyone else, but appetizing smells wafted from their kitchens. Molly stopped in relief near one of them. The cheerful activity and good smells eased her soul.

"Hey, Cookie!" A young man dashed around the corner of a tent and nearly ran into her. She sidestepped and froze. "I got some fresh greens for the pot. Least ways, they're sorta fresh. But listen ta this. Everyone at the supply tent is talkin' 'bout the queen. Seems she's sleepin' with that bastard, Fuller! Kin ya believe it?"

The cook quit stirring his pot and took the vegetables from his helper. As he examined them and cut out the rotten parts, he replied, "No, I can't, and nor should you, Billy Berg. Think on it. Fuller's an evil little rat. What would Queen Flora want wi' the likes of him? An' here's another thing. By my count, the queen's well over eight months pregnant. If you knew anything about pregnant women, you'd know that sex is the furthest thing from their minds when they're that far along."

"But that's what everyone's sayin.'"

"If everyone was sayin' the sky's green would ya believe 'em? Use yer head for somethin' besides waggin' yer chin, boy. Now get along with ya. I need more wood for this fire."

Asmodius jumped back just as a rock exploded on the wall behind where his head had been. The cat streaked into the maze of tents.

I will catch up with you later, Molly. I'm attracting attention and have no wish to become an entrée. Stay out of trouble.

Molly spun around and saw two men who had just come out of their tent.

"Dang, ya missed 'im. He would 'a fed the whole unit fer supper. After 'im. He went that way."

She put out her foot and tripped the first worker as he ran past and the second one tripped over him.

"Josh, ya clumsy oaf. Now lookit. We'll never catch 'im."

⌒

A few hours later, Molly huddled miserably at the base of the first watchtower. The whole camp was growling over the queen's supposed infidelity. The mood was ugly. She had watched from a distance as a group of stern-faced soldiers all but dragged the queen out of the end tower and back to work after her midday meal.

The tower was almost deserted now. If she sneaked up to wherever the queen stayed, she could wait there for her to return from work. With a shudder, she moved her mind into the forbidding structure and began to explore. There was a guardroom and what felt like a prison on the first floor. The prison was empty now, but the stench of fear and human waste remained. Two soldiers argued in the guardroom.

Another soldier on the second floor guarded the door to Lord Fuller's office and living rooms. They were lavishly furnished with heavy mahogany furniture upholstered in velvets and brocades. The floors were covered with thick, hand-knotted carpets. Silver and crystal candelabra bearing beeswax candles were everywhere. Heavy velvet curtains smothered all the windows. Even though Fuller had bought the best of everything, the rooms felt soulless and offered no comfort. Insatiable desire and bitter dissatisfaction wove through the tapestries and twined around the gleaming chair legs.

She moved her attention to the third floor and found the queen's apartment. It was a spacious room that occupied the top of the tower. Open windows to the east and west caught the freshening afternoon breeze. There was a bed, a writing desk, a comfortable chair, a soft wool rug, a small table with a lamp and wash basin, a chamber pot, and an armoire. The furnishings were exquisite and perfectly placed. But sadness and longing languished in the shadows left by the weak afternoon light. The room wrenched at Molly's heart and she sighed, startling a soldier leaving the guardroom.

He spun around. "Hey, wot are ya doin' here?" She melted farther into the tower as the man drew his sword and came toward her. His frightened eyes passed over her, searching for the intruder that had been there just a moment ago. "Friggin' place is haunted. I knew it," he muttered. "Glad I don't have night duty." He sheathed his sword and walked quickly toward the other end of The Wall.

Molly checked on the tower's two remaining occupants. One soldier sat in the guardroom playing at dice, one hand against the other; and the second remained at Fuller's door. All she had to do was sneak past the two guards and up to the queen's room.

The door at the base of the tower was ajar, supplying much-needed ventilation. Molly was able to squeeze through without moving it. The dice-playing guard paid no attention. She began climbing the stairs. The wretched things squeaked. Placing her feet close to the risers helped a little, but not much. She came around the curve of the stairway and into view of the second guard. He was white as the ghost he feared, and he was staring straight at her. But instead of challenging her, he clutched his sword in front of him, shrank back onto the landing, and plastered himself against the door. Sweat stood out on his forehead and his trembling free hand formed the Damian two-fingered sign against evil. Molly hurried past.

Several steps up from Fuller's door was another door. This one opened in the opposite direction and probably led out to The Wall, but Molly wasn't going to push her luck with the guard by opening it to see. She climbed up and around the tower, out of the guard's sight, and came to the door of the queen's chamber. She tried the door. The latch moved soundlessly, but as the door opened, it creaked in a way that would have done any haunted-house proud. A pitiful moan of fear echoed up from the guard below. Molly let herself in and closed the door. Moments later, she was hidden in the armoire, doing her best armoire imitations to cloak her presence.

The door creaked open and tentative footsteps entered the room. The soldier had guts—he was doing his job. He searched the room, even the armoire. "I don't see nuthin', so I don't have ta report nuthin'. If I told anyone about this they'd laugh me outa the army," he muttered to himself, and left the room, closing the door firmly.

Molly stayed huddled in the queen's armoire for the rest of the afternoon. It was cramped, but it was the sweetest-smelling thing she had encountered in hours. Finally she heard footsteps on the stairs and the door opened and closed. Footsteps moved across the room. Molly peeked out through the slightly open armoire door.

A woman in a plain, green dress was slumped in the chair. Her hair was pulled back in a simple twist. Dark shadowed eyes stared vacantly out the window. With a ragged sigh, she began to stroke her huge belly and croon a sad, sweet melody.

Shit! That's Queen Flora. What's Fuller done to her?

The queen stopped humming, sat up straight, and looked at the armoire. "Whoever is in there, come out immediately."

Molly dropped her invisibility and nearly fell out of the armoire—her legs had fallen asleep. She managed an awkward bow.

"Greetings, Molly Adair. Although you are not the same Molly Adair who left our palace four months ago."

Molly was amazed. "You saw through Asmodius' glamour. No one's ever done that."

"This is my kingdom. It is a part of me. I see it for what it is—all of it. Now, to what do I owe the pleasure of this visit?"

"Your Majesty," Molly said, bowing again. "You're in danger. I've come to warn you and see if there's anything I can do to help."

The queen's tired, violet eyes showed not even a hint of surprise, only a shadow of sadness. "Tell me more."

Molly paced back and forth to get some circulation back into her legs and work off her nervousness. "Someone has been spreading the rumor that you're, uh, like sleeping with Lord Fuller." She stopped, clasped her hands together, and looked anxiously at the queen.

"Ah, that explains the hostility. But how could anyone possibly believe that?"

"Don't know, Your Majesty, but most of the folks out there do believe it and they're furious with you. They loved you and trusted you and now they think you've let them down—right when they need you most."

The queen's face turned gray and fear flickered in her eyes. "This is even worse than you know. If the people lose faith in me, I'm useless. If I lose the people, I lose the kingdom."

There was a knock at the door. "Supper, Your Majesty."

Molly slipped back into the armoire as the queen unlocked the door, took the tray, and pushed the door closed. The soldier retreated down the stairs in a thunder of footsteps and Molly continued her pacing as the queen placed the tray on her writing desk and sat down. "Fuller must be the one who started the rumor. Oh, I'm such a fool. I should have acted sooner. I think he's planning to take over the kingdom, and he's just taken the queen. The game's over."

Molly watched in anguish as Queen Flora crumpled back in her chair in defeat. "I had the power to stop this. When Fuller and Wicket proposed this scheme, I hated it. I knew that it wasn't right for the people or the land. The truly courageous thing to do would have been to say 'No.' But because I didn't say that one little word, the High Priest's predictions have come true. My child is in danger and we've lost the kingdom."

Kneeling in front of the dejected queen, Molly clutched the hem of her skirt and pulled on it insistently. "You can't just give up. Your people need you. And what about the king and that little prince that's gonna come any time now? Fuller will kill them both if he comes to power." She pulled on the royal skirt yet again. "You gotta suck it up. You haven't lost your powers—you knew I was in the armoire, even though I hadn't made a sound; and you saw through Asmodius' spell. You're still the Queen of Damia no matter what these soldiers believe. And that evening after the High Priest told his vision—didn't Dama herself tell you that everything would be all right? You must at least believe *her*!"

The queen drew a shuddering sigh. "That's true, I'd forgotten."

She frowned at Molly. "How did you know that? And how did you know my child will be a boy?"

Oh geez, stupid, stupid. "Uh, I just knew, Your Majesty."

Queen Flora snorted in a most un-queen-like manner, sat up straight, and smoothed her hair back. "I sense Asmodius' sneaky paws all over that answer. Now, what can we do to help Alex?"

Molly breathed a sigh of relief and got to her feet.

Quick footsteps sounded on the stairs.

The door to the queen's room slammed open and Lord Fuller stood in the doorway. He was a blackness that pulled everything in and gave nothing back. The entire room seemed to tilt toward him as he stepped into it. The gold crown on his head gleamed red in the late afternoon sun.

His flat, reptilian gaze pinned Molly's feet to the floor.

Oooo! Molly Molly—that one needs killing—let's do it. C'm on, c'm on! Flick howled.

Hush.

"Good evening, my dear," Fuller said, shifting his attention to the queen. Molly sagged with relief.

"I came to let you know that our little secret is all over the camp. Several of the guards saw you tip-toeing down to my rooms in the middle of the night. You weren't very discrete, you know. They've been telling the whole camp about it." He turned toward Molly once more. "But it seems you have company."

Molly cringed.

"Who is this brat? I thought we decided that you were to have no visitors."

"You decided that, Fuller, not I. And this 'brat' is one of the kitchen boys who sneaked up to ask if I was really being unfaithful. Let him leave. He's no threat to you."

Fuller reached into his pocket and held a silver coin up between his thumb and forefinger. "Don't you believe a word she says, boy. Your queen is a ruined woman. This is for you if you will go out and spread the word. The kingdom deserves to know."

Behind Fuller's back, the queen was nodding and making shooing motions. Molly's heart filled with love for this valiant woman. No way was she going to leave her alone with this monster.

"Never!" she shouted, glaring up at Fuller. Queen Flora winced and put her hands over her eyes.

"Then I'll have to kill you." he replied, smiling in anticipation.

Molly shook with terror, but her training kicked in. She eased into a relaxed fighting stance doing her best to maintain the image of a frightened child. It wasn't difficult. He had a sword, and he moved like he knew how to use it. His reach was a bit longer than hers, and his empty eyes told her she could expect no mercy.

Fuller moved languidly, savoring the moment and feasting on her fear. He drew his sword with a practiced hand and then looked at her waist. His eyes gleamed, like a cat's when it plays with a mouse. "But let's put some sport into this. You have a knife. I'll give you time to draw it and defend yourself like a man."

Thank the Gods for Asmodius' glamour. It would give her a much-needed second or two.

Molly reached for Flick.

16

The Tower

ower jolted through her and the presence of Brigga surrounded her. Flick jumped into her hand and the world clicked into slow motion.

She gazed into Fuller's eyes as she parried a slash to her left arm and saw surprise flicker through them when their two swords met with a clang. His lips tightened as he began a series of quick slashes and lunges. Molly countered them all and nicked his arm. She worked her way inside his guard and Flick slashed his chest as he leaped back. Redoubling her efforts, she moved in for another thrust and saw fear blossom in his eyes as he backed away.

Their swords danced and clashed in a quick, deadly rhythm.

She lunged. Fuller just managed to smash her sword away and jump back. Reaching out, he grabbed Queen Flora and shielded himself with her body. Molly gasped as her next slash barely missed the queen, slicing a neat opening in her green sleeve that revealed a hairline scratch dotted with red.

Fuller bared his teeth in a vicious grin and backed to the door. "You'll never make it out of the tower alive, you little bastard."

The queen caught Molly's eye and dropped to the floor.

Molly seized her chance. Flick whirred through the air, and barely slowed as it glided through Fuller's neck.

The grinning head stayed put for an eternity, and then slid off. Molly felt Brigga yank her aside as two arching fountains of impossibly red blood from the great neck arteries missed her by inches and splattered on the wall behind her.

There was a thud and Molly looked down to see Fuller's rapidly glazing eyes staring up at her with an expression of such horror and hate that she shuddered and looked away. Fuller's fallen crown rolled in drunken circles. Molly and the queen watched it intently as the headless corpse collapsed.

Why are you here? I thought you weren't going to help me if it wasn't an assignment from you, Molly asked.

Ah, but this be an assignment, the invisible goddess replied. *Queen Flora asked me to protect her and her unborn child and she donated generously to one of my temples. Lord Fuller's wife be also expecting and asked me to protect her from her husband. She hadnae any money to donate, but her prayers were desperate. I have answered both women's prayers quite nicely, dinna you think?*

The circling crown tipped over and began an ever-quickening wah-wah-wah-wobble until it lay still on the floor.

She'd just killed someone. Shouldn't she be feeling just a little bit sorry?

Or guilty?

All she felt was relief. She was alive. And so was the queen.

She ignored Brigga's rhetorical question. *Next time, tell me when I'm working for you.*

I will. I wanted to see what you would do on your own.

You did well.

The unexpected praise calmed her, and she wiped her bloody sword on the dead man's indigo velvet tunic.

Mmm mmm. That was one evil man, Flick said. *I will have many grisly tales to entertain me!*

A chill gripped Molly as she remembered the magic swords some warriors carried in WarCraft Universe. *Don't tell me you've eaten his soul. That's just wrong. Even* he *doesn't deserve that!*

What would I want with that bastard's soul? It's stories I love, and his whole life story sang in his blood. It was deliciously awful, but it ended well!

Molly sagged with relief and sent a surge of affection toward her blade.

Flick, you are a ghoul.

Sheathing her sword, she turned to the queen, who was staring over Molly's shoulder. Her eyes were round with shock and amazement and then the queen bowed. "Thank you, Great Lady," she said.

My pleasure, Your Majesty, Brigga replied, and her presence faded from the room.

The queen turned to Molly. "And thank you. You are her agent, aren't you?"

"Yes, Your Majesty," Molly replied. "She made me an offer I couldn't refuse. We need to get out of here. Can you get us past the guards?"

"I'll try."

They stepped over the body of their fallen foe, avoiding the blood that had splashed everywhere, and Molly led the way down the stairs. The guard at Fuller's door was gone, but another was coming up the stairs to take his place. "Here now, where d' ya think you're goin'?"

Queen Flora glared regally, "Move aside, and let us pass."

"I ain't movin' for any royal whore. You get back up there where you belong."

How could he speak to any woman like that, let alone his queen? Angrily, Molly reached for her sword, but the queen was quicker. She grabbed her elbow in a tight grip. "No, Molly, don't," she whispered.

Molly did the only thing left for her to do. She was a few steps above the man, so it was a simple matter to swivel to the side and kick him in the chest. He fell backwards, his armor and sword clattering noisily down the spiral staircase.

The door onto The Wall stood open just behind them. They could run across to the next watchtower and escape. She led the queen through the door and out onto The Wall.

It was clear.

They were going to make it.

Molly was frantic to escape, but it was slow going. The best speed the queen could manage was a quick waddle. They were halfway to the next tower when a group of soldiers strolled out of it. She looked back and saw two guards come running out of the queen's tower, waving their arms and yelling a warning to the soldiers ahead. "They've killed Lord Fuller, stop them!"

Trapped.

She looked over the battlement. In the red-gold glare of the late afternoon sun, a swarm of men and horses was flowing through The Gap. Even at this distance, Molly could feel the ground tremble as thousands of feet hit the earth in perfect unison.

The Dalotian army had arrived without warning.

Below, in the Damian camp, Molly saw that a whole army of Damian soldiers had just arrived, but they weren't ready for battle. They were pitching tents and cooking dinner.

Wonderful! Just freakin' fabulous! They were gonna get captured just in time to see the Dalotian army smash the Damian army and take over the kingdom. Molly growled in frustration, and her heart thudded with fear as she watched the soldiers run toward them.

There was a deafening clap of thunder. The soldiers skidded to a halt and looked up in terror as the sky split open and revealed a monstrous black dragon. In perfect unison they turned and ran back to their respective towers as the dragon tossed his head and roared a roar that shook the earth and rattled The Wall. Neon blue light sizzled around him, and his bat wings filled the sky. The rogue dragon's wicked, red eyes glared down at Molly. "I'M DYING AND I'M TAKING YOU WITH ME, BITCH."

Molly turned to the queen and pointed to the tower they'd been headed toward. "Run!" she screamed, and turned on her heel and ran back the way they'd come, hoping against hope that it would leave the queen alone.

So the dragon had belonged to Fuller. Excellent. She'd killed two nasty birds with one stroke of her blade.

She gasped in pain as the dragon grabbed her and jerked her skyward.

"AND THE LOVELY QUEEN AS WELL!"

A frantic scream pierced her heart. Shit.

She twisted around in the scaly, sharp hand and glimpsed the queen's wheat colored hair peeking over the top of the dragon's other black fist.

Her fear evaporated, replaced by simmering rage.

She wasn't going down without a fight.

RIADA!

Another blinding flash of light and another clap of thunder, and there, suspended in the dazzle like a black shadow, was her dragon. Light in every color of the rainbow writhed along her wings and extended neck ruff, and sparkled gold and silver on her ebony scales. She threw back her head and roared.

Molly shrieked with terror as torrents of relentless, mind-numbing power coursed through her. She felt wings pulling at her shoulder muscles as they pushed at the air, pulling her higher and higher. The world snapped into crystal focus. When she looked down at the tiny Dalotians, she could see the sweat running off each face, and every single hair in every single beard. Her fingers and toes flexed and sword-sized talons slid out.

She was her dragon!

She reached for her enemy and roared again.

Yes, Molly Adair, we are inseparable. And we are in great danger. Be still. I have a battle to fight.

Riada pivoted and rammed her adversary with outstretched talons. Even though Fuller's dragon was twice as large, the blow sent it spinning through the sky. Molly, clamped in the rogue dragon's hard, scaly hand, squeezed her eyes shut as earth and sky cart wheeled around her. The hot-metal reek of her captor's blood as it cascaded down its arm burned her lungs. The sky thundered with roars and the fury of dragon wings as the blue dragon steadied itself and lunged upwards toward Riada, who was rocketing up through the clouds.

It caught up with her easily, dodged a vicious tail swipe, and zoomed in for the kill. Molly watched in horror from two perspectives as enormous, cruel talons streaked toward her dragon's heart.

They closed on empty air.

Riada had jumped. She was now above and behind the blue dragon.

Almost tenderly, Riada opened her jaws wide and clamped them down on her adversary's neck. There was a deafening howl and the world exploded around Molly.

Fuller's dragon was dead, and Molly was headed in that direction. The wind whistled in her ears and tore at her clothes as she tumbled headlong toward the Dalotian army. She screamed a scream that tore at her throat and emptied her lungs as she watched the ground zoom toward her.

Then she was perched on her dragon's back, clutching the hard raspy scales and sobbing with relief. Riada had jumped again.

Another jump.

The queen appeared next to her. Her eyes were wide with shock, her face was deathly pale. She smiled weakly at Molly, fainted, and began to slide off the dragon's back. Molly, breathless with fear, grabbed her, got Riada to tilt the other way to stop the slide and dragged the queen back to the broad place between the dragon's wings. "Your Majesty! Wake up," she cried, desperately patting the queen's ashen cheeks. *Oh dear Goddess, please don't let her die.*

Riada's muscles rippled under her scales as she spread her wings and caught an updraft. Molly and the queen were pressed flat against her back as they began a tight spiral up through the low-lying clouds and broke through into sunshine. Her glittering scales heated up until they felt like warm beach sand. The extra heat and Molly's frantic ministrations finally brought Queen Flora to consciousness. She looked around dazedly. "Am I really riding on a dragon?"

"Yes, Your Majesty, it's my dragon, so you're safe, at least for now. The one that nabbed us belonged to Fuller, and it's dead."

"Ah, yes, of course," she murmured, staring down at the tops of the clouds. "I've always wondered what it would be like to fly." And she fainted again.

They began a tight spiral down. Molly, suddenly weightless, her heart pounding in her throat, grabbed a dragon scale and clutched desperately at the queen to keep them from falling off. The Dalotian army was advancing again, but stopped abruptly and congealed into a quivering mass when the dragon roared down through the clouds. The first thing Riada did was slap the section of The Wall next to the queen's tower with the tip of her tail. It exploded into a scatter of blocks.

"Not The Wall!" Molly yelled.

"Oh, come on, Molly, you know you hate it and everything it stands for. Let's have some fun."

"But the people...."

"Oh, they're long gone—at least if they have any sense."

Indeed, the Damians were putting as much distance as possible between themselves and the dragon. The Wall was deserted. Riada laughed and flicked her tail again. Another section of wall fell like so many toy blocks. The queen's tower was just ahead. Riada bugled and clawed at the air with her wings, gaining altitude. The queen stirred awake in Molly's arms, grabbed onto a dragon scale and peered over Riada's shoulder.

"Watch this!" her dragon said. "Hang on." Huge bat wings snapped full of air like parachutes pressing Molly and Queen Flora against her back. Then Riada folded them back and they began a dive that sent Molly's heart into her throat and left her weightless once more. Just when Molly was sure they were going to crash into the tower, the dragon stretched her wings. They caught the air with a deafening CRACK!

Molly and the queen were squashed into the dragon's back as she pivoted feet first into the tower.

BAM!

A hundred blocks exploded out toward the Dalotian Army. With mighty sweeps of her wings, Riada flew upward once more, roaring with delight. She glided slowly down to The Wall and began dancing along it on tippy talons, mashing it flat like a bully smashing sandcastles at the beach. When she arrived at the second tower, she flew up and kicked out the top part, turned in a graceful arc, and kicked out the bottom.

Queen Flora threw back her head and laughed with joy as her nightmare disappeared into rubble. "Don't forget the other end!"

"I wouldn't dream of it, Your Majesty." Riada flew the gap between the two ends of The Wall like an avenging angel and repeated the process on the south end, flattening it into oblivion. By the time she was finished, both Molly and the queen were howling with glee. They were safe and the horrid Wall was gone.

They soared back up into the evening sky. The view was awesome. Far off in the distance, the River Selene wound its silvery way down towards the sea and the fields and forests glowed in the red-gold light of a late-summer evening. Warm, sweet air rushed over them and Molly relaxed into the ecstasy of flight.

"Oh dear, the Dalotians are advancing again!" said the queen.

"Shit! OK, we'd better do something."

Riada swooped and plunged in the warm air a few more times, just because she could, and headed for the Dalotian army.

"But don't hurt anyone." she said.

"Aw, Molly, that's an army. They've got bows and arrows and, yup, those are catapults; and I bet they know how to use them. How am I supposed to stop something that big and with that many teeth without hurting it?"

"I have an idea."

Riada snorted and began flying in a holding pattern over the Dalotians while Molly draped her arms around her neck and explained the plan. The army skidded to a halt as the dragon whirred menacingly above them.

Riada pivoted and flew two soccer field lengths toward the crumbled wall and flamed a neat, black line between the two armies—from one end of The Gap to the other. She settled on the Damian side, belched a huge gout of flame into the glowing red sky, and roared.

The Dalotian army understood at once. The ranks did an abrupt about face and marched rapidly away to put more distance between themselves and the dragon. Then they broke into organized chaos and began constructing a fortified encampment.

Molly and the queen watched in dazed silence from Riada's broad back, and Molly wondered what to do next. Queen Flora solved her problem.

"I am exhausted," she said. "Getting down from your dragon seems impossible right now, but her back is warm and probably the safest spot in my kingdom. I will sleep for awhile."

As Molly watched the sleeping queen, she thought about what she had just done. Her world had shattered today with The Wall. She had encountered unimaginable cruelty and greed; and she had killed again. Molly shivered in disgust as she realized that this killing had been satisfying. Even worse, if it hadn't been for the queen, she would have killed again just because a guy was rude and in the way. But Lord Fuller's eyes still haunted her. Even when he was alive, they had been flat and dead with no trace of human kindness or pity. Would hers look the same way in a few years?

Tears streamed down her cheeks and dripped off her chin onto her folded hands as the reality of what she had become sank in.

A black shadow flowed out of the rubble of the fallen wall, swarmed up the dragon's scales, and onto Molly's lap. Golden eyes gleamed into hers and a raspy tongue licked a tear off her cheek.

Ah, here you are. And just look at this mess. I distinctly remember telling you to stay out of trouble!

Molly stared at the cat. And then she laughed. She laughed 'til the tears came once again. And she pulled his warm, furry body into a fierce embrace and kissed him repeatedly on the head.

Her maniacal laughter echoed through the Dalotian camp.

Soldiers shuddered and made the sign against evil.

17

The Star

ing Alexander I of Damia sat at his desk and swore softly. His beloved wife was in the clutches of a dragon and he was trapped in his tent planning a war. He had no idea whether she was safe or even alive.

His crown hung from a knob on the back of his chair and his hair stood out in angry spikes. Lanterns cast dancing shadows across the jewel-tone carpets and creamy, white tent-canvas. A red glass, oil lamp burning on a blackthorn wood altar to Mardoc at the back of the tent added another set of shadows that flitted and cavorted gleefully as if anticipating tomorrow's battle. The camp was in an uproar. Generals and a horde of officers and scouts had been dashing in and out all evening bringing problems, complaints, and information.

General DeWeis stood at the open entrance and scratched on the canvas.

"Enter."

"Your Majesty, the catapults are misplaced. They need to be on elevated ground, and dispersed across the line."

Alexander gestured to a rough map of their encampment on his desk. "Where do you want them?"

The General stepped forward. "Here, here, and here."

"But there's a mess tent there and a cavalry picket there…"

"Well, they'll have to move."

And so it went.

Nothing had gone right.

The north arm of the Dalotian pincer movement had spotted them in time to retreat into the safety of the pass just north of The Wall. Instead of the solid victory he'd anticipated he'd been forced to leave behind a whole division to make sure it didn't sneak back through.

He had arrived at The Wall that afternoon with his diminished forces just in time to see the rest of the Dalotian army come streaming through The Gap, and his queen grabbed up and carried into a vicious dragon fight. She and a boy had reappeared, riding on the back of the smaller dragon that had completely destroyed The Wall. He could still hear their jubilant laughter as his amazing wall tumbled to ruin. The beast had halted the Dalotians and Flora appeared to be alive, but for how long?

A corporal scratched at the entrance.

"Enter."

"Your Majesty, a scout has arrived with news."

"Send him in."

The scout stepped in and bowed. He was covered with dust and his hard face was streaked with sweat. "The rest of the Dalotian army is a day's march from The Gap, Your Majesty."

"Did they leave any troops at the pass?"

""No, sir."

"Well done, Corporal. Get some rest."

As the scout hastened from the tent, Alexander continued to lay his plans. Each piece of information allowed him to fine-tune them a bit more. If only he had a better idea of the size of the Dalotian army. Because the plain was flat, it was impossible to

see how far back it extended. The scout he'd sent to find out hadn't returned.

He stretched 'til his sinews cracked, raked his fingers through his hair, and gazed at the two heads stuck on pikes just outside the door. Torchlight highlighted their ghastly features and the crows had already picked out their eyes. Fuller's severed head and body had been found in the rubble of the first tower, and a flying block had killed Wicket as he ran from the tower at the opposite side of The Wall, slowed down by the bags of gold he was carrying. So far, these were the only casualties.

But even this was unsatisfactory. Arriving to find one's enemies already defeated was well and good, but where was the fun in it? He had been looking forward to the pleasure of defeating the traitors himself. Instead, here he was crouching behind a bunch of rubble, dealing with a situation he didn't really understand, facing what looked to be most of the Dalotian army, listening to rumors of his wife's infidelity, and agonizing over her safety. He cursed again, this time loudly and vehemently.

"Cheer up, my love. It's not as bad as you think!"

With a joyful gasp, King Alexander looked up to see Queen Flora standing in the torchlight between the two heads. Her dress was plain and grimy, her hair was disheveled, and she was white to the lips with exhaustion, but she was the most beautiful thing he had ever seen. He swept her up into his arms and kissed her.

"Flora! Oh, my life. I got here as fast as I could," he said as he carried her into his sleeping chamber. "You need to rest, but first you must tell me about the dragon and what happened to Fuller."

A shadow with two golden eyes flitted in after them and curled up under the altar.

Some time later, a kinder, gentler king emerged and signaled to an aide to follow him into the night.

—

Molly paced back and forth on Riada's broad back and glared at the stars sparkling in the velvet black sky. They didn't care that these two armies were going to rip each other apart tomorrow.

Asmodius had told her that Alexander was even arming the workers. Amelia's husband was a tailor, Jackie's father was a farmer and the boy who had been grabbed up with her by the soldiers on The River Road probably was too. And what had Billy Berg, Cookie's gossiping helper, been before King Alexander's soldiers had scooped him up to work on The Wall? What did they know about fighting? They would be slaughtered along with thousands of other helpless husbands, fathers, sons, and brothers.

And for freakin' what?

As far as she could see there was nothing to fight about—The Wall was down.

"Lady Adair, permission to come aboard?"

Molly looked down from Riada's shoulder and saw a young soldier frantically backing away from her dragon's intense stare. King Alexander I was standing in front of him, ignoring the dragon and looking up at her.

Damn. Now what. How're we gonna get him up here?

No problem.

King Alexander raised his eyebrows as scales the size of serving platters jutted out to form a curving stairway up the dragon's side. He climbed, trying not to think about what would happen if the beast retracted them.

When he reached the top, the young lady bowed. "Welcome, Your Majesty. How can I help you?"

He looked at her in amazement. Flora hadn't exaggerated. The awkward girl had become a warrior. It was obvious from the way she held herself and the way she moved. If he had a thousand more of her, Damia would be invincible. "You can destroy the Dalotian army," he replied.

"I won't do that, Your Majesty." She actually had the audacity to glare at him.

And she wouldn't. One look into those smoldering gray eyes was enough to convince him that even a direct order would be a waste of time. He bit back an angry reply. "Then, perhaps you would be willing to fly me over their encampment."

She pointed to a place just above the huge wings. "If you kneel there and hang on to her scales, you can look over her shoulder." She helped him get settled and went over to the beast's other side. With a terrifying lurch, they were airborne.

The dark shadows of the Altaspinas swelled up on either side of the broad valley, and a brilliant full moon hung suspended over it. The Dalotian encampment flowed like a river of flickering campfires back into The Gap. The army was larger than he had imagined, but, thank the Gods, his was larger. And there was the king's tent, all lit up like a Solstice tree. "Can you fly lower and make another pass through here?"

His heart raced as the dragon carved a tight spiral down and flattened both riders onto its back as it leveled out. Soft night air whipped at his clothes and hair. This was really quite marvelous. As terrified soldiers ran for the doubtful protection of their tents, he noted with grudging approval that the encampment was well organized. He couldn't have done better himself.

"We should be getting back, Your Majesty. The longer we fly, the less time we have before my dragon must let go of her form. There's a ley line running through The Gap and that's why she's been able to stay this long, but she'll start to fade tomorrow morning."

"Very well. We'll begin fighting early in the morning, and your dragon can leave as soon as the charge begins."

"Why do you have to fight at all?" Her words were reasonable, but he could feel the rage behind them. "As far as I can see there's nothing here to fight about. The Dalotians came down to keep you from building The Wall, and The Wall's gone. Can't you all just go home now?"

The dragon settled down on the Damian side of the line and the king stared at Molly in confusion. Why was she so against tomorrow's battle? Ye Gods, she was a warrior herself. "We must fight them because they are Dalotian scum," he said with exaggerated patience. "If we show any weakness, they'll come sweeping over our borders like a plague of vermin."

She jumped to her feet, put her fists on her hips and glared down at him. "They don't look like scum. In fact, they look a lot like Damians."

Alexander stood. He had better things to do than argue with this angry young woman. "Thank you for the reconnaissance flight. It was most helpful. Good night, Lady Adair."

"Good night, Your Majesty." Stair-steps formed from the dragon's scales and he made his way down.

—

Back at his desk, the king repositioned three catapults, moved two stringers of horses to a safer position, and checked over everything once more to make sure all was in order for the upcoming battle.

Then he stretched and knelt in front of Mardoc's altar. He lit a stick of incense, eliciting an annoyed sneeze from Asmodius, and pulled out his boot knife. Pricking his finger, he rubbed the tiny drop of blood into the blackthorn wood. "Great and powerful Mardoc, grant us victory tomorrow."

Shadows danced on the canvas as the candle flame flared brilliantly and the incense stick popped, sending a cascade of sparks over the dark, gleaming altar.

An excellent omen. They were sure to win.

Dismissing the remaining aides, he headed for bed.

As he slipped between the sheets, he remembered that The Wall was down. He looked into the beautiful face of his sleeping wife and rested his hand on her belly and the life growing there. Flora was one of the most down to earth people he knew and she loved her kingdom with a passion. And she loved this unborn child. Why would she destroy a thing that would bring safety to both?

Wrenching his mind from the beguiling caress of sleep, he remembered the appalling treatment his people had suffered at the hands of his Lord Treasurer; and how all the land for miles around The Wall was dead and blighted. The people and the land, these were the things that mattered to his queen. And The Wall had destroyed them both. But it was almost finished and Fuller was dead. Couldn't she have just left it? The priests could have figured out some magic to set it right.

And, as he lay in his warm bed, listening to her soft breathing and feeling the fluttering movements of his unborn child, the answer floated to the surface of his mind. She had destroyed it because the presence of a wall assumes the presence of an enemy.

He looked up at the graceful curve of the tent top and rolled his eyes. All that work and he had arrived at the obvious. Of course there was an enemy—Dalot. It had always been the enemy because... well, because it was.

But what if it wasn't the enemy?

What if it was an ally?

He sighed and surrendered himself to sleep.

⁓

King Alexander sat outside his tent munching a spiced meat roll, drinking a cup of coffee, and thinking. The hours before dawn were his favorite time of the day. No one needed answers or orders and no one had anything to report. The soft morning air was as fresh as it got in a military camp; and there was a feeling of anticipation as the Earth lay shrouded in pearl gray light.

He now understood that two ravens, a girl, and sheer luck had given him a chance to make a lasting peace between Damia and Dalot. He would be a fool if he didn't at least give it a try.

By the time his drowsy aide came trudging toward him, he had it figured out. He sent the young man on a series of errands that turned the sleeping camp into a hive of activity.

⁓

Molly shivered in her sleeping bag between Riada's forelegs and watched the growing light chase away the stars. She could feel her dragon fading and she dreaded the upcoming battle. Would they expect her to fight?

"I'll miss you," she said. Riada had been a source of comfort and sanity through the long night, helping her see the benefits of her new life instead of just the problems. She'd had little sleep, but she felt grounded and at peace.

Riada's dazzling eyes regarded her impassively. "I will be with you even though I won't be visible."

Molly stroked the smooth scales of her dragon's forehand and marveled at their iridescent beauty. "Yeah, but it won't be the same. Hanging out with a real, live dragon is awesome."

Quick footsteps approached. Molly peeked over Riada's foreleg.

It was the king followed by two guards.

And he was smiling.

She struggled out of her sleeping bag and vaulted over her dragon's leg. "Good Morning, Your Majesty." She bowed.

"Good Morning, Lady Adair. You will be pleased to hear that I intend to negotiate a truce. Unfortunately, it may take awhile. How long can I count on your dragon's presence?"

Molly grinned and sunlight flooded The Gap. "I'm not sure, Your Majesty, maybe through the morning. She'll stay as long as she can."

"Excellent." And he was gone as quickly as he'd arrived

⁓

By midmorning, a white pavilion straddled Riada's black line. It had been pitched well upwind of the sulfurous-smelling dragon, but still close enough to ensure that its occupants could not ignore its ominous presence. Alexander had briefed his generals on his plans, and given orders for battle in the event that negotiations failed. The Damian army was in battle formation, and he had dressed in the finest attire his aide could assemble. The crown on his head felt very heavy.

A Damian soldier, bearing a flag of truce, stood beside the pavilion. The front line of the Dalotian army, marked by a line of shields that glinted in the sun, stood one bow-shot ahead of him. Looking fearfully at the black nightmare, the messenger cleared his throat and shouted, "Hear ye! Hear ye! King Alexander I of Damia respectfully requests the presence of King Louis III of Dalot in this pavilion within the hour."

The Dalotian army passed the message back into their ranks with a wave of chatter.

A thick, expectant silence pressed down over both camps.

Nearly an hour later King Louis's messenger approached. In a loud voice, he announced to all, "King Louis III of Dalot begs the patience of King Alexander I of Damia, and requests an afternoon meeting."

Alexander smiled grimly; it was exactly the reply he would have given if he were in King Louis's boots. However, it was unacceptable. If he waited until afternoon, the dragon would be gone and there was a chance that the rest of King Louis's army would arrive from the pass to even the odds. He composed a reply and made sure the messenger had it word perfect.

The messenger returned to his place by the pavilion opposite his counterpart.

"Let it be known that Alexander I of Damia is not a patient man," he thundered, "But he will wait one more hour for King Louis III of Dalot to present himself at this pavilion."

The dragon leapt into the air, sparkling neck ruff and gleaming talons extended. It soared over the Dalotian encampment to the king's tent, roared a bone-shaking roar, and settled back down on the Damian side of the line.

The reply bounced back. "King Louis III will honor King Alexander I with his presence within the hour."

Less than an hour later King Alexander guided his horse through the rubble of the fallen wall and headed for the pavilion. All his generals had opposed the truce. Why give up a chance to smash the Dalotian army? Two of them rode beside him in tight-lipped silence, and several foot soldiers and a scribe followed. Ahead of them the silver line of Dalotian shields parted, and King Louis and his generals and foot soldiers approached. The only sounds were the clop of the horse's hooves and the occasional clink of the soldiers' chain mail.

Soon both kings and their generals were seated in the pavilion on opposite sides of a table, sizing each other up. Their scribes were busy shuffling papers at their own tables.

Louis III was a surprise. He wore his silver armor like a second skin and moved with a cat-like grace. His midnight blue tunic and black leggings were functional, yet beautifully cut. Intelligent, blue eyes, set in a face tanned to parchment, regarded King Alexander shrewdly from under a thick cap of golden hair.

"Greetings, King Louis," he began.

"Ah, King Alexander, greetings." King Louis smiled, and laugh lines crinkled at the corners of his eyes. "Yesterday's events were highly unusual. You have some explaining to do, and I'm sure it will make a fabulous tale." He settled back in his chair like a small child awaiting his bedtime story.

He's having too much fun, Alexander thought. He gave his counterpart an icy smile and replied, "I didn't arrange to meet with you to swap stories, Your Majesty; but since you ask, I will recount the events that led up to yesterday's excitement. It all began with my Lord Treasurer, who wanted to build a wall..." He told the Dalotian king all about Fuller's deceit and how he had countered it. Then he began on Molly's story.

"Stop a moment." Louis leaned forward. "How did you discover what I was planning so quickly?"

Alexander grinned wickedly. "Let's just say two little birds told me." He continued his tale and ended with: "And so The Wall is destroyed, and your other army is safe, and I suggest we call a truce."

King Louis stared at him; his pleasant face a wooden mask.

The seconds dragged by.

Alexander began to wonder if he'd made a mistake. He wasn't good at diplomacy. It was all he could do to keep from jumping up and demanding "Well? What do you think? Answer me!" Instead, he sat back in his seat and waited for his answer, as if the outcome didn't matter to him at all.

It was the most difficult thing he'd ever done.

He hadn't realized until today how weary he was of fighting.

The stocky, bull-faced Dalotian General shifted impatiently. "Your Majesty, his troops are ill prepared and exhausted from their march south. This is our chance to finally conquer Damia!"

"I am aware of that, General Blum," King Louis replied.

The older Dalotian General glanced nervously at the dragon. "They seem well prepared to me, Your Majesty."

It was almost past noon.

How long would that cursed dragon be able to keep its form?

More seconds passed.

And then King Louis reached his hand across the table. Stifling a sigh of relief, King Alexander took it and gazed into his eyes. The Dalotian king was probably thinking the same thing he was: "Can I trust this man?"

King Louis, still grasping King Alexander's hand, cleared his throat and said, "I agree to a truce. There is no reason for a battle. If you agree not to rebuild The Wall, we will leave you in peace."

King Alexander replied, "I will not rebuild The Wall, and I will honor the truce." The scribes scribbled down the kings' promises and traded copies so each could read what the other had written and verify that that was indeed what had been said. With a flourish, they whisked the documents over to the kings to sign.

Even though the negotiations had been mercifully brief, the opposing armies had begun to fidget and mutter amongst themselves. They resembled two giant mastiffs snarling at each other and straining at their leashes. When the kings' messengers emerged from the pavilion and shouted, "Truce, stand down!" a giant, silent sigh wafted through the still air, followed by a fierce intake of breath and a mighty roar of gladness. The ranks dissolved into joyful chaos and flowed back into their camps to celebrate.

The dragon leapt into the air and hung suspended above the two armies, its wings outstretched and its ruff extended. Everyone cringed. It roared; and the earth shook. With a flash of light and a clap of thunder, it disappeared. Not even its brimstone reek remained. A slim, still figure stood alone on the black line, then turned and trudged back toward the Damian camp. Alexander shuddered to think what he would have been doing today if that tiny warrior hadn't decided to visit the queen.

But there was still much to be done. The king signaled his messenger to have refreshments sent out, and then turned to King Louis. "This truce is only a beginning, Your Majesty. I would like to fashion a permanent peace. Our constant fighting saps both our kingdoms and leaves us vulnerable to our common enemy, the Norsemen."

King Louis's mouth gaped open in a most un-kingly manner.

General Blum looked like he was about to have apoplexy, and hissed into his king's ear, "Never! Your Majesty, remember the Battle of Tronlin! Our fallen heroes must be avenged!"

The older general looked thoughtful.

King Louis's mouth snapped shut. "Impossible! Our countries have been at war off and on for centuries. Atrocities have been committed on both sides that will never be forgiven."

"So what is your solution?" asked Alexander, banging his fist on the table. "Continue fighting until we wear each other down to nothing and the Norsemen come marching in and conquer us both, raping our women and plundering our fields and cities? Ye Gods, man, we must do something and now is the perfect opportunity!"

Louis blinked, and Alexander actually saw the moment his mind clicked into gear and began evaluating the problems and possibilities.

There was one quick glance at the black line.

Thank the Gods for that dragon.

The fair-haired king settled back in his chair and opened his fists, leaving his hands palm-up on the table. "The question is: Can we convince our people to forget their grievances and become allies?"

General Blum growled. "It will never happen, Your Majesty."

The food arrived and Alexander snatched a goblet of wine and a chunk of sausage and thought about Louis's question. That, of course, was the nub of the issue. All along the border petty disputes were constantly erupting—bubbling up out of carefully tended cauldrons of remembered killings, maimings, rapes, and humiliations. Many escalated into skirmishes.

How to change the mind set of two nations?

"We need to find people who understand these things......." He sat up as if he'd been stung and slapped the table. "Yes! There *are* people who understand these things—the priests! And they're always nattering on about love and peace. It shouldn't be hard convince them to finally get serious about it. All we have to do is make a few well-placed donations with the promise of more to come."

King Louis threw back his head and laughed, "Finally, a good use for those pesky priests! If they can't change our peoples' attitudes, no one can."

Two crystal goblets clinked together.

18

The Moon

olly and Riada flew high in a cloudless blue sky. She felt the warm air flow against Riada's wings and the sun warm her scales as she watched the world spread out below them. Far in the distance, another dragon appeared, and it was moving in fast. Friend or foe? They streaked toward it, senses alert. Soon they could see that it was a red dragon of about the same size as Riada. Green sparks danced along its folded neck ruff. They circled each other gradually moving closer. Its rider was a woman.

Just as Molly recognized her mother, her soul told her that this would be the last time she would see her. The thought saddened Molly, but she was grateful for this last chance. She had so much to tell her. She stood and waved as the red dragon glided in beside them. Her mother grinned and tucked a lock of hair the exact same color as her dragon behind her ear.

Oh geez, whenever she did that, Molly knew she was in for a lecture.

Her heart sank.

What had she done wrong this time?

"I just wanted to let you know how much I love you and how proud I am of you," her mother said.

Those amazing, powerful words, the words Molly had been waiting for all her life, soothed every cell in her body, infusing her with warmth and comfort. But as she stood suspended in the joy of finally knowing that her mother really did love her, alarm jolted through her brain.

"Ah, I see that you need to leave," her mother said. "Good bye, my darling." The red dragon flicked one wing daintily and they were gone—like they'd never been there at all.

Riada also disappeared, and she struggled out of sleep and into consciousness just in time to see what looked like the poster-boy for the Nazi Youth Movement push aside her tent flap and walk toward her. The wonderful smell of coffee swirled from the steaming mug in his hand. No threat. But if he had been, she'd be dead by now. The warrior's assessment of the situation quickly gave way to the sixteen-year-old's, and she wasn't too happy either. A thin line of drool cooled her chin. She'd been sleeping with her mouth open—probably making disgusting noises. And her hair, no doubt, was a total nightmare.

Wonderful.

She sat up and wiped the drool off her chin.

"Ah, good, you're awake, Milady. The king requests your presence at the celebration feast tonight."

"Huh?" Oh, geez, this guy must think I'm a dork.

As if reading her mind, he continued, "You don't look like an assassin. Are you sure you didn't just trip and hack Fuller's head off by mistake?"

Molly's temper exploded. Who did this jerk think he was, waking her up in the middle of an amazing dream and then standing there and insulting her? In one quick movement she had Flick in hand and was leaping out of bed. Coffee splattered on the white canvas tent wall as the officer sprang back in wide-eyed surprise.

Shit, all I've got on are my undies and tank top. Well, too bad. She slashed viciously at his chest and snagged a button off the fancy uniform.

"Brigga's blades, watch where you're wavin' that thing!"

Molly growled.

Another button went flying.

"Begging your pardon, Milady," the soldier said, holding out both hands in surrender. "You do know how to use a sword."

Asmodius appeared. *Molly, stop it! Now!* She was about to smack the soldier with the flat of her blade, but her traitorous hand sheathed it instead.

He was bein' a jerk.

The multiverse is full of jerks. Are you planning to run around bashing all of them with your sword? Flick wasn't forged for that kind of nonsense. Apologize at once!

Asmodius was correct, as usual. With another heartfelt growl she retrieved the officer's buttons, and said, "I'm sorry. I'm cranky when I wake up."

He gave her a look that had "No shit, Sherlock!" written all over it, but confined himself to saying, "I will remember that. Apology accepted." He glanced over at Asmodius. "That black devil scares the stuffin' out of me, but Her Majesty says we're to be nice to it. I wish it would go away."

Asmodius glared evilly and yawned, displaying a set of wicked fangs. He leapt up on Molly's bed and curled into a gleaming black ball.

"Oh, is it with you?" the young man asked, averting his eyes and handing Molly a silky cotton bathrobe.

"I don't think he'd see it that way, but yeah, he's with me," she said, hastily pulling on the robe. It fit perfectly. "This is way cool. Where'd you find it?"

"Uh, let's go back to before I got you all riled up." He stood tall and made a sweeping bow. "Milady, allow me to introduce myself. I'm Corporal Gavin Shears, and I will be seeing to your needs. The quartermaster found out that my father's a tailor, and that I know a little bit about women's clothes, so he made me the queen's servant, and she asked me to help you as well. That robe was the queen's. I shortened it for you."

"It's just what I needed, thanks." She pulled the robe more tightly around her. "Uh, aren't there any women who could help me?" She sank down into The Chair, which had morphed into a wicker easy chair with chintz cushions.

"Not unless you count the camp prostitutes, and I don't think you want one of them!" Molly smiled as she remembered Amelia. "Just think of me as your valet," he said. "We need to get busy. I'll send one of the kitchen boys in with some food and then a few tubs of hot water. I'll be back with your gown after you've bathed."

A few minutes later there was a scratching sound on the tent door.

"What?"

"Yer midday, Milady."

"Good. Come in." A boy carrying a plate of rolls, meat, cheese, and pickled vegetables pushed aside the tent flap and stood staring at her like she'd sprouted horns.

"Thanks," she said, scooping the plate out of his hands and stuffing a piece of sausage in her mouth.

She looked up to find he had shifted his avid gaze to Flick. "What?"

"Di'ja really hack Fuller's head off with that sword? It's a real beauty. An' wot's it like to ride a dragon, an' knock down towers, an' save queens? I wish I could do stuff like that!"

Molly stopped in mid-chew and stared at the boy. He was looking at her like she was some kind of superhero or something. But she felt like just plain Molly. Her hair was still a mess, she was still too short, and she still did dumb stuff, like picking fights with handsome men who brought her coffee in bed. "What's your name?"

"Andrew, Milady."

"Well, Andrew, mostly I was scared. And I'd be dead by now if I hadn't had some really good teachers and lots of help. But it felt great, and I'd do it all over again if I had to."

"Er, yeah. I'll be back in a few minutes with yer bath water." Andrew was still staring at her in awe as he backed slowly out of the tent.

Molly was clean, fed and in a much better mood when Gavin scratched a warning on the tent flap and entered, carrying a marvelous gown. "This is one of the queen's. Because of her, uh, condition, it was way too big, so I've cut it down. I need to try it on you and pin it to fit. Father always said I was hopeless with a needle, so it won't be anywhere near perfect, but I'll do my best. And, uh, maybe you should do something with your hair," he said, making vague finger motions around his own well-kept locks.

Molly went over to the dressing table and mirror and sat down. The last time she'd done anything with her hair was when she'd chopped it off before she left the palace. "Yeah, it's a mess. But I don't know how to cut hair."

"Begging your pardon, Milady, but I don't think you could make it much worse."

Molly laughed. "OK, I'll see what I can do. Call me Molly and I'll call you Gavin, alright?"

"Fine by me." He pulled a knife out of his boot and came toward her. Molly reached for Flick but relaxed when he set it on the dressing table. "Here, you can use this. Don't cut yourself."

Molly snorted. "Not likely."

But just a short time ago it would have been quite likely—and it wouldn't have been an accident.

Gavin smiled. "I'll leave and let you put on the gown. Turn it inside out. You can cut your hair after the fitting."

It was white crepe silk, simply cut, with a plunging neckline and long flowing sleeves. Asmodius would be scandalized. Queen Flora would have worn an elaborate overdress with it and tons of jewelry, but its simple elegance was perfect for a warrior mage. Molly slipped it over her head and called Gavin, who arrived with a box full of pins.

They bickered good-naturedly over the hemline and how snug to make the bodice, and Molly's heart thudded happily every time Gavin's hand brushed against her and every time he touched her ankle to get her to turn while he was pinning the hem.

When he left, she looked in the mirror and scowled at her tangled mass of curls. She looked like a street urchin. No wonder the dashing corporal treated her like his little sister. Raking her fingers through her hair she tried to plan her attack. All that the fashion 'zines had said about cutting your own hair was "Don't!"

Maybe if she just evened it up.

She pulled a small bunch out from her head and flattened it between her first and second fingers. Gavin's knife glided through it with a whisper. It was so sharp she could have shaved with it, but her legs would probably have been a bloody mess. Good thing her dress was full length and she didn't need to.

He returned a few hours later with the finished gown, a pair of white slippers, and a small velvet box. "Here's your outfit, and this is a gift from the queen. She says to wear them with the dress."

Molly opened the box and gasped. A moonstone necklace and earrings floated on the black velvet lining. The stone in the necklace was a two-inch diameter disc set in simple silver. The earrings were crescents shot with opaline fire.

When he'd gone, she slipped on the dress. It was far from perfect, but from a distance, the slightly uneven seams and the tiny bloodstain where he'd pricked his finger hardly showed. The shoes were tight, but wearable. She slid Flick through her belt, smoothed her hair, put on her jewelry, and pronounced herself ready. When Gavin came to check his handiwork his jaw dropped. He looked so comical that Molly laughed out loud. "What's wrong?" she asked. "I couldn't look that bad!"

"Oh no, you look good. I mean, really lovely. I would never have thought it—uh, begging your pardon."

"I guess I did look awful. But this dress is perfect and the moonstones are fabulous. You must have gone crazy today with two of us to dress for a banquet in the middle of a military camp."

Gavin smiled and her stomach did flip-flops. "Actually, the queen's not going."

"How come? This is really important."

"Her Majesty is aware of that, but giving birth in the middle of the banquet wouldn't be proper."

"Oh geez, I didn't realize she was that close. And she actually took the time to help me?"

"I think she did it so you wouldn't embarrass the king. He couldn't have the young lady who saved his queen and killed the traitor looking a fright at the celebration feast, now could he?"

"Yeah, you're right, that would've been bad. But if she's not going, I should thank her for the dress before I go."

"Allow me to escort you, Milady." He placed her hand on his forearm and led her out into the warm summer evening, her pulse racing at his touch.

—

Queen Flora was tucked up in a huge bed with satin sheets and soft wool blankets. Her eyes were too large for her face, and dark smudges pooled under them. Her hands moved restlessly over the blankets and she shifted constantly in search of a comfortable position. But she smiled warmly as Molly entered the tent. "Don't you look marvelous! That dress is perfect. Do the shoes pinch?"

Molly curtsied. "Thank you, Your Majesty. I love the dress. The shoes'll do just fine for the evening, but I wouldn't want to hike in them. The necklace and earrings are beautiful, thank you. It was kind of you."

"It was my pleasure! I can't go to the banquet, but I enjoyed planning an ensemble for you. It took my mind off things."

There was a musical jingle of harnesses and the clop, clop of horses' hooves, as a wagon pulled up outside the tent. Quick footsteps approached.

Asmodius poked his head through the tent flap. *Your Majesty, the midwife is here.*

"Enter, please."

The flap swept aside and in stepped Madame Rue. Her blue cloak rippled and sparkled around her and her black hair writhed like a nest of serpents. She curtsied deeply as she greeted her queen. "Your Majesty, an honor."

"I am glad you are here." the queen replied and nodded toward Molly. "Madame Rue, this is Molly Adair."

Ebony eyes held hers in their gimlet gaze once more and shuffled through her soul. "Hello, Dearie. You've been busy, I see. And you're nearly there now, aren't you?" She took off her cloak, poured it onto a nearby chair, and rolled up her sleeves. "Now leave us. The queen and I have work to do this night and so do you."

Molly turned to Queen Flora, curtsied, and said, "Best wishes, Your Majesty, I'll be thinking of you."

"Have a nice trip, Dearie!" Madame Rue cackled as Molly left the tent.

King Alexander sat beside King Louis at the high table decked with white linen and garlands of late summer flowers and looked out over the score of Generals assembled there. Molly's table was front and center, and she sat among the hard, fierce looking men like a white rose among thorns. Clusters of golden stars floated up near the ceiling of the pavilion filling the air with a soft glow that stripped years from the soldiers' weathered faces.

He signaled to Father Elysius. The rumble of conversation ceased and every one stood. The priest approached, bowed to the monarchs and blessed the gathering. Then he bowed again to the kings and hurried out of the pavilion. Alexander watched his exit with a sigh of relief. He was glad the good father had insisted on coming. Flora would need all the support she could get tonight.

And with that thought, came a stab of anxiety. What if there were "problems"?

Straightening his shoulders and shoving aside his fears, the king stood to address the gathering. "Gentlemen and Lady," he began, smiling down at Molly. "We have come together this evening to celebrate the beginning of a new era, a time of peace and goodwill between the sovereign nations of Dalot and Damia. Together we will achieve an even greater level of well-being for all, and present a united front to our enemies."

A cheer went up from the generals. They were tired of dealing with the incessant border skirmishes. And besides, there would always be Norsemen to fight.

King Louis stood and put his hand on King Alexander's shoulder. In front of him were six bottles of chilled, golden wine. "My wine steward has reminded me that whenever we go on campaign, he always brings a few bottles of Dalot's legendary Peace Wine—just in case. It was created to be imbibed in celebration of an honorable truce. The story goes that back in the mists of time, the great mage, Lysios, who was also a wine maker, enchanted a batch of wine made from his finest Crespa grapes and presented it to the king. He promised that it would help ensure a lasting peace between Dalot and any country its king desired—if that country was also willing. No one in living memory has tasted this wine, but it is reputed to be fabulous. Of course, if the enchantment has failed, it may be awful."

The king's wine steward was a portly man with twinkling eyes. At King Louis's signal, he bustled over to the bottles and opened one. He poured a small portion into King Louis's crystal wine stem.

Like the showman that he was, the king held his glass up to the light and examined the wine's color and clarity. He sniffed it hesitantly. Then he smiled and took small sip. "Ah, this is wonderful stuff! Steward, pour us all a glass and let us drink to Peace!"

As the steward moved from table to table, the wine's complex aroma tripped enticingly out of the bottles and permeated the pavilion. Soon everyone had a small portion of the glowing, golden wine.

King Louis raised his glass and said, "Here's to a lasting peace between Dalot and Damia."

He and King Alexander clinked glasses and all the generals clinked glasses with as many other generals as they could reach. And of course they all wanted to clink glasses with Molly and mutter things like, "Good job, m'girl!" and "Well done."

At the end of the toast, the entire tent was suffused with a luminous aura of peace. Laughter rang out as the men began to mix and mingle and discover friendships where before there had been only mistrust and hatred.

The first course was just being brought in when Molly collapsed to the ground with a small sigh. The last bit of wine arced out of her glass and fell on the ground beside her, forming a string of golden beads that clung to the green blades of grass.

Silence sliced through the gathering.

King Louis smiled.

King Alexander looked from the fallen heroine to his beaming ally and grieved. How could he have been so gullible? Molly and her dragon had been the threat that had insured this peace. He should have protected her instead of placing her within the grasp of his enemies. He had trusted where he shouldn't have; and a brave, beautiful soul had died because of his foolishness. "Poison! Generals, to me." He grabbed his fellow monarch and held his boot knife tight up against his throat.

"Wait, curse it, you don't understand!" yelled the king of Dalot. But he held perfectly still.

Cries of rage and horror shattered the silence as tables were overturned and generals leaped to defend their respective monarchs. They knocked trays of soup out of the servers' hands and into the faces of their opponents. Fistfights broke out and boot knives flashed. The lovely banquet became a melee worthy of the roughest tavern in Bontare.

Asmodius bounded out from the shadows. He put his face next to Molly's and sniffed. Then he stood over her still form and raised his hackles, howling and spitting like a demon from the abyss.

Everyone froze.

He looked over at King Alexander. *She's alive, Your Majesty, but she is in a deep trance.*

King Louis continued, "She's not dead, she's in a trance. She will be fine in the morning."

Asmodius sniffed her wineglass and several others that had been tossed down near by. *Her wine was enchanted by someone who was very good at that sort of thing—no surprises there. However, it is exactly the same enchanted wine everyone else drank. I am puzzled.*

King Louis shifted and muttered between clenched teeth. "If you will put your little pig sticker back in your boot, call off your men, and sit down in your chair like a civilized being, I will explain everything."

King Alexander breathed into his ear, "Fine, but this better be good!" He tucked his knife away, retrieved Louis's platinum crown, and replaced it with only a slight bit more force than was necessary. "At ease, generals. Lady Adair is alive, but deep in trance. King Louis will explain. Corporal Shears, carry Lady Adair to her tent."

As her tent flap swished closed behind Gavin and Molly, Asmodius slipped in behind them and settled in the shadows, watching as the corporal laid Molly's small, limp form on the bed, gently pulled off her uncomfortable slippers, and draped a soft, wool blanket over her.

When he'd left, the big cat leapt up beside Molly. After a brief but intense consultation with The Chair, he curled up and prepared to follow her out into the worlds.

Back in the pavilion, King Louis was explaining: "There is another property of the Peace Wine that I didn't mention, because I didn't think it would apply. If someone with talent and training in the Magical Arts drinks it in celebration of a treaty, he or she will fall into a trance and venture out into the worlds where all the futures lie. The adept will observe a possible future of the two countries involved. What this means is, that in a few hours, we will have a better understanding of how to weave our way through all the shifting futures and maintain a lasting peace. This is a blessing I had not hoped for."

⌐

Molly was floating in an ocean of warm, dark water. If she held still, it was impossible to tell where the water stopped and she began. She expanded into a weightless, limitless being. She contained everything and she contained nothing. She would have been happy to float in that still infinity forever, but she began to glide through the water. It caressed her like a fold of Madame Rue's cloak. She flowed onto a beach and lay on the firm sand, gazing into the cool, white light of the full moon floating in a black night sky. To her right, a wolf howled; to her left a dog barked. Far in the distance two towers shone in the silver light. She stood and moved toward them through fertile fields...

Beyond the towers, the land became a barren wilderness. The air grew cooler as she climbed toward the distant mountains. Pale moonlight shone eerily on rocks and boulders, casting sharp shadows that occasionally morphed into fantastic shapes that scuttled off into the darkness...

She was walking along a mountain ridge. Looking out over the land to her left, she saw a river running through a broad plain. The fields were fertile and cattle grazed in lush pastures. Mighty forests cloaked the hillsides. The land on her right had only small, fierce rivers that roared down sparsely forested mountainsides, through a coastal plain covered with fields of yellow wheat, and into the sea. Sheep dotted the foothills, and mining towns clung to the sides of the mountains. Mills huddled next to the swiftly flowing rivers, dipping their water wheels into the racing currents. Damia and Dalot...

She came to a great encampment, hidden among the rocks and boulders. Hundreds of ragged soldiers huddled in the bitter wind around scores of tiny campfires. She moved through it like a ghost. No one noticed her, and when she spoke to a soldier, he shivered and pulled his coat tighter against the wind. A young man dressed in light armor strode into the center of the camp to address to his troops. He looked like King Alexander, except his hair was the color of ripe wheat and his eyes were vivid blue. Beside him stood Queen Flora. She looked sad and her hair was streaked with gray.

"Gentlemen, our scouts have reported that my father's army will enter the pass tomorrow. He must be stopped before he reaches Dalot. At dawn, we will rise and defend The Peace!" The men leaped to their feet and jabbed at the air with their fists. "Huzzah! Huzzah!"

She gasped in horror and began running.

Something rumbled gently in the distance, and she ran toward it.

Asmodius appeared in front of her, purring. *It's time to return now. You've been dreaming. Remember your dream. King Alexander and King Louis will want to hear it. Follow me.*

He led her down a moonlit sand dune and into a wine-dark sea.

And then, ever so slowly, she awoke.

Moonlight shining on white canvas gave Molly the vague impression that she was floating in the middle of a glowing white egg. She stretched luxuriously, sat up, and found herself facing King Alexander and King Louis. They looked slightly embarrassed, but eager to hear what she would say.

Eyes widening in astonishment, Molly checked to make sure she was fully dressed, then collected her memories and faithfully recounted every detail of her dream.

When she had finished, both monarchs stared at her in shocked disbelief. They talked it over, but no matter how many questions they asked her or how many ways they interpreted it, the nightmare continued to squat malignantly between them. Finally the kings thanked her and left.

19

The Sun

he sun rose the next morning to a mighty roar. The entire army was yelling, and banging pots, and blowing bugles. Fearing trouble, Molly grabbed up Flick and headed out to investigate. She ran into Gavin as he arrived with her coffee. It was like hitting a wall.

"Oof!" he said, and put out a hand to steady her. Not a drop of coffee spilled.

Molly looked up into his marvelous blue eyes and cringed in embarrassment. Gods, he was so freakin' gorgeous, and she was such a spaz.

"What's the hurry? Was this what you were looking for?" He smiled into her eyes and offered her the coffee.

"Um, yeah."

"Great news!" he continued, handing it to her. "The queen just had a baby boy—Damia has an heir!"

So that's what all the yelling was about. "How is Her Majesty?" Molly sipped her coffee and tried to look cool. She still wasn't used to sitting half dressed in a bedroom with a man who could send her pulse racing just by looking at her.

"She's doing well. That old witch that came to help sure knows her business. Not a real friendly sort though. As soon as the babe was out and safe, she got in that gaudy wagon and just seemed to disappear."

"Yeah, she's good at that."

"So, what do you want for breakfast?"

"Uh, don't worry about getting me breakfast, I'll stop at the mess tent. I want to explore the camp." She sank down in The Chair. "Thanks for the coffee."

He grinned, making her stomach do flip-flops. "I wish I could go with you, but I'm on duty. I'll see you at midday."

After he left, Molly finished her coffee and collected her wits. "Will the kings be able to keep the peace?" she asked The Chair. "I mean, it'd be great if they could, but it doesn't seem real likely. But my dream said that they'd succeed. At least for awhile."

I'd rather talk about what's going on with that corporal.

Molly felt herself blushing furiously. "That's none of your business, now answer my question."

The Chair snickered. *Both King Louis and King Alexander are savvy rulers. They understand that if they make peace profitable for enough people, then peace will prevail. And, given enough time and skillful encouragement, most people will eventually stop seeing their neighbor as the enemy. Also, there's that Peace Wine – never under-estimate the power of a bit of well-placed magic. I suggest that you go out in the sunshine, get your breakfast and see for yourself what King Alexander and King Louis are doing to bring about peace.*

It was one of those fabulous summer mornings where the sun shines down like honey and covers everything in a golden glow. A warm breeze was blowing in exactly the right direction to keep down most of the stink of pit toilets, and the delicious aromas coming from the mess tents helped cover the rest. The camp was no longer gray. Bright banners flew from tent poles; and the workers had shrugged off their dreary uniforms and put on their regular clothes.

Molly strolled through the maze of tents enjoying the warmth of the sun on her shoulders and the sights and sounds of an army at peace. With Asmodius' glamour still on them, she and Flick attracted very little attention and Molly was able to move about freely. She found long lines of chatting workers and soldiers threading between tents. The lines converged on a row of official-looking men seated at a long table surrounded by bags of coin. A bored guard standing behind them told her that the king had been so horrified at the ordeal his people had suffered that he had decreed that everyone would receive twice what was owed him. The paymasters were using Lord Fuller's ill gotten gains to supplement the workers' wages.

The kitchens were bountifully supplied, and breakfast ale flowed from casks in almost continuous streams. There was so much to celebrate: the birth of a royal heir, the peace treaty, the death of the hated Lord Treasurer, the destruction of The Wall, and the fact that they would be home in time to bring in the harvest. Men strolled around the camp, greeting old friends and making new ones.

Several mess tents and a few dozen tables from both camps had been moved out to the black line. Soldiers from both sides were there, socializing as they ate and drank. Knowing that all mess tents were not created equal, Molly checked out each one. Sure enough, there was one that was more crowded than the others—light, fluffy scrambled eggs, fried veggies, crisp bacon, freshly brewed coffee, and sweet dumplings to die for. She was not surprised to see Cookie and Billy Berg hard at work behind a stove and chopping board; trading jokes and insults with their patrons, Damian and Dalotian alike.

Molly enjoyed her breakfast and watched the simple magic of good food and friendly conversation doing its work. The few arguments that happened were quickly broken up. By late morning the ale casks had disappeared, but the celebration continued.

She wandered over to the scatter of blocks that had been The Wall. Engineers from both sides were measuring and planning the foundations for two temples, one to Dama and one to her husband Dalot, which were to be built from the surrounding rubble. Workers with measuring lines and sighting rods were sent scuttling here and there as engineers from both sides waved their arms and argued over site location and entrance alignment. A few Dalotian and Damian priests were voicing their own ideas when they could get a word in.

A bouquet of cheerful sunflowers towered over the flowers at the high table of the pavilion where the feast had been held. Molly strolled around the tables listening to the generals exchanging ideas over plates of sausages and tarts and copious cups of coffee. The magic of the peace wine was still in the air, calming arguments and encouraging friendships.

At one table, officers discussed strategies for guarding caravans through the passes; another table discussed protecting their northern borders and coasts from invasion; and another table decided how best to enforce tariffs and trade agreements and develop and encourage commerce, especially by the sea routes now accessible to Damia. Over in a corner, the kings talked with Father Elysius and top ranking priests from both sides about how to convince the temples to preach kindness toward their neighboring country.

Most remarkable of all, Molly noticed that the land around the ruined wall was coming alive. Green grass was sprouting in the low traffic areas and flowers were already blooming among the stumps surrounding the camp. Birds sang on tent posts and fought raucously for crumbs around the mess tents. The queen was content and in communion with her land once more.

But the scorched line dividing the camps refused to grow anything, and remained as a sharp, black reminder of yesterday's events.

—

At noon King Alexander helped his queen onto a wagon filled with silk covered cushions and bright tapestries and pulled by a pure white stallion decked out in flowers. The monarchs processed through both camps, followed by drummers, pipers, and dancers.

Flora looked tired, but radiant. Her hair gleamed and curled around her crown of stars and her violet eyes shone with a joy that danced into the crowd. As Alexander relaxed beside her, pure happiness filled his heart. Nestled in his arms, and sleeping peacefully, despite all the noise and hubbub, was his son, the future king of Damia. The king gazed into his precious face and prayed that Lady Adair's foretelling belonged to another future.

As they proceeded through the camps, the Damians went crazy with joy, and the Dalotians gave them many enthusiastic huzzahs. King Louis came out to greet them and offer his congratulations and best wishes.

20

Judgement

The next morning Molly sat on her bed, dressed in her tunic and leggings. The Chair was a pack once more, and Flick was at her side. She had tossed and turned all night trying to decide if she was really in love with Gavin or if she was just in love with the idea of being in love.

But the river was calling her.

When Gavin came whisking through the tent flap with her coffee and saw her dressed and packed up, the smile evaporated from his face. "You don't have to leave, you know."

"I know. The king asked me to stay. But this isn't where I belong. I've got a journey to finish. I can't stop now; I'm almost to the end."

He handed her the mug and said, "I'll get you an audience with the king and queen so you can say your good-byes. Meet me in the mess tent."

She had just finished picking her sausage roll apart when Gavin appeared beside her. "They'll see you now." He squeezed her shoulder. "Good bye, Molly." She watched him walk away through a shimmer of tears.

The soldier on guard duty showed her into the royal sleeping quarters. Queen Flora was propped up in bed holding her son, and King Alexander was sprawled in a chair nearby. They looked tired, yet supremely content. In their simple clothes and informal surroundings, they looked like any other wealthy couple that had just been blessed with their first offspring. Molly's heart warmed with affection for them as she bowed.

"Your Highnesses, I've come to say good bye and to thank you for your hospitality."

The king rose from his chair and took her hand. "Ah, Lady Adair, we are the ones who should be thanking you. Thousands of soldiers owe you their lives; and with your help, we were able to negotiate peace between Damia and Dalot. These are priceless gifts that can never be repaid; but allow us to give you something to show our appreciation. We first thought of land, but then we realized that you probably wouldn't be staying. Only a few of Asmodius' clients do. And so we decided to give you these."

He picked up a small, leather pouch from the bedside table and poured a rainbow of glittering light into his hand. "These are gems of the highest quality. They should be sufficient to make you a wealthy woman anywhere in the multiverse."

Molly looked at the beautiful stones in amazement and then into the smiling eyes of the king and queen. "You don't owe me anything, you know. I did it because I care about you and this kingdom, and because I'm Brigga's agent. I mean, I sort of had to do what I did."

"We understand that, my dear," replied the queen, "but that doesn't make what you did any less valuable to us. Please, take them as a token of our appreciation and esteem."

Alexander poured the stones back into the pouch and handed it to her. "May the Gods bless and keep you, Molly Adair."

Molly bowed again. "Thank you, Your Majesties."

She stepped out of the tent and almost tripped over Asmodius.

Are you ready to go? he asked.

—

The noise and odor of the camp faded into the distance as she headed south once more. The air was warm and soft and the breeze wafting up from the river was tinged with the salty tang of the sea. The world around her pulsed with life and excitement. She kicked at a small rock. What right did the world have to be happy when she was miserable?

She was walking away from a guy who had looks to die for and was actually nice.

And she was walking away from a place where she was a freakin' national hero.

What was she thinking!?

And she missed Riada something fierce.

Several hours later she reached the river. She stripped off her clothes and plunged into the cool water. Swimming halfheartedly against the current, she was able to hold her place next to her pile of belongings and Asmodius, who was snoozing under a bush. The Selene was broad now and flowed regally between sandy banks lined with river willows. There were islands, formed as the river slowed and dropped its burden of sand and silt. She remembered from the maps that more islands would soon form a marshy delta. This side would narrow down to a small stream and eventually flow into the sea.

The river worked its magic. After her swim, she was not only clean, but also more content with her choice.

"Do you think Grandmother's worried about me?"

She's probably frantic.

"And if I don't make it back, what's she going tell people?"

Let's just hope you make it back.

⟶

Another few days of hiking brought her to the coast. She stopped at the dune line and watched what was left of her beloved river glide, all bright and unsuspecting, across the beach and into the tossing waters of the sea. It made a sparkling blue path that went through the breakers and green seawater all the way to the horizon.

Now what was she supposed to do? The river continued, but she couldn't follow it.

A small rowboat appeared on the riverbank. It was the exact same blue as the river. A painted eye on one side of the bow stared at her and winked, and there was probably another one on the other side staring out to sea.

"I'm supposed to get in that boat, aren't I?"

At this point, that's about all you can do.

"But it hasn't got any oars or a sail. If I get into to it, I'll drift out into the ocean and starve to death or drown in a storm."

Maybe, maybe not.

"Well, what else could happen?"

I don't know. You'll have to get in the boat and find out.

Molly stared out over the relentless waves. As each one neared the shore, it built up into a mountain of jade green water and toppled over into churning rows of snow-white froth that threw themselves at the beach and surged over it in hissing whispers. As each wave slid back into the ocean, she felt its cool fingers pulling at her, calling her into the depths.

Molly shivered. She loved her new life and wasn't at all ready to die. But there was one thing she was now quite sure of: just staying alive wasn't living. If she remained here, safe and sound on shore, she would die a small death every time she wondered what might have happened if she'd had the guts to get in the boat and finish her journey. With a sigh, she threw her pack into the boat, pushed it part way into the water and held it steady for Asmodius to jump in.

I can't go with you. My job is done. May the Gods be with you, Molly. He patted her foot with his paw, leaped into the air over the riverbank...and disappeared.

Molly screamed in agony. "ASMODIUS! Don't leave me. I need you. Come back, oh please, come back!"

Abandoned.

Again.

First by her parents, then Tamerlane, then Brigga, then Riada, then again by her mother, and now Asmodius was gone. It was too much. She leaned on the side of the boat and wept deep, wrenching sobs until she was sure she had cried enough tears to sink it.

Ahem.

"What?"

He's not dead, you know, said The Chair from the bottom of the boat, which had remained dry, despite her best efforts.

"I know, but he's gone," Molly wailed.

I've noticed. However, crying will not bring him back, at least it hasn't yet. You have a journey to finish. Asmodius worked hard to get you this far. The rest is up to you.

Molly collected herself with a few last, shuddering sobs. She blew her nose, splashed cool river water over her face and climbed into the boat. She felt weak and used-up, but The Chair was right, she had a journey to finish.

The moment she sat down, the boat pulled away from shore and glided out to sea. There were a few tense moments as it threaded its way through the breakers and plunged bow first through the ones it couldn't avoid. Eventually they were past them, moving rapidly away from shore.

The water slapped and sucked at the sides of the boat.

Gulls cried endlessly.

Molly stared at the receding shoreline.

The color of the water changed from sparkling river blue to sea green, and the constant lurching and pitching lulled her into a sort of waking sleep.

Time passed...

She awoke from her stupor, thirsty and ravenously hungry. She fished the chalice out of her pack and dipped it into the ocean. All through her journey it had provided her with fresh, clean water. Would it still work? She took a sip, and sweet water filled her thirsty mouth. The plate was useless, however. No matter how hard she concentrated, she couldn't make even one French fry appear.

Then she had to pee. She hung over one side and almost tipped the boat over. Recovering her balance, Molly went to the back of the boat and hung out there. After a few false starts, she managed to get most of it in the water. She was careful to hold on tight. She doubted that the boat would stop for her if she fell out.

The gulls had disappeared.

She tried asking Brigga for help, but the Goddess didn't answer.

She didn't dare call Riada.

The water had partially appeased her empty stomach—but when it realized that that was all it was going to get, it knotted up in stabbing hunger pangs. To keep her mind off her complaining insides, she thought back to all the places she'd been, and all the people she'd met.

The boat continued out to sea as her mind drifted back through her journey.

The wind picked up, cooling the air and fluffing the wave tips into whitecaps.

Dark clouds scudded in from the west.

The waves grew bigger and sea spray wet her cheeks.

There's water everywhere and it smells funny. I don't like it, Flick said from beside her.

"It's sea water, and it would make you rust even faster than fresh water. But I won't let any of it touch you."

She picked up the pack. "Can you change into something waterproof?"

The Chair morphed into a waterproof bag large enough for her belongings and Flick.

The wind howled and cold rain dumped down in sheets. Molly grabbed the chalice and began bailing for all she was worth. For every chaliceful she poured out another poured in. The tiny boat wallowed in the high seas. As it was climbing up the face of a monstrous wave, she made the mistake of looking up and found herself facing a wall of gray water. As she stared into its cold depths, huge faces appeared and stared past her, like she was no more important than a sardine. Enormous shadows glided behind them. The boat reached the windblown crest and teetered. Molly gasped as she caught a glimpse of endless mountain ranges of angry gray water, tops whipped to white froth by the wind. Then she plunged screaming down the other side. After that, she kept her eyes on the inside of the boat and concentrated on keeping hold of it, hanging on to her belongings, and bailing out sea water.

Night came and darkness enveloped her. The wind howled like a thousand drowning sailors and the rain lashed over her.

Time passed...

Molly's arms turned to lead and then to jelly, but she kept holding on and bailing until the rain died down to a patter. Now all she had to do was hang on.

Dawn pinked the horizon, but the wind continued to churn the clouds and whip up the waves. Searing pain shot through her arms and hands as wave after wave after wave jolted the boat. By midday, however, the sea had relaxed into a rough chop and Molly collapsed into sleep.

On the third day Molly woke up with the morning sun blazing into her eyes. She dragged herself up off the bottom of the boat and onto the seat, grabbing at the sides as her aching head spun and her eyes tried to focus on the endless, heaving waves. Her hair and clothes had dried stiff with salt and her lips were cracked and painful. Fortunately her stomach had given up complaining. She rinsed off with fresh water from the chalice and drank and drank.

Are you OK?

Oh geez, she'd forgotten all about Flick. She pulled her sword out of the dry-bag.

You were so frightened and I couldn't see.

"I'm alright. Could be better. But *you* need a good cleaning and a coat of oil."

Flick hummed sharp, silver songs as Molly worked.

She slipped Flick into the dry bag, went through the forms in her head, and sat back to do some serious thinking. If she didn't do something she was gonna die out here—and it would be a slow death. She'd read somewhere that if you drank plenty of water you could live for a month without food. She'd been out here almost three days and no angels or Gods or dragons had appeared out of the sky to take her home, but there was another possibility.

"Chair, can you take me home now? I mean, we're really at the end. There's nowhere else to go."

No, I'm sorry. The dry bag on the bottom of the boat managed to look contrite, but firm. Molly hadn't expected it to help her, every other time she'd begged it to send her home it had always insisted that it wasn't allowed to.

So...

The only way to get home from this world was to jump, but she'd only done short jumps, and always to places she could see. But Earth was probably in another universe. Maybe it would still work if, instead of looking at where she wanted to go, she just pictured it. But what if she got lost part-way there? Would she become a ghost wandering the multiverse forever, leaving her body to feed the fishes and Flick to disintegrate in the sea? She pushed away the ugly thought, grabbed The Chair and Flick, pictured her room in Portland and reached for it...

Nothing happened.

Shit.

Fear started winding its way through her; and even though the sun was hot, a cold chill crept up her spine. She shuddered as she imagined her body sinking slowly through miles of cold, blue-green water. Just like her parents...

Stop it!

This was insane. The last time she'd freaked like this was in the corpse tree. She didn't have Asmodius here to remind her to chill, but she could still do it.

She stilled her mind, or at least she tried to. But every time she created a quiet, empty space in her mind, her brain rushed in to fill it with all kinds of thoughts. It was even worse than last time, because lack of food made her brain even busier. But it wasn't like she was in a hurry. She had twenty-seven more days. So she sat cross-legged on the bottom of the boat with her back against the seat, feeling the gentle rocking of the waves, listening to the endless parade of thoughts and letting each of them go—until she noticed one that was actually helpful. She remembered that prayer worked well here. Dama had healed Asmodius for her. But Dama probably wasn't the best goddess to ask about sending her away from Damia. Maybe just ask the multiverse? And then she would have to continue meditating so she could hear the reply.

OK, so...

"Multiverse. I need to go home. Please help me." She concentrated as hard as her food starved brain would let her on sending that message up into the sky and beyond. And then she sat and meditated. There was nothing else to do.

She stopped occasionally to drink water.

Time passed.

Molly reached out and melded with the world around her. She became the gentle, restless waves, the infinite sky, and the intrepid, blue boat. She was everywhere and everything.

The sun began to set, splashing the clouds with gold and pink.

And the world stopped.

Nothing moved, there was no sound, no soft breeze caressed her skin, and no waves slapped at the side of the boat. A web of luminous lines appeared all around her and she somehow knew they were the living links that connected everything to everything else in the multiverse. A flash of movement in the vast stillness caught her eye. Someone was coming toward her. Day-Glo-orange high-tops and green leggings flashed in the sunset.

With a cry of joy, Molly waved her arms over her head. "Tracy! Over here. It's me!"

Tracy danced through the shining clouds—graceful and calm. "Hey, you've finished."

"No! I'm just starting. I need to go home!"

He stepped into the boat and floated cross-legged opposite her. His clothes were no longer in filthy tatters, just a bit worn and smudged. The feathers in his hair swayed gently in some otherworldly breeze. As she gazed at him, she noticed that there was a definite Mollyness about the way he moved and held his head. And those eyes. They looked just like hers.

Of course!

"You're me!" she gasped in surprise.

"Nah, you're *me*!"

She stared at her other self in amazement and thought back to Tracy's first appearance in her life. They'd been sitting opposite each other in her bedroom in Portland. And then…Oh geez, she'd single handedly sent herself into this mess. Her loopy, starved brain thought that was hilarious and she rolled on the bottom of the boat laughing hysterically. When her laughter had tapered off into an occasional giggle she said, "Whatever, we need to go home or at least one of us is gonna die."

"That's easy," Tracy said.

The shining web surrounding them warped and twisted and they were suspended in radiant blackness.

"Right now we're everywhere and nowhere. All places and times are present here. Pick where you want to go...and go."

Molly pictured her room in Portland...

...and fell in a tight spiral, leaving behind dizzying tracers of neon bright colors that sparkled with her laughter.

21

The World

olly sat in the blue plush, overstuffed chair in her new bedroom. The late summer sun poured through her window, lighting up the statue of Xena, Warrior Princess on her nightstand and glinting on her upraised sword.

Molly grinned.

Not only because her treasure was back, but also because she was sure the tiny warrior had just winked at her.

The patchwork quilt on her bed glowed like a mass of jewels, and in the middle of that riot of color was a gleaming black mound. As if her notice had somehow alerted it, the mound shifted and two golden eyes appeared, blinking sleepily.

"Asmodius! You're here!"

In two quick leaps, the big cat sprang onto the floor, and into her lap. He patiently submitted to a series of rib-crushing hugs and joyful kisses. When he had had enough, he wriggled out of her embrace, and stalked away. Was that a nearly inaudible *har-rumph!* that she heard as he made his exit?

With a jolt of panic she began searching for Flick, and sighed in relief when she found it tucked in The Chair's seat cushion. Holding her breath, Molly drew Flick from its scabbard. The fabulous sword was still a fabulous sword. The patterns still flickered and danced along its blade, and it still radiated the same fierce, bright energy.

"Flick?"

Hey, Molly!

Had she heard it or just imagined it?

"Chair?"

I'm here, Molly.

She slumped back onto her friend in relief. Asmodius had been right yet again. There was magic in her world. Not like in Damia, but enough.

Footsteps pattered up the stairs.

"Molly?" Her grandmother appeared at the door. Tears streaked down her cheeks, but her face was shining with happiness. "I'm so glad you're back." She held her arms out hesitantly.

Molly smiled and threw herself into those waiting arms.

Her grandmother smelled of love and oranges.

Acknowledgements

Writing a novel was not something I had planned to do. My diploma says "Master of Science" not "Master of Fine Arts." Learning to write has been a fascinating, all consuming, later life adventure. I am so grateful to my editor, Jessica Page Morrell, for her brutal honesty, sound writing advice, and enthusiastic encouragement. Without her talents, Forging the Blade would never have been published. I would also like to thank the following wonderful people who were kind enough to read at least one of the many versions of the manuscript and brave enough to offer constructive criticism:

Karen and Dick Seymour
Charla Teufel
Faylyn and Alexandria Herseim
Catherine Evleshin
David Bennet
Ron Root
Samuel/Grim
Kier Salmon
Linn Prentis
Renee Moxlow
Michael Howard

Many thanks to Michael Bell, master swordsmith and founder of Dragonfly Forge in Coquille, Oregon, for patiently explaining the properties of steel and how they relate to Japanese swords and then allowing me into to his forge to watch him create a katana blade. It took him four grueling, awesome days. Yes, he starts with a foot-long length of steel cable. And yes, a blade really does come alive when it is completed, heated to red hot, and plunged into water. Any errors and omissions in the forging process in the story are, of course, mine. And much gratitude to my husband, two sons, and daughters-in-law for their love, encouragement, and support. It means the world to me.

About the Author

C. LaVielle began her grown-up life as a biologist because she is fascinated by people, plants, and animals and what makes them tick.

She became a wife, a mother, and a healer specializing in tarot divination and energy work.

She traveled to many marvelous, mythical places—from pyramids to temples to standing stones to cathedrals.

And became, at last, a writer.

She has discovered that magic is real. And it makes fantastic fiction.